THE SHOUT
A novel about a lifeboat crew and harbour life

by

Chris Snell

Published under license from Andrews UK

1

One huge wave lifted the stern of the coaster, propeller and rudder, out of the froth and oil just as Bill Hawken tried to swing the Tamar Class lifeboat into a better position. The bronze screw must have been about five feet in diameter. With no medium but air to resist, the prop picked up speed. Even above the scream of the wind and the bombardment of wave against hull, the noise of unregulated energy penetrated the darkened space of the Tamar's wheelhouse.

'Christ!' Bill was a man rarely moved to profanity, but this was the worst sea, as coxswain, he'd ever put the crew into. Visibility was practically nil and navigating the boat was a nightmare. He increased thrust instinctively, on dual throttles, at the same time steering the craft in a desperate broadside away from the steel plates of the grey painted hulk hovering above him. The boat's mechanic, Chris Pascoe, seated back from him, silently thanked the designers for saving his back as his chair cushioned the abrupt change in pitch and rotation. It took almost the full twenty centimetres it was designed to travel, leaving its occupant free to focus on the boat management system captured on the screen facing him. The blue fibre glass hull of the RNLI Carrick Maid hit another monstrous wave, sweeping it side-on back into the path of the descending propeller.

'Look out, she's coming down.' Pascoe didn't need to voice the obvious, as he braced himself against the seat's harness. In the gloom the crew caught a glimpse of the rudder flapping. The reason the coaster had put out a mayday call in the first place.

They weren't going to make it.

The leading edge of the first blade to hit them scythed into the side rail at the stern of the rescue craft. They felt a shudder and the tug of metal being ripped from decking as the rail wrapped itself around the propeller descending on them like a huge kitchen blender. The lifeboat pitched upwards and veered away from its nemesis, but stayed uncharacteristically bow high, with a distinct list to port. The upward bias wasn't normal, but the crew, conscious of the change, had more pressing responsibilities to contend with than any unease about the attitude of the boat. With the kind of instinct developed over years of navigating these coastal waters, they somehow felt the change wasn't threatening. Intuition took precedent over anxiety in a carefully selected and trained crew.

Trust in the coxswain had developed, along with respect, otherwise too many shouts would have ended in disaster. Their immediate concern was Dog Tooth Rock. Even in this heaving sea the boat had picked up speed in response to Bill's earlier hand on the throttle. The rock was visible in the spray-laden gloom, as the surge of wave breaking against its seaward face gave it a luminous, white apron of water. Thousands of tiny bubbles acted like a skirt of minute lenses, collecting and magnifying what little light penetrated the scene. Dog Tooth had claimed a number of hits over the centuries, but this time the granite hazard would not be shattering any hulls. The lee-shore was about a hundred metres or so from the duel being enacted between rescue boat and coaster and Dog Tooth was the only outcrop in the vicinity they needed to worry about.

Bill brought the craft around, this time alongside the starboard flank of the distressed vessel, at the same time keeping an eye on the demarcation between the cliff top profile and the only-just lighter backdrop of sky. Another huge wave lifted them above the decking of the coaster and deposited them obliquely across its gunnel. The boat teetered not knowing whether to slide forward onto the deck or slip back into the sea. The crew braced themselves for what seemed eternity as the rescue craft swayed and twisted on its keel. As coaster and boat together dropped into a huge trough, a peculiar lull in the motion left them in a kind of limbo. Bill had throttled down the racing screws as the rescue craft started to roll on the gunnel. He could see one of the coaster's seamen above them at the end of the side deck outside the bridge. A counter-wash from the port side of the coaster hit the bow of the little boat and flushed it back towards the sea. Its keel pointed up at forty-odd degrees. The boat's radio operator looked instinctively back through the rear door to the grey turbulence they were about to plunge back into.

'Bloody hell, we've got her screw embedded in our stern.'

'Hell, no wonder she's ridin' bow high,' the mechanic shouted above the screech of the keel as it scraped across the larger ship's edge. By this time they were about three metres above the water.

The force of re-entry could blast the rear door inwards and they knew it. The coaster rolled on its starboard side, putting the rescue craft nearly horizontal. By this time they were practically level with the sea as their hull disengaged totally and re-floated, a free agent. Heads and shoulders slumped in relief. Arrested breathing gave way to welcome volumes of fresh oxygen.

'That was a pretty close one, nearest we've been yet,' Dave Lobb swivelled in his seat as he voiced the thoughts of all of them.

'Look, I'm going to stand off for a spell,' Bill Hawken didn't need to agonise over the decision, it was an obvious choice to take.

'She's past the rock and without a prop this current and wind will take her out past Deedmans Head to open water. We can afford to wait a while for this sea to drop now, then move in to grab the crew. Any fault with that? Falmouth Coastguard report the wind should be easing up soon.'

The volunteers knew there was little chance of pulling any one off the ship the way things were going, added to which a repeat of the previous episode risked everybody's lives, on boat and ship. At least time was on their side. They still had more than three quarters of their four and a half thousand litres of fuel left and riding seventy or eighty metres back from the coaster posed no danger.

'I'll check out the stern damage, see if we're getting water into the refuge area,' Chris Pascoe called across to Hawken, 'that OK?'

'Go ahead. I'm reminding you to attach the safety cable, you need it this time, but check the refuge area first before going to the back. If the deck isn't punctured by the blade and below is not taking any water don't risk going out there for now. Otherwise, use some of that stop-foam stuff on the underside to seal any gap between blade and deck, if it's more serious.'

'OK Bill.'

Pascoe unbuckled his harness, removed his lifejacket and slipped out of the chair. He grabbed at a hand hold as the boat took another broadside. Waiting for the next fleeting lull in the motion of the boat, he made it to the refuge hatch and went down the short stairway to the lower reaches of the hull. Everything was securely anchored one way or another, but he gave little attention to equipment that he knew would remain held by ties tested by seas worse than this.

He took a torch from its cradle above one of the seats. Getting through the small doorway in the rear of the compartment was a bit of a challenge. The clumsy boots and immersion suit restricted movement, a lifejacket would have been an even greater hindrance, a life threatening danger if for some reason it became inflated below deck. Flashing the torch into a cavity just about big enough to take a couple of people, he could make out no penetration of the decking above, nor any water sloshing around his feet. Satisfied he turned and made his way back to the cockpit.

'No hole Cox and from what I can make out, without going there, the prop is locked fair and square into the rear railing. Parted from her shaft at the key way.'

'OK. We've had confirmation a tug is on its way from Falmouth. They've established salvage rights with the master. We're to stay in place and give whatever assistance we can when they get here. ETA twenty to twenty-five minutes. Tide's on the turn, so won't drift far. It'll be light in less than an hour.'

Chris Pascoe put on his lifejacket and buckled himself back in place as the crew settled into the more comfortable regime of a passive stand-off. Able to relax some, the crew speculated about the seaworthiness of the disabled vessel. About the issuing of forged Board of Trade certificates and the tragedies it caused when dodgy owners risked all for the sake of profit. This might not have been the case at this time. But the combination of a malfunctioning rudder and shaft sheared between bearing and prop, bore the classic signs of an unseaworthy ship falsely registered as seaworthy.

'I reckon the shaft must have been in advanced state of fatigue for it just to lose a prop like that. Seen it before in dry dock. Oxide inclusion in the shaft surface and the thing just goes from there. You can see it in the fracture. Surface smooth at the source of the break, series of crescent arcs as the break widens, then crystalline fracture when she finally goes,' Jean-Pierre Pascal spoke with no trace of the tone that irritates when someone is exercising superior knowledge, or trading in sophistry for the sake of impressing. He was just stating facts as he perceived them. His English was pretty nigh perfect. From a Breton village near Brest, he had married a girl he'd met as a boy when his parents regularly took part in twinning visits to their

6

host village. A graduate in ship design from the Ecole Nationale Supérieure, Brest, he'd managed to get work as a lecturer in the faculty of ship design, at the University of Falmouth and had proved himself a 'safe pair of hands' on a number of hairy call-outs.

Dave Lobb swivelled in his chair, 'The tug's just showing up, on and off the radar. Reckon it's about half a mile away.'

'OK. Tell him we've spotted him. We'll head round to the bow of the coaster. Radio its master. Ask if he's in contact with the tug and tell him his screw is embedded in our stern. Tell Falmouth Coastguard we're moving in again to check for any major superstructure damage. Might as well tell them, too, that we've got the coaster's screw stuck in our stern.'

Bill Hawken did a quick scan of the various functions on the screen and peered through the window into a slightly less mountainous sea. It was getting lighter. Wind was dropping. A good fifty metres from the ship's starboard side, he positioned the lifeboat mid-on at right angles. He could just make out the deck area as it tilted towards the boat. Repetitive wave sequences, like a pendulum with a period of about five seconds, gave him about a two-second window of inspection each time. There were no loose, rogue structures, that he could see, ready to release further complications into this particular version of hell. He reversed back a few metres, headed for the bow and traversed the port side. Satisfied there was nothing else worth noting he peered in the direction the tug should be arriving from and positioned the rescue craft well to the stern of the disabled vessel. Back to back and separated by a hundred metres of heaving water, he peered ahead, watching for the tug's lights, handing control to Andy Cornwell, the relief helmsman picked for this shout. It gave him a break and allowed him to focus better without the distraction of having continually to reposition the boat. Coming out of a trough he caught a glimpse of a light before the sixteen metre hull slid back down into the next gulley of water.

'Got her in view. Radio her. She probably picked us up on her radar near enough when we spotted her. Tell her we'll stand close until sea permits a crewman to catch a line from her. I reckon we're going to wait an hour before either ship will risk putting a man out on deck.'

'Right cox.' The crew then hunkered down, waiting for the seas to abate and for the welcome first light to bring some respite from the eye-straining darkness.

Some little while later a new voice roused the crew from whatever each was thinking. It was one of the Coastguard duty officers.

'Bill, what's the score? Culdrose are still on standby. Do you reckon you're going to need their Sea King?'

'Don't know. Way things are, we can afford to wait. Coaster's not shipping water, so no immediate danger and we're well clear of Dog Tooth Rock. Seas pretty bad still, but not like when we arrived. Tell 'em to hold.'

'OK. Keep us in the picture.'

Bill swivelled round in his chair. 'I reckon Robin,' he referred to the tug skipper, 'will give us a shout any time now, about going in. Light enough to see a line being tossed.' Sure enough, within the next few minutes the tug's master radioed the rescue craft.

'I'm going to risk tossing a 'streamer' to the ship. Same drill? The master speaks good English. Over.'

'Yep! I'll take up position at 2 o'clock off the Mixim's bow, ready for MOB. It's still pretty dodgy even though the big ones are abating. He's managing some semblance of navigation, without the rudder, using his side thrusters. I'll follow your moves. Over.'

The two smaller vessels took a little time to position themselves. Instructions proceeded between tug wheelhouse and coaster. A couple of seamen appeared on deck and picking what hand-holds offered greatest security, played a game of cat and mouse with the pitch and roll of the ship. Reaching the bow, they waited for the ball and line from the tug. Tug and coaster were lined up with wind direction as best as conditions allowed. One of Robin's crew was positioned astern, attached to a safety line, swinging the ball, ready to increase its momentum for a throw. An opportunity presented itself as coaster sank into a trough and tug rose, simultaneously, on a high swell. The ball arched well above spray and decks of both vessels, but a gust took it sideways back into the drink.

'That looks like Mick Treloar tossing the line. He's the only bugger with a swing strong enough to span the gap. Look, I'm going to pull in closer to the ship. Those two don't look happy up there. Radio Robin and the coaster. Tell 'em we're positioning off her port anchor. You still OK with the wheel Andy?' Bill swivelled in his chair and faced the crewman he'd handed control to earlier.

'Yep! All set.'

'Right. As soon as Dave gets acknowledgement, take her in.'

The replies came within seconds. Bill watched Andrew Cornwell and did a quick take on his stance and facial expression. Satisfied there was no hint of indecision, he focused on the bow and the two seamen fighting the lunge of the deck with each wave surge. They alternated handholds with whatever protruding piece of steel provided a grip. One of them wasn't quick enough transferring to a second grip. A pitch to starboard swung him back, loosening his one hold on a piece of piping. His back thumped into the casing of the hydraulic motor that operated the anchor winding gear. Winded, he let go of the piping. At the same time the bow dipped as a rogue wave swept across its deck. The rescue crew watched, knowing what was going to happen next. The stunned crew man was like a rag doll, limp, limbs uncoordinated. It was probably this which saved him from fracturing bones, since rigid resistance is the most likely cause of damage in a fall. But this did not save him from the cascade that washed him up over the ship's gunnel and down into the swirl below. Andy Cornwell didn't need direction from Bill Hawken. He accelerated into the gap between tug and coaster. Two crew members left the safety of the wheel house and shackled themselves, one to the port the other to the starboard exterior guide rails, ready to lunge forward for a grip on the ditched seaman.

A white face bobbed up and down in the water, a few metres off the hull of the coaster.

'I'm leaving this entirely up to you Andy. Don't hesitate to trust yourself.'

'OK Bill.' Andrew took the boat as close as he dared to the ships grey plates.

'Bloody hell, he's getting close to the side thruster.' Andrew voiced his comment at the same time swinging the dark blue hull of the Tamar through a ninety degree turn, heading between victim and impeller. Bill had already noticed the warning image of a thruster stencilled above the location of its duct. The two men out on deck had spotted it too and were prepared for Andy Cornwell's manoeuvre. They were now positioned down at the sunken level of the side decks ready to grab and haul.

'Hell, he's gone down again.' The white face, in spite of a buoyancy aid, had disappeared beneath the surface just as the Tamar's bow was within a couple of metres to the left of the dazed seaman.

'There can't be enough suction this far out from the hull to pull him into the mincer if it's on reverse thrust. He's gotta surface.' Andy was talking to himself half in hope and half to the rest of the mob in the wheelhouse. Bill stared through a cockpit window and did not reply. Anything could happen. The sea did not oblige the hopeful. But he was a pragmatist and believer in a man's survival instinct. Sure enough the seaman reappeared, but he was too close to the coaster's hull. If the lifeboat moved in he risked being crushed between the two craft. Mike Traherne was at the starboard side. The only course open was to toss a line to the now alert seaman. Mike could see the man was losing energy, partly through the cold and partly fighting to keep his head above the constant buffeting of the choppy sea. Like the tug line, the first attempt failed. Mike pulled in the rope and waited. The Tamar rose a metre or so above the trough in which the struggling seaman was treading water. This was the best chance for a second throw. Any longer and the victim risked being sucked below the waterline. The rope uncoiled through the spray and landed across one shoulder of its target. The seaman had enough energy to half loop it below one shoulder and arm pit. Mike tested the line. The man moved a few inches towards him, managing to signal with an arm up. That was enough for Mike. He hauled in the line, at speed, ready to slacken off if the need demanded. His quarry reached the blue hull, but was washed a metre or two towards the stern by a wave. The danger now was the starboard bilge keel forming the open propeller duct of the rescue craft. The risk was small, but nonetheless still a risk, that his foot could be pulled into the propeller. Andrew Cornwell needed to maintain a thrust of sorts and daren't throttle down too low. Mike Traherne hauled back on the line as the subsiding wave gave him some respite. He was a strong man, but his arms were beginning to tire from the effort of managing the rope.

The seaman got a surge of energy as he again neared the lowered gunnel of the boat. He kicked out and made a frantic single breast stroke towards the safety of the Tamar. Mike let go the line, took a firm hold of the nearest rail post and reached out over the water. His gloved hand managed to grip a strap of the floatation aid on the back of the gasping seaman. He pulled the man across the rim of the boat, his legs now almost clear of the water. This was the hardest part when the full weight was no longer assisted by the water's buoyancy. Mercifully, the boat rolled back down into another trough and the added buoyancy enabled Mike to slide the man wholly on to the side deck. He hurriedly tied a makeshift loop around the shoulders of the gasping seaman, then fixed the slack line more securely to the boat's superstructure. Mike then made ready to instruct his charge as soon as the man had got his wits back and he could check for body injury. His fellow crewman had by this time arrived to give assistance. Satisfied there were no fractures to main limbs, they managed to get him on his feet and took advantage of each counter-surge to bring him into the relative safety of the rear deck. Dick Trueman, an A&E doctor at the local hospital and also crew member, was waiting in the aft area ready to examine the exhausted seaman.

The three crewmen got him out of his storm gear, such as it was. The medic confirmed there were no breaks, but would need to check for internal damage. There was no blood being coughed up. That the seaman was gasping was an indication no ribs were broken. The pain from a broken rib-cage would have prevented normal lung function. After a series of what Dick termed 'field tests', he pronounced the rescued seaman fit enough for the journey back, without the need for an airlift to Truro hospital, by the standby Sea King.

Back on the coaster a third seaman was already in the bow ready to assist the remaining crewman to catch the tow. The thrower on the tug had by this time got the feel of wind gusts and the rhythm of the surges on the soles of his deck boots. He waited as coaster dipped and tug rose and released ball and leader in a smooth under-arm throw. The missile performed the classic trajectory of a parabola, arching above spray in a period of gust-free wind to land across the anchor winding capstan. The two on the coaster made a secure hitch of the trace on the safety rail surrounding the winder before hauling in the heavy tow rope from the tug. This they did at each fall of the bow, resting as the coaster tilted back up again. Apart from the possibility of a tow line parting, the next risk would be the tow post it was attached to. If it had been merely welded like a stub to the deck top plate, rather than a post sunk into the hull and securely fixed to the deck below, there was a danger the stub would be ripped from rusted, flimsy welds, or worse, pull the plate from the deck, leaving a gaping hole for water to flood into. Fortunately, apart from other glaring omissions in its architecture, a weak tow post was not part of the ship's structure. The tow cable was secured and both men retreated to the safety of the coaster's interior.

With sea conditions a picnic to the earlier sup with Satan, the trio set off to port. Bill Hawken put the rescue craft to the landside of tug and coaster. They made good passage. With a Sou'Westerly wind assisting them and waves no longer mountainous, the journey time back wasn't a lot longer than the outward pull, even with the dragging mass of the coaster. Bill Hawken and his mob accompanied the two vessels to the Fal estuary with no further scares and with task completed, headed into the calm of the marina to tie up and shed their gear in the warmth of the lifeboat station.

'I'll do a quick check of the mission data,' Bill addressed the crew, now freed from their survival kit, 'and write up a brief set of notes before going home. The rest of you – great effort! Thanks again. Get back to your families. See you here Friday.' Bill accessed the SIMS – Systems and Information Management System – to check that a full log of the mission had been automatically recorded. Handling the Tamar class boats was a much easier game than those he'd crewed in the past. The single system was clear in the way it presented information. Through an intuitive control-console design and boat systems management, it had done away with a multiplicity of separate stand-alone systems that made for a tiring and dangerous exchange of movement in the tight wheelhouse. He had known crew members to break an arm or suffer other injury whilst swapping operational roles in a pitching and rolling vessel. Satisfied that the information of the last few hours had been fully logged, he went to the small office overlooking the marina and called his wife. Pulling the office laptop out of hibernation mode, he accessed a template that allowed him to type in quickly, other details of the shout. A final 'Comments' section gave him cause for reflection. He wrote simply, 'We set out with two propellers and came back with three!'

2

Out of season The Chisel and Adze, the crew's local watering hole, was free from high-heeled, East-ender type women, with skirts too short for their age, sipping glasses of Chardonnay and loud-mouthed, shaven-headed, gold bracelet, tattooed cockneys bragging about their business intellects being – in so many words - superior to those of the locals. It was the favoured gathering place for any one and every one with an affection for harbour politics. The annual Sea Shanty Festival kicked off from there each year. Serious yachties drank there. The local sea fishing club met there. In short, it was a most satisfying hostelry in which to sink a pint. Three of the county's breweries were represented at the bar and the cider from a local orchard, exclusive to the pub, was said to be the best in the South West.

Friday night was the time when the crew would gather there, after the weekly meeting at the station, whether or not there had been a reason to celebrate a successful rescue. But if a rescue had taken place that week, celebrate they did. Bill Hawken drank lemonade, normally. If a Mayday was called he was totally alcohol-free and in a position to lead those volunteers who had stood down, giving the other crewmen an opportunity to enjoy a pint. Occasionally he would appoint a relief coxswain to stand by so that he could celebrate in full. Tonight was such a night. Always it would be a crew member who had done at least one shout, as cox, under his surveillance. Someone who, on a number of practise runs, had already undergone a successful coxswains assessment under the qualified eyes of two RNLI inspectors.

This Friday was a particularly jocular evening. News of the 'Kitchen-blender Coaster', as the propeller-embedding escapade had come to be named, had become global. A video of the propeller in its new setting, still wrapped in the lifeboat's rail, had already taken over twenty seven thousand hits on the station's web site. The popularity of the crew was never an issue and tonight's clientele were eager for first-hand accounts of the rescue. The warm, beery fug, with occasional whiffs of smoke from unseasoned logs of apple wood, sizzling on the open fire, encouraged the drinkers to delay going home. Chris Pascoe told and retold the story, until the account was beginning to take on the dimensions of a Norse Saga by the middle of the evening.

Bill sat looking at the flames licking the grey bark of one of the logs. His mind was replaying the actions and rehearsing alternative outcomes that, thankfully, did not come about earlier in the week. An image of the screw's blade impaled in the deck changed his train of thought. He wasn't sure how maritime law affected the salvage rights concerning the prop, but he was pretty sure a good price for it could be exacted from Lloyds. In theory, the RNLI couldn't claim, but the coaster would need a new screw and castings in naval bronze were expensive. He was pretty sure all that needed doing to the old screw was grinding out the slight dent in the leading edge of one blade and keying it back on to a new shaft. Lloyds insurance money would help cover the cost of repairing the lifeboat. But as far as he was concerned – whatever the big wigs at HQ, Poole decreed – the orphan prop was going to stay locked up in the lifeboat station and he would brazen out his case until they assented to the claim covering repairs to 'his' boat. And in any case, barring total condemnation to the scrap yard, it was pretty certain the coaster would be repaired in one of Falmouth's dry docks. Labour costs in Far Eastern yards might be cheaper, but materials were often of a lower specification than advisable, which might have been the cause of the debacle in this instance - a previous repair or refit with duff steel. The quality of machining and fitting was always a gamble. Semi-skilled workers could butcher a job to functioning perfection. The hidden flaws performed their task like a computer virus, programmed to cause maximum havoc well after the vessel had been delivered back to its owners, or sold on to an unsuspecting new owner. The sooner international maritime law tightened up the lower standards of inspection and certification of ships plying under flags of convenience, the less frequent would be occurrences like the latter. Still, that wasn't the RNLI's problem, except that they had to deal with the consequences when it landed up in British water.

'Another one, Bill?' Dave Lobb, appearing at the table, broke in on Bill's reverie.

'Just a half. Thanks Dave.'

Dave returned after a couple of minutes and put a fresh glass down on the table in front of the older man. The two raised their glasses without voicing a salutation.

'Somethin' troublin' you Dave? You a ... ', Bill searched for words, 'you've been a bit ... a ... a bit quiet the last few weeks. Anythin' wrong?'

Dave Lobb put his glass down. 'Well, yeah. Got a bit of a problem over the slipway where I bring my catch in. Bleddy owner of the holiday home overlooking the ramp is causing problems. He's complaining that the gulls frighten his dog when I'm unloadin' the lobsters.'

'Frighten his dog? What sorta bloody dog's he got? Never heard that one before. It's Cornwall, not the middle of the Sahara desert. These wealthy Londoners with their four-by-fours hogging the roads know what they're buying into when they come here. 'mazes me. They'll be complaining about the sand and seaweed next. Tell him to piss up his kilt.'

'Wish I could, but not as easy as that. The ramp belongs to the cottage and seems he can stop me. Threatens to make a legal issue of it and if he wins, I pay costs and whatever else is awarded. Found my pots tossed over the jetty edge one morning. That's what he's like. The guy's some sort of TV celebrity, all glitter and sequins.'

'Oh that one! I've heard about him. Uses the name Gary Gaylord doesn't he? Wasn't there some business over him and some young lad he raped? Kid committed suicide so the case never got resolved.'

'Yeah, that's the one. The guy has friends in high places who supported his denials. Evil lot of bastards.'

'Thing is, that jetty's the property of the Duchy, I'm pretty sure and for the use of fishermen storin' their gear. The boys won't take kindly to that kind of intimidation. There must be some way out of it.'

'Don't know what and I can't afford to take legal advice.'

Bill took a swig of ale, 'There was a similar issue with a fisherman at Port Goss, 'bout twelve years ago. Janner Truscott. Wasn't gulls, but some dispute about laying up his boat under the kitchen window of somebody's holiday home, down by the quay.

16

Area of bare ground used by fishermen ever since anyone can remember.'

'How'd he sort it?'

'Well, the bloody thing blew up into a full-blown war. This guy, the holiday bloke, got some of the other owners involved. They dragged the boat down to the water one night and set her adrift. There was some not too veiled bragging about it in the harbour pub, by the parties involved, but nobody could prove anything. Janner was lucky. The incoming tide beached the boat in a sandy cove just up from the harbour. One of the local kids out in the woods, above the cove, found it, recognised it and told Janner. He left it where it was for a few days. Got help to drag it up the beach first and tied it to an oak bough whilst he figured out what to do.'

'What'd he do?'

Bill chuckled. 'Trapped two or three cages of rats, for starters, over a period of days. Got them used to humans by feeding 'em daily, over a number of weeks. Then, one night, one weekend, he got a length of small-bore down-pipe and let half of 'em slide down it, one by one, through the letter flap. Must have been about twenty or so. He hung about for a while. There was a god-awful scream, apparently, from the bloke's wife. Rats running everywhere. One or two on to the bed. She felt movement on her chest. Thought it was the kitten they'd brought with them, switched on the bedside light, so it later transpired and was staring straight into the eyes of a rat on her pillow, standing on his hind legs twitching his nose at her, grooming his whiskers. Rodent catcher brought in. But a week or so later Janner let another cage-full in and – here's the cunning bit – let the population from two more cages into two of the other second-home owners the same night. Created the impression that the area was overrun with rats. Two of the properties were put up for sale that same week. Janner managed to get a mortgage and bought the first one using his own cottage as collateral. The irony is he advertises it as a holiday let.'

'Bears thinking about.'

'Some of the boys'll give support if you need 'em, pretty sure. I'll have a word with them if you like. That OK?'

'Well, fine, but don't want to cause any nuisance. They've got their own problems.'

'You know 'em well enough. They like a scrap when some bugger's tryin' it on, 'specially when it's a bloody emmet tryin' to throw his weight about. Anyway, stow it for now. Enjoy tonight. I'll give it some thought. We'll come up with somethin', sure to.'

'Thanks. It's been good to get it off m'chest.'

A few chords from a guitar warming up were a prelude to the opening bars of 'Wild Colonial Boy'. Five or six locals launched into a polished rendering of the song and followed it with a raft of sea shanties.

Time was signalled by a couple of pulls on the lanyard of a ship's bell, belonging to a naval ship long since decommissioned and cut up in some hell-hole of an Indian breaker's yard. The solitary drinkers – there were a few, surprisingly nearly always the first to go - downed their pints and filtered through the various small groups wrapping up whatever topic of conversation was being addressed at the time. Bill took his empty glass over to the bar and headed for the door, stopping briefly to greet the odd person here and there on his way out.

3

Over the next few weeks the sea gave everyone a quiet time. It was calm enough, even, for a few coastal fishing boats to venture out in the hope of catching a crate or two of turbot, a fish which commanded a high price in the market. Graham Hodge was one of these. His brother Tim occasionally doubled as navigator on the lifeboat and Graham, as soon as he was old enough, had started training to join him. A couple of years on a vocational course, in nautical studies, at Falmouth Marine School, gave him a deeper insight into the marine environment than his youthful games round the harbour, after school.

Graham's vessel was a fairly recent acquisition. He'd equipped it with expensive electronic aids, more than the norm for a shallow-sea fishing boat. As a consequence he was forced to take greater risks in order to pay off the bank loan financing its purchase. The bank manager had put him into the hands of a roving employee, based in Plymouth, who negotiated the maritime, commercial loans from the bank. An Indian with a glib tongue and annoying inflection of speech characteristic of those Indians who affect to sound sophisticated, those who try to be more 'Briddish' than the British. This particular employee paid monthly visits to the Cornish branch, supplementing it with extra calls to finalise loans as and when necessary. His name was Naht Patel. He had a M.Sc. in business studies, let everyone know it and was very conscious of what he thought was his superior status in the world of commerce. He was also avaricious and the bounds of his avarice extended beyond the reaches of Her Majesty's Revenue & Customs.

His manner varied, not surprisingly, according to the age and perceived social class of his clients. With Graham Hodge he adopted a superior, slightly officious tone. This did not go down well with the young fisherman, but he needed a loan. However, what surprised the latter was the ease with which he secured that loan. Patel even suggested the sum should be inflated by a further twelve and a half percent in order to cover installation of navigational and shoal detection equipment to a higher technical specification. The deal between bank and client being sold on the premise, again suggested by Patel, that more sophisticated equipment would lead to bigger catches and, therefore, bigger profits. The inexperienced young fisherman should have smelt a rat there and then. But lacking financial acumen and knowing little about the world of business plans, his signature committed him to a heavy dose of debt. He was taken in by Patel's spiel. No way was he going to be able to service the loan, even on peak catches. But Patel knew this right from the start. When Graham Hodge missed two consecutive monthly repayments Patel called a meeting.

'Right. So you are in difficulties? It looks as though the bank will have to foreclose, sell the boat and recoup its losses.'

'But it's my living.' Hodge countered. 'All my savings went into the deposit.'

'The bank is not a charity. You should have thought about that before you bought the boat.'

'Can't you hold off 'til next month? Weather should begin to improve and catches pretty well guaranteed.'

' 'fraid that's not possible. Terms of the loan.' Patel injected an abrupt tone of finality into the conversation, deliberately cranking up the level of dismay in his client. He enjoyed the power his authority gave to inflict terror on defaulting clients. Patel knew and Graham Hodge knew, that once his boat was seized no way could he save enough, for a long while, to put down on another. He would have to crew for a larger trawler at a lower level of income – that is, if he was lucky enough to find a boat needing another hand. Jobs were few and each year saw even fewer in that line of work.

'Must be something you can do,' a note of desperation crept into Graham's voice.

Patel leaned back on his chair, fixed a cold gaze on his client, then bent forward, palms together, resting his elbows over the open file on the desk. He brought his mouth into contact with the index fingers and focused on a point on the desk between the two of them, brow furrowed. It was a pose calculated to convey an impression of benevolent reflection. He let the cornered fisherman stew for a few seconds.

'There might be a possible way out,' he watched the defeat melt from his victim, 'but I will need time to look into it. I have a friend who might need some jobs done.'

'What sort of jobs?'

'Private transport. Non-taxable.'

'But I don't have a car.'

'Who said anything about a car?'

'You mean the boat?' The sickening realisation dawned in his mind. He'd been set up right from the start and could do nothing about it – for now. It was Hobson's choice and the choice was a poisonous one. Drugs or illegal immigrants, or both!

Patel said nothing, just smiled imperceptibly then stared expressionless at the reluctant conscript.

'I'll be in touch.'

Closing the thin file in front of him he got up from the desk, held the door and avoided any eye contact with his client as the latter left cheated and angry.

Back at his parent's home his anger calmed to a more rational level. Graham figured he was unlikely to be the only one caught by Patel. So instead of defeat, his mind began to focus on retaliation. Whilst he might be young he didn't lack spirit and the set-back acted as a goad, a lesson well received. There were people he could trust.

His girlfriend's father was based in the Maritime and Coastguard Agency. The office was adjacent to the lifeboat station and he knew all the staff. He had listened to many stories of joint operations with the UK Border Agency. Stories of illegal immigration and various modes of trafficking. An ever changing catalogue of cleverer, more ingenious ways of smuggling bodies and contraband in. But by far the commonest, most successful was the simplest – a fast boat being met mid channel by another under cover of darkness. His boat would be the stooge boat, the one running the greatest risk of interception. The cargo would be taken up the coast into the lower reaches of the river Tamar and offloaded onto a small quay in a quiet creek, somewhere, shielded by trees overhanging the water either side. Contraband or people, it was then a short journey in a lorry or 4 x 4 to the outer reaches of Plymouth. Immigrants weren't choosy about accommodation. A few hours in abandoned dockyard buildings, awaiting conversion, demolition or re-commissioning by the naval authorities, made ideal repositories for the once sea-sick chancers speculating on a future in England. Off-loaded that close to

Plymouth, it was easier to melt into the demimonde of exploited labour in a large city than to avoid the conspicuous existence of directionless wandering in a small seaside town.

Graham telephoned his girlfriend, Alex, a teacher in a local school. Although a graduate in mathematics and philosophy, unusually, she elected to teach in the primary sector rather than seek glory in the upper levels. On teaching practice she had discovered that younger pupils responded to puzzling challenges, particularly paradoxical puzzles. Not oppressed by a sterile educational regime, they developed sharper, lateral-thinking skills. The space between their ears was not yet a fixed map of categories, like the baggage of a book of Latin declensions with its redundant and often identical case endings. She recognised the stultifying effect that some educational practices had, turning young minds, effectively, into Bonzai trees with rigid constraints atrophying shape and form. It had been a revelation to her to discover that Newton, although he was expected to publish in Latin, actually recorded his thinking in English.

It was late afternoon and Alex had finished teaching. She checked the caller before answering.

'Hello!' The way she modulated her voice conveyed the pleasure she felt at hearing from him. 'This is a pleasant surprise. You don't normally ring this early.'

' 'wondered if you were free this evening. 'bit of an issue over the boat. The guy handling the bank end is a bent bugger. Don't want to talk on the phone.' Graham's use of the word didn't offend Alex. She had grown up used to the many contexts in which the Cornish displayed an almost fond affection for the many and versatile uses of the word. It reminded her of her grandfather who had coined the phrase, 'Bugger my old boots,' whenever he had felt the need to express surprise – real or feigned - in support of some raconteur's utterances. After her grandmother died, she would visit and do a bit of baking for him. Free run of his kitchen was a novelty. She enjoyed not having her mother looking over her shoulder tut-tutting about departures from her way of handling the mechanics of haute cuisine. He appreciated her visits. It was no surprise, then, that he left the harbour-side cottage to her in his will.

'Fine!' She paused, 'Bad?'

'Bad enough! Are you at home?'

'Yes.'

'OK. Shall I call about sevenish? 'bring a take away?'

'Come earlier if you like.' The inflection in Alex's voice summed up her pleasure at the expectation of more than just a social call.

'Six thirty, then.'

'OK. See you.'

4

The route to Alex's cottage was down a cobbled alley just wide enough, in the old days, to take a horse and cart laden with barrels of herring. The building had originally been a granite-built shed shared by a number of fishermen. It was used then to store any amount of chandlery and other gear. Crab and lobster pots, stinking barrels of rotting fish for crab and lobster bait, sails, oars, spars, rope, pulley blocks and all the other paraphernalia that go to service a fishing port. The rope, in those days, was hemp, rough to the touch. Some of it would be new. But piles of the stuff, too weak and rotted by sea water to take any load, would lie about waiting to be used with tar to re-caulk the hulls and decks of clinker-built boats. Nothing was thrown away merely because it had outlived its primary use.

A multi-paned bow window replaced the large double doors that once gave access to the shed from the slipway. The latter was still visible. The heavy granite blocks, from which it was constructed, were now coated with various marine algae and the odd colony of mussels. The slipway had been used to drag boats into the shed for essential winter maintenance. Fortunately, because the stones were too large and difficult to access, they had not been removed. They provided an interesting contrast to the granite building they complemented and a historical pointer to the shed's former life.

The interior had been partitioned and fitted out to make a comfortable, well-equipped dwelling. Somebody had welded an ancient, eight ounce cannon shot to an equally robust steel bar, fitted a hinge assembly and fixed it to the door. A bronze plate protected the oak panels from the hammer blows of the knocker. Graham had only given it a couple of bangs when Alex's distorted grin framed itself in the six-inch, bottle-end window set in the door. Sliding back a bolt and releasing the Yale catch she let him into the cottage. Three or four days of abstinence had given them both an appetite. Graham managed to drop the carrier bag with the takeaway onto the waist-high shelf in the alcove as Alex wrapped herself around him.

He barely had time to say, 'Bloody hell', before she had stifled any further utterance, smothering his lips with a full-on mouth to mouth, forcing her tongue into the warm, welcoming juice from his throat. Both his hands pushed her T-shirt up over her breasts as he disengaged from her mouth, lowered his head and ran his tongue upwards, below the breast and up across each nipple in turn. She straightened her body thrusting her cleavage into his face as he gently forced his knee between her legs. Letting go, he slipped out of his anorak and they both turned to the stairs. Half way up he slipped a hand up her skirt, along the calf of her leg, to the top of her inner thigh. She gave a shriek of surprise and pleasure.

By the time both were at the mezzanine floor, he had loosened his belt. Alex dropped backwards onto the foot of her bed, propping herself on both elbows, showing the outline of her parted knees below her skirt. She wriggled further up to lie back on the pillow as Graham, now only in his shirt, followed her onto the covering. Her T-shirt lay ruffled around her throat like a large choker, half across her right shoulder, with that arm through a sleeve, the other free. Passion changed, as if the bed had exerted some kind of influence on energy levels. The rush took on a more leisurely pace. Each became conscious of the comfort of soft bedding. Graham gently stimulated Alex until her body shuddered and he could no longer restrain himself. With one smooth movement he crossed her thigh and launched himself into the depths of blissful oblivion, thrusting a number of times in unison with her naturally timed rhythm until, with one great cataclysmic orgasm, they took in great lungfuls of air, simultaneously giving expression to their passion with words and groans of full, sexual gratification.

**

Alex had a couple of bottles of Tribute unopened on the table and place mats, serving spoons and cutlery set out ready for the takeaway. The contents, now only warm, were put into separate dishes and reheated. Graham opened a bottle and shared the contents. Both of them, unlike the common practice of their peer group, preferred glasses.

'So, what's the problem?'

'Patel wants to re-possess the boat. He damn-well knew, all along, I'd have a problem paying it off. But he's willing to 'adjust' the account if I use the boat for smuggling in drugs or immigrants.'

Alex paused from serving the rice, 'Tricky! Knowing you, I know the way your mind is going next. You're going to suggest we involve MCA and the Border Agency or Customs.'

'Well, what else is there? The police would be OK, but they would function at a narrower level and the Agency would be involved, I would guess, anyway. But it would all be a bit fragmented with too many loose ends. The Agency and Customs would engineer a different scenario with a wider net. Through them, I reckon, there might be a chance of some kind of reward for closing down a smuggling ring. Government has a scheme, I believe, whereby they give substantial pay-outs for that kind of information. I bet he's got other boats in tow, so t'speak.'

'You want to have a word with dad?'

'Well, what d'you think? I thought he'd know best.'

'If the guy's that much involved, he's not going to leave himself open for entrapment, and you'll probably have to put yourself at risk, one way or another. I've heard dad's friend in the Border Agency say these people are pretty ruthless. They cripple defectors. Your friend Patel will know this and won't run any risk to himself. Anyway, let's get on with this. You've got a bit of a breather. If he's made this overture, he's already made an assumption you're easy meat. We'll have a word with dad.'

The two made short work of the takeaway. Alex took the dishes to the sink.

'Like some fruit before coffee? I've got a ripe pineapple that needs carving up and trimming, unless you want the remains of a Camembert.'

Graham got up and joined Alex in the galley kitchen, 'Piece of cheese would suit me fine.'

'Get it out then. Bit of baguette in the cupboard. Don't bother with a plate for me, I've eaten enough.'

Graham opened the fridge door to look for the Camembert. He cut a small wedge, not bothering to find a plate and consumed the lot in two bites.

'Pig!' Alex grinned as she watched her boyfriend help himself to second slice. 'I'll ring dad now. Shall we ask him over?'

'Might be an idea. Better to be prepared before this guy contacts me again.'

'OK, hand me the phone.' Alex dialled.

'Hello! Dad? ... Graham's here. He's got a bit of a problem. Need to sort something out. Have you got a minute. ... No, can't really talk over the phone. OK, see you later.' She put the phone back in its cradle.

'He'll be here in five or ten minutes. He's just on his way out somewhere. I think he'll suggest having a word with Bob Treloar, Border Agency. You met him at our place last summer, at the barbeque.'

Graham nodded, 'I remember him, fairly thickset with mop of blond hair.'

'That's him. Wicked sense of humour. A bit wary of the danger of employing non-whites, other than for translation purposes. There've been a few problems with non-nationals turning a blind eye to passport irregularities with some of their compatriots. Although he keeps his nationalistic beliefs to himself. I'll get some coffee ready anyway. Dad'll drink a cup any time of day or night.' Alex fetched filter and ground coffee from a cupboard and charged her machine with water, ready to switch on. The two settled down on the Langham settee that faced out across the estuary. A two-masted Cornish lugger, anchored out in the middle, was catching the remains of the evening sun.

'Pretty sight. Never tire of looking at that boat. She's a picture when rigged up. Sam Markham takes her over to Brittany regularly and brings back wine, for his own consumption. Buys it from a negotiant who supplies one of the ferry operators. Gets a good deal.'

'I've wondered who she belongs to. He's the owner of the chandlery isn't he?'

'Yeah. Bit of a hobby, the chandlery, that is and the boat. Has mining interests ... 's where his money comes from. Couldn't live the way he does on the business from the chandlery. Was a director and shareholder, still is, of an Australian mining company, large outfit. Various other interests he's got a finger in too. I crewed for him

27

couple of years back, when he was let down last minute by a lad who broke his leg, just before a trip across to Roscoff. Donates quite a bit to the RNLI and knows most of the local crew. Tim knows him. Did some casual work restoring the inboard engine for him just after he bought the boat. Asked my brother if he knew anyone wanting a trip to Roscoff. That's how I know the boat.'

'Sounds a good man.'

'He is. Doesn't brook fools. But he's got a sense of humour. Some of the local business men don't take to him. Pretty outspoken at Chamber of Commerce meetings, apparently.'

'I'll switch on the coffee. Dad'll be here any time.'

The door knocker sounded just as she went to sit back down.

'Good timing,' she was addressing a tall man. Goff Jago was six feet two. Of a swarthy complexion, he betrayed the ancestry of Phoenician traders common to the shore millennia earlier. Traders who valued the pickings from the rich tin seams and in return brought spices and other coveted goods to barter. This was where Alex got her hazel-eyed, dark beauty from.

'Hello Graham, good to see you.' Goff held out his hand. He and Martha, his wife, had always liked their daughter's choice of boyfriend. Graham was by this time around the back of the three-seater and shook hands with the older man.

'Hello Goff, sorry to pull you away in between shifts.'

'That's OK, I'm on my way to a lodge committee meeting, so was going this way anyway.'

'Sit down you two, I'll bring the coffee in a jiff.'

'What's the problem?'

Graham briefly outlined the background to the story and the threat posed by Patel. Alex sat diagonally across from the two, having placed mugs half filled with black coffee on the low oak table in front of the settee. A small jug of milk allowed Goff to dilute the contents of his mug to that of a colour resembling milk chocolate.

'Hmmm! Bit of a bugger! You're right though. This is a job for the Border Agency and Customs. Should be able to work something out,' he took a mouthful of coffee, 'and the sooner we move, the better. Leave it with me. I'll be seeing Bob this evening, as a matter of fact. He was involved in a similar game last spring,

28

only it was a light aircraft using St Merryn airfield, rather than a marine smuggling setup. The RAF stopped using it in the mid-fifties and the airfield was sold off two or three years later.'

'Did they get them?'

'No. 'plane was flying in and out to no particular timetable of drops. The gang discovered they were under surveillance and stopped using the site. There was no evidence concrete enough to make arrests. The plane was sold on and that was the end of it. Bob Treloar will be glad to get his teeth into this one I'm pretty sure. Just leave it with me.'

'Again, sorry to drop this on you, but it's a relief just to unload it.'

'You're right to bring it up. We'll sort something.' Goff downed the rest of the coffee and sat forward on the edge of the settee.

'Tell Mum I'll be around tomorrow evening,' Alex got up as her father rose from his seat, 'and thanks Dad.' She gave him a peck on the cheek and followed him to the door.

'Well, that wasn't so bad. I knew he wouldn't be anti, you can relax now. Out of your hands in a sense, apart from the action, that is.'

' 'have to admit it's a load off my mind. Just a matter of waiting. Anyway, that's enough about my problems, how's your day been?'

'So, so. If you really want to know, the head's being a bit of a pain. Too full of education theory and low on leadership. Bragging, so I hear from outside sources, that in the first two years she's been in the county she's turned the school around. In fact what's happening is experienced teachers are so pissed off they're leaving and she's replacing them with misfits from some obscure supply agency she seems enamoured of. Thinks setting up 'after-school' clubs and the like makes up for not achieving academic targets. Parents are beginning to complain.'

'What's her name?'

'Robyn Brown.'

'Is she the one who looks like a bull dike?'

'Well, since you put it so delicately, yes I suppose she does.'

29

'Thought Cornwall had a 'closed county' policy of recruiting teachers.'

'No. That finished some time ago. Trouble is, governors are made up from good ladies of the parish, wives of JPs, National Trust types, you know the sort, with nothing much to do but be busybodies under some pompous, equally ineffective chairman. There are two or three who are worth their salt, but the majority get taken in by forceful candidates, like the head, who are good at self-promotion, but low on expertise.'

'Worth applying to another school? Deputy headship or something?'

'Haven't had enough experience. Three years in a first school isn't really long enough. But I'm getting so pissed off I'd almost consider a total change of career.'

'Like what?'

'Dunno really.'

'Not getting broody are you?'

'Hell, no. That's about the one thing I am pretty certain about. I like kids, as long as they behave properly and I don't have to bring them up. You know that. No! What I had in mind was the police force or – don't laugh – volunteer crew on the lifeboat, that would let me keep my job as a teacher.'

Graham looked at Alex and sat back against the settee, still facing her, 'You're serious aren't you?'

Alex nodded, 'Need to do something or I'll end up assaulting the head. Mary Kessel is talking of handing in her notice at the end of this term, that's just between you and me. She's being targeted by the head. Can't take any more of it. Probably one of the best teachers the school has ever had. Taught you didn't she?'

'Yes. Could explain anything. If you didn't get it one way she could spot the problem and sort it out a different way. But watch out, if anybody got caught causing a distraction she'd have them out in front the class and make them get down on their hands and knees and crawl back to their desk. You wouldn't think it would work, but for some reason even the most hardened misfits made sure they never repeated the mistake of upsetting her. Anyway, back to what you said, are you sure spewing your guts up, to rescue some Burke of a yachtsman, is going to calm your restless spirit?'

'Don't be crude. I've never been more serious. In fact I've been checking the internet and quite a few crews around the country have women.'

'Well, if you say so. Never considered it to be an exclusive club, so t'speak. Would be a first for Falmouth. Maybe that's the answer. Don't think the police force is quite your thing. Shift work would interfere too much with your other interests.'

'You, you mean?'

'Well, no, but since you say so, it would disrupt things a bit. No, I was thinking more of your History of Art classes and other hobbies you get enjoyment from.'

'That's alright then. All's forgiven. D'you want to stay the night?'

'Now that's a better career move. Count me a supporter and if you do get accepted for training by the RNLI you can fill in as an extra hand on my boat.'

'Cheeky sod. I'll expect man's wages and a share of the catch.'

5

Friday, three weeks later, saw the crew back in the boat house. Repairs carried out on the boat and a full sea trial completed. The practise had been a short two hour run giving one of the deputy coxswains a test in navigation using charts and compass and no electronic aids. Bill had taken them out into a fog and then switched off the system at the navigator's station. Handing control over to the temporary cox he gave him instructions to brief the navigator and sat back to observe, having retained full electronic control at his own station as a precaution. The exercise had gone well. Bill allowed his mind to drift over the conversation with Dave Lobb the previous week. There had been a series of confrontations over the years with second home owners. Livelihoods had been threatened. Nobody had yet been injured, but there was a growing mood of anger and inclination to react with something stronger than just words.

The lifeboat skipper knew there would be support for any kind of retaliation bar murder and serious injury. A plan of harassment in the form of failures in the services and frustrating malfunctions of other features in the property's systems was, in his mind, the best way to deal with the problem. If that failed, something more drastic could be considered. The easiest was blocking the sewage outlet so that the sludge backed up and overflowed into the shower tray. Fixing the electricity supply, midway through a dinner party, exasperated the most passive of owners, but then, the passive ones rarely caused problems. Dumping manure into swimming pools really stirred the shit, he smiled to himself as he connected metaphor with image.

Finishing a quick inspection of the crews' storm gear, now hanging in an orderly row on hangers, he turned to Dave Lobb, 'Still no let up with your dog owner?'

'Well, haven't been out, so the boat's been pulled up into the yard and causing no upset. But he won't let up. He's a nasty bugger. All smiles and smutty humour on television, but a vicious little shit underneath. Another bunch of pots has been chucked over the jetty. He seems to know which gear is mine. None of the others has been touched.'

' 'tell you what we could do. I've been thinking about it. There was a local farmer, one year, pissed off with a family continually leaving gates open and letting their dog worry his sheep. Spread a load of acidic pig slurry on the roof and windscreen of their BMW 4X4. Local police were contacted, but there was no way proof of origin could be connected with the farmer. He lifted a couple of buckets of sludge into the back of a pickup, from a local piggery and just dumped it on top. What sort of car has this bloke got?'

'White Ferrari. Soft top.'

'Just the bloody job. Tip a load of shit in when the hood's down. We'll teach the bugger. And if that doesn't work we'll start on the cottage. The local police aren't that enamoured of him, I gather, so I don't think there'll be any high priority given to investigating any complaint. Mike Traherne's father keeps pigs. Mike'll be glad to get a bucket or two. Pig slurry really cuts the cake, 'specially if it's got plenty of urine in with it. Smells to high heaven. Can't get rid of the smell, particularly if it soaks into the leather upholstery.' Bill laughed, 'We'll sort the bugger out. You goin' to The Chisel?'

'Yeah.'

'Right. I'll be along later. Need to sort out a few more things here first, but won't be that long.'

Dave Lobb zipped up his anorak and exited through the side door to the outer office and on into the street.

***

The crowd in The Chisel and Adze was quiet for a Friday, but sometimes it was like that. It wasn't a particularly small crowd, but occasionally the mix reflected a more cerebral bent, especially if the Café Scientifique bunch decided to meet there. They alternated between ale houses, cafés and local tapas bars for their meetings. Their membership comprised physicists, chemists, one or two geologists from the local geothermal project, a number of amateur scientists, the odd psychologist and a sprinkling of electronic, IT engineers and the like who worked in prosperous little start-up businesses on the local industrial estate. A few came along with their

33

partners just for an evening out, having no interest in any specific scientific discipline, but happy to listen to a range of discussion, scientific, political or philosophical.

One of the group was a GP, Norman Varcoe, who also doubled as a second relief medic for the lifeboat. It wasn't common for a doctor to be a crewman as well, that Falmouth sported two was doubly unusual. He greeted Dave Lobb as he came in. The GP had stitched up a nasty wound, in situ, during one particular rough sea rescue. Dave Lobb had gashed his cheek on a bracket, used to secure the lowered radio mast when the boat was docked. The fisherman expressed his gratitude by bringing Varcoe the occasional crab or lobster.

'Couldn't make it for the launch, managed to let Bill know before he left. Had an urgent home call to attend. How'd it go?'

'Hello Norman. Fine. Tim Hodge got the blind navigation shot. Had to bring us back on chart and compass. Did a good job. Bill superimposed his track on the screen. Hardly any deviation, apart from occasional zig-zag correction due to current drift.'

'Pretty good, considerin' the double hazard of fog an' darkness. What 'you havin' ?'

'Pint of Tinners'll go down well. Thanks.'

Norman Varcoe nodded to the barman who was already expecting an order and within earshot.

'Pint of Tinners it is.'

Dave lobb watched as the beer foamed its way up the side of the glass. He could never understand how the younger drinkers could stomach the fizzy lager that age group seemed to favour. Chemical crap that lacked body and character in his opinion. Sleeve filled, Norman retrieved his drink and the two moved to an unoccupied table away from the Sci group.

'Bill mentioned your problem over the slipway. I know the guy. Was called to his place one day and had to make an emergency call for an ambulance. Young lad OD'd, probably cocaine. Needed hospital treatment. Can talk about it because not mentioning any names. But that wasn't all. He was haemorrhaging from the rectum. Needed stitching up. There were about three or four other men lounging about the place looking pretty uncomfortable and one other young lad. Both boys must have been somewhere between fourteen and sixteen. Anyway, it had all the marks of a pretty sordid set-up.'

'Couldn't do anything about it I suppose?'

'No. The casualty didn't want to bring any kind of charge when approached later. Filed my notes, at the time and mentioned it, in passing, to the local DCI. Know him well. Calls me about the occasional assault victim down at the nick, or to take a blood sample from the odd drink driver. He'd like to see the bloke inside, doing a long stretch. That rape case that fell through, d'you remember? Made the police look incompetent. Wasn't on his patch. London, somewhere. But the CPS and police were hamstrung when the victim, under age kid, committed suicide and a watertight alibi from people in high places got our celebrity friend off the hook. If he's treated to some vigilante justice, I don't think the local police will galvanise themselves to catch the instigators. If anything, they'll tie him up in lengthy questioning on the pretence of doing a thorough job.'

'You reckon we could apply a bit of robust persuasion?'

'Well, if a few of the crew got together and wore balaclavas he'd have a problem identifying anyone. Also, he might not necessarily tie it down to his feud with you. In fact, he's more likely to believe it's a response to his other activities.'

'Yeah, that's a point.'

'I'm willing to give a hand. The sooner something's done the better, as far as I'm concerned. Could tranquilise him, but keep him aware of what's happening. Shove a Burgundy bottle with a broken neck up his ass and leave him to come to in a public lavatory somewhere.'

'God, you're a sadistic bugger.'

'Poetic justice! Look, you don't know the half. People like him don't just satisfy their deviant sexual urges, they engage in sadistic, group sexual orgies, torturing vulnerable kids unable to fight back. Talking about torture, if you really want to know what the world's like, when I was doing a short service commission with a team of medics in Kuwait, time of the Iraqi invasion, I saw some pretty brutal behaviour. Was with a patrol in the early part, when we were flushing out squads of advance commando units. We got scent of some activity in what seemed to be a non-combatant area of one of the more opulent suburbs. Rounded a corner and came across a couple of Iraqi jeeps. Keys still in 'em. They were outside a house with a short drive in a gated compound, much like any of the other neighbouring properties.

Gate was wide open. Crept up to the door of the house – again, wide open. We could hear screaming, a man. Went round to a side window and saw half a dozen men in combat clothing, two of them dealing with the owner, one forcing his head up to watch a woman being tied to a sun lounger dragged in from a terrace outside. The bloke only had a vest on and was bleeding down the legs. He was tied by the wrists to a banister, with his arms stretched up in the form of a Y. His legs were forced apart and separated by a curtain rod, with ankles secured each end so he couldn't kick or move. They had slit open his scrotum and exposed his balls. Hadn't actually castrated him at that point, but I reckon that was the next stage of their enjoyment. The second of the two was crouched down and in the process of sliding a thin-bladed knife up inside the outer skin of the bloke's penis.

The captain in charge of us, had put two men at each of three different exits. He and two others were at the window. A second pair were with a jeep. As soon as they heard stun grenades go off they were to drive one jeep up to the door and block it. As soon as the captain smashed the window, with his rifle butt, the two of us with him were ready to toss in a grenade each. One would have been enough, but we had to take no chances with a miss-fire. The rest of our mob were to go in and execute the six Iraqis. No prisoners! It was a bloody massacre. The woman had fainted by this time and her husband reduced to a gibbering wreck. None of our mob got hurt. The bloke was lucky. I stitched him up and gave him some morphine. He would recover, but no sex for a couple of months I reckon. So you can see, the bottle treatment for our paedophile friend would be punishment to fit a crime he thought he'd got away with and no remorse on my part.'

Dave Lobb pursed his lips, but feeling encouraged by the support, felt a weight slip from his mind. At that moment Bill

Hawken came through the door. He nodded to the two and joined them with a lemonade.

'We've been talking about the aggro over Dave's lobster pots.'

Bill took a swig and nodded in a summative kind of way, 'Bastard needs dealin' with.'

'Yeah. Can't we sort it next time he's down? Us three and one more should be able to handle him. What d'you say?' Varcoe fixed the other two with a stare, swinging around as he did so to give added emphasis to his suggestion.

'Depends on whether he's got any of his gay cronies with him,' Bill countered.

'Who'd you think we should ask?' Dave looked at the other two.

'Chris Pascoe. He's pretty hefty, could almost handle him on his own.'

'That's what I was thinking. Got a pair of hands on him like a gorilla. Talk of the devil ... .' Bill nodded towards the door. Their fellow crew mate blocked the entrance like a piece of granite outcrop. The three at the table rearranged their chairs to make space for the boat's mechanic. Pascoe ordered a drink, passed a few pleasantries with the barman and then made his way to the trio. Wasting no time they drew their bear of a crew member into the subject of their discussion. Having played rugby for Cornwall and knowing something of the lifestyle of their intended victim, he warmed to the prospect of a scrap.

'Look, I know we could be had for queer-bashin' if we're caught, but I've had just about enough of homosexual humour bein' rammed down my throat by some of these buggers.'

Doc Varcoe laughed at the unintended pun.

Chris Pascoe continued, 'Camp television comedians and the like pushing their anal innuendo at us. I know I like a good joke that's near the bone sometimes, but I'm sick of the bloody mob of perverts that get paid from our license fees.'

'So, how serious do we get about sorting the sod out?' Bill waited.

'I'm in favour of not just tinkerin' with the property, but roughing the swine up so he's in no doubt about shiftin' from the

37

County and I don't just mean a few bruises,' Varcoe made his point again.

'OK! I reckon tie his ankles, gag him and dangle him over the quay with his head in the water. Lift him up and down a few times, give him a bit of time to think whilst we pause between duckings. Terrorise the bastard. Then we drag him up the barnacles against the wall. Have to rope his arms together. I tell you what, we could hang him from the crane the yachties use.' Pascoe leant back and waited for comment.

'Should be easy enough. He's only a stone's throw from the quay. Nobody's about much after tennish, so we can slide the bastard out through the lower garden gate right by the crane. There's a stack of pots and other gear that'll block anybody seeing us from the land side. If we strap him to a plank first that'll stop him thrashing about and attracting attention. Easier to handle too.' Dave Lobb could visualise the whole scene.

'OK, next time he's down we'll catch him. Just need to keep an eye out for the Ferrari. Somebody's sure to notice when he's about again.'

Each one in the party could sense the collective feeling of unspoken agreement. The remainder of the session was spent in general conversation of harbour politics.

6

Graham picked up the phone, 'Graham Hodge here. Hello! Ah, Mr Treloar. Yes, was expecting a call, but surprised it's so soon ... ,' Graham listened, '... fine, I understand ... nobody other than Alex and her father know. Haven't told my parents. ... down at the MCA office ... yeah, I know it, next to the lifeboat house. Thanks for calling. I'll be there sharp.'

Two days later Graham let himself through the office door. He recognised Bob Treloar immediately, standing talking to three other men in navy blue sweaters and navy, uniform trousers.

'Come on in.' The young fisherman stepped into an inner office containing a couple of desks. Each desk held a screen live with shipping movements superimposed on satellite maps.

'These are two colleagues from The Border Agency, Phil Eltons and Mike Grenville and Jim Smith from Customs.' Bob introduced the three men. The atmosphere was friendly, but there was an air of expediency about the gathering communicated by the business-like way the two Border Agency men launched themselves off the desks they had been sitting on, as if they already knew what Bob was going to say next.

'Help yourself to a mug. We'll go into the briefing room. More comfortable.'

Graham pulled a mug from the shelf indicated by Bob Treloar and filled it half full from the glass flask sitting on a hot plate. A splash of milk toned down the strength of what looked like used-car sump oil. The aroma left no doubt the brew came from a high roast bean. He took a sip and appreciated the gratifying effect the brew had on his taste buds before following the others into the windowless briefing room. Windowless, that is, except for a metre-square Velux window of the type let into garret roofs.

The four of them settled at a table large enough to seat a dozen comfortably. Mike Grenville opened the session.

'Bob's told me about your problem. First, let me say that you are bound by the Official Secrecy Act, as some of our surveillance techniques are not public knowledge. Secondly, you will be in some danger. I am obliged to tell you that, but we haven't lost anyone yet and we're well practised in this kind of surveillance and arrest scenario. That's the formal bit over. Welcome to the team.'

Graham nodded, 'I'm ready for whatever you suggest.'

'OK then! First up, do you have anyone with you on your fishing trips?'

'Most times. My brother Tim, if he's got a day free will come out with me. Also one of my old school mates, if I go out on a Saturday or Sunday.'

'Does Patel know?'

'Only that occasionally I have casual help and no full-timer. He doesn't know who.'

'Good! We can try to put one of our men on if you gain their confidence after a few trips. You'll have to suggest it and imply the helper isn't averse to a bit of illegal trading. In the meantime you can be pretty sure he'll place one of the lower gang members with you to start with. If it's trafficking, it's pretty sure to be someone who speaks the language of the mob you'll be picking up. Although, more than likely, it'll be English. If it's drugs, then they'll just rely on you. We want to permit enough transfers in the hope that eventually we get a lead to the top. Does Patel know you have a girlfriend?'

'Not as far as I know. Don't ever remember mentioning Alex to him. Why?'

'Could be used as a threat. Insurance against you suddenly turning.'

'So how'd you actually catch them? I mean physically get your hands on them. If the transfer people have high speed launches and you've lost them in the past how d'you expect to intercept them?'

'That's the uncertain bit. As soon as there's a chase they're on their mobiles and relaying our moves. But we've a new tactic that's worked in practice. Two of our boats - they look like trawlers - span the stretch of water either side of the transfer location. In fact they send out AIS signals showing a false fishing identification registered to a local harbour. Our fast interceptor goes in. If the delivery launch makes a run for it, it'll go for the gap between our trawlers. That's the theory. Then we catch 'em, literally.'

'How'd you mean?'

'Simple. We have a submerged cable rigged between the two boats. Then all we do is sail on courses near enough a hundred and eighty degrees to each other. The cable lifts from the water and a heavy duty mesh suspended from it traps the getaway launch. It's worked well in trials.'

Graham nodded, 'Any firearms involved?'

'Our mob, yes. Mainly small arms. You? No, but it might be a good idea if you can have a distress flare handy, or better still a Very pistol. We can provide them. What we'll do is make the whole operation look like a chance encounter. You'll be arrested to give your cover authenticity. The transfer crowd will be tried in separate court appearances, Patel on a day different from the others and on a day different to your hearing, which in your case will not actually occur. That's to minimise still further any suspicion of collusion on your part. The circumstances of your involvement will only feature in a normal, but confidential, internal report of the action. No details of your arrest will be logged in any criminal data records. You will just be referred to as Trelawney. Patel will be deported to serve a sentence in an Indian prison. But this is way in the future. Pure speculation. It'll take a number of trips to gain intel on the hierarchy, but if after, say, three trips we're no wiser, then we take 'em on the next one.'

'What about my boat?'

'Initially she'll be confiscated along with the getaway launch. The latter will be sold, that's if it doesn't sink, to help clear the bank debt on yours and together with the reward money you'll come out of it the owner of a fully paid off fishing vessel. Maybe some cash in hand. OK?'

'More than OK. It would have taken me some time to clear the debt on her.'

'Well, that's about it. Any other questions?'

'None that I can think of.'

'You can always contact here if anything comes to mind. Best to be cryptic about it. Say you want to speak to Bob Treloar and give your name as Trelawney. We'll want to have a look at your boat. Maybe early one morning. Never know who might be keeping an eye on you. Although, pretty unlikely. I guess Patel will be nearest and he'll be controlled from the Midlands, I should think, or the Continent.'

'Next week will suit me. Weather forecast rules out fishing then. That too short notice?'

'Should be alright. I'd like to get one of the armed team to look her over with me. Take some photographs of deck, hold, bow and stern, etc. and note your navigation and comms system. In fact, Mike, you'll be about then. That suit you?'

'Could fit it in. We're doing some snap checks on a few of the larger cabin cruisers, some yachts and some of the small trawlers. Whatever's about in the marina.'

'Thursday's probably best for me,' Graham offered, 'should be dry. Sea still too rough outside the estuary, though, for fishing.'

'OK, that settles it. We'll get in touch closer to the time. Pete, d'you think Graham should have some training of any kind?'

'Might be a good idea. Would also suggest we equip him with a flotation aid with a concealed microphone. Won't function if he's in the sea, of course, but moving about the deck during transfer we might pick up tactical info.'

'Can the two of you liaise on that?'

'Both looked at each other and nodded mutual assent.'

'Oh, just one other thing, take note of any calls that are made from your boat. We might need to fake some messages at some point. OK? Right let's call it a day.'

7

Alex woke feeling troubled. Today was likely to bring a showdown. Monday's staff meetings always kicked off with a diatribe from the head. Today's meeting would be more vitriolic than usual after the announcement made on Friday that she was bringing in a Year Level Coordinator to displace Mary Kessel. Sprung totally out of the blue, in a special meeting called at the end of the day's lessons, it left everyone gobsmacked. The departure of one member on maternity leave, at the finish of that week, had given her the opportunity to appoint the niece of a friend. The meeting was conducted with a clear order not to interrupt and that no discussion would be tolerated concerning the appointment.

Arriving at school early, Alex knew there would be a knot of Mary's friends chewing over the recent fiasco generated by their beloved leader.

'Good morning,' the greeting, with a hint of cynicism, came from Sylvia James, one of the few colleagues reckless enough to challenge the head over policy.

'Good morning.' Alex nodded to the group looking up at her from their seats around the low table.

'Looks like you've debated the latest. Any suggestions, apart from strangulation?'

'Plenty. There's enough support for a signed protest to the education authorities, with copy to the governors.'

Alex nodded, 'I'll support that. Things are beginning to slide. Bumped into Lucy Phillip's mother in town on Saturday. She's concerned about Lucy struggling with her maths under the latest 'star' appointed by the head. Says she's having to explain even straightforward stuff of a standard that Lucy would have sailed through a year ago.'

'Seems to be an epidemic,' another of the group observed, 'had a phone call from the mother of one of mine, too. Never been contacted at home, ever. Same sort of anxiety. What did you say?'

'Not a lot. Just was careful not to give any cause for a 'Defamation of Character' claim. But I did say there had been other complaints. Suggested she write to the head. "Already done that" she told me.'

'You must have asked her what the response was,' one of the others queried.

'Yes. The head told her the girl was inattentive in lessons.'

'What? How can she say that? I know the girl. One of the quietest and eager to please I've ever had in a class.'

'I think the best thing is to contact those parents,' Alex suggested, 'and get them to enlist the support of other parents. There'll be others. Suggest they write to the governors with a copy to the local education authority. We can match it with one airing our own disquiet. Something's not ringing true over the way these recent staff have been appointed. The deputy head has never been asked to sit in on any interview. Not even been any observation of teaching skills offered by these new ones.'

'I agree. Never been in a school where so many staff have left over so short a period, nor seen such offhanded treatment of good teachers and I've taught under a number of heads in my time.'

'OK,' Alex scanned the faces of her colleagues, 'shall I contact Mrs Phillips and ask her to speak to those parents she knows are concerned and tell her we will give support? Give me the name of the parent who rang you and I'll pass it on to give her some confidence, as a starter.'

'That's about the best course of action, but tell her to keep it under her hat about our separate action. Don't want madam to be forewarned and prepared.'

The arrival of another staff member signalled the end of the discussion. Chairs were rearranged to face a long table. Alex sat by a young female teacher who had been appointed in the same term as she had been. Janet Capstick was slightly built, with an elfin-like face to match an elfin-like figure. The two had got on well from the start. Janet lent towards her colleague, 'I've got a bit of a problem. Need to talk to you, in confidence. About work.' The pitch of her voice indicated the matter carried some urgency. 'Been preoccupied all weekend with it.'

Alex thought for barely a second and turned to face her, 'OK, what about after school, today. We could go to Provedore for a coffee. D'you know it?'

'Yes. Often go there for a hot chocolate and churros early on a Saturday. They put on tapas evenings towards the end of the week as well. Love the atmosphere there. 'bout the best place around for an espresso I know of, too.'

The conversation was cut short as the head marched in, followed by the deputy and a new face. All three sat down, separated from the staff by the long table. Placing her iPad with its gaudy cover on the table, Robyn Brown peered over the top of an equally gaudy pair of frames. She stared around the room, mentally registering any absentees, then turned towards the new face and back to the staff, 'I want you to welcome the new Year Level Coordinator, Marlene Mugford.'

No "Good morning", no "I hope you all had a pleasant weekend", just wham, bang, "this is what you're getting." Nobody moved. Any staff she had appointed and who might have entertained any loyalty towards her, could sense the hostility emanating from the rest and sat staring ahead, faces expressionless. The freeze was broken as Sylvia James lent forward, chin up from her chest, palms on her legs, fingers pointing in and elbows pointing outwards in a hostile pose, 'What about Mary Kessel's position and the effort she puts into making our work seamless?'

The head stared icily at her challenger, 'That may be your opinion, but I have different measures of competence by which I judge performance.'

'Such as?' Sylvia wasn't going to let this one go. 'From what I hear this appointment smacks of cronyism and a number of us are concerned that educational standards in the school are suffering as a result of your decisions, since you took over. As a representative of the ATL I have to say professionally and as a teacher concerned not only with the wellbeing of the members, that I also have an ethical responsibility towards the children's educational wellbeing. In fact I would go so far as to say that is an even more important responsibility than protecting the interests of the staff.'

The head, by this time, was beginning to realise there was more than just resentment in the air. Issues of protocol were being raised that rested uneasily in her limited brain. She was not as sharp as Sylvia, but stupid enough not to know it. Cunning? Yes, in a self-interested way that was totally blind to the consequences of her actions, but not sharp.

'I stand by my decision based on Miss Mugford's references and will tolerate no further discussion of the matter.'

'Excuse me? I thought Cornwall Education Committee's guide lines were that in no circumstances no appointments should be made without candidates being observed giving at least one lesson delivery. You are in breach of that directive.'

Obviously thrown by this accusation, Brown picked up her tablet and faced her deputy, 'See that Miss Mugford is taken to her new class. Then see me in my study.' Without further comment she pushed her chair back and swept out of the room. The staff held by the tension generated by the stand-off between Brown and Sylvia James, seemed to recover the mechanics of breathing simultaneously. There was a positive atmosphere of triumph as people looked at each other and erupted in a chorus of nervous laughter. A number of staff got up and went to congratulate Sylvia. Alex smiled across at her and nodded meaningfully.

**

Provedore was quiet. Students and lecturers from the Falmouth College of Art, frequently to be seen there, had not finished the afternoon session. One table was occupied by a serious looking man, with the air of an intellectual. Studying the screen of a thin laptop, he tapped in a few words every few seconds, checking the result occasionally before continuing. Alex and Janet made their way to the table in the far end of the cafe, away from the door. A postgraduate student, Alex recognised from previous visits, was serving behind the short counter. She remembered Alex.

'Hi! What would you like?'

'I'm having a cappuccino, can you put an extra shot in? Janet, what will you have? My treat.'

'I was going to have tea, but I think a dose of caffeine, the same as you, would suit me fine. Thank you.'

'So, not happy with work?'

'No. Bit of an awkward problem. The head has been making advances and I'm not sure what to do about it.'

'What?' Alex's voice registered shock at this disgusting revelation. 'That's not on. Have you told anyone else?'

'No, but the girl I share a flat with knows about it. It's got pretty bad. She turned up one evening late, drunk and demanded to be let in. Kept hammering on the door. She only went when my flat mate threatened to call the police.'

'God, that's awful.'

'Yes, she's made it clear I'll get a bad reference if I try to leave.'

'OK! Has she conveyed her intentions on paper, or through emails?'

'Well, she has sent me a birthday card with rather suggestive Lesbian content on the front. Also emails.'

'Have you kept any of them?'

'Yes, all of them and printed them. Since that phone hacking business with the newspapers and the incriminating issue of emails that were flying about, I realised it was important to save them.'

'Good. This is a matter for Sylvia. Are you in the ATL?'

'Yes. One of the first things I did when I finished training.'

Alex took a sip of coffee, 'How suggestive are the emails?'

'One of them is inviting me to a hotel for a weekend. There is another where she says she would like to – God, it's so embarrassing.'

'No, don't worry, I think you know you can trust me.'

'Yes I know that. I wouldn't have told you in the first place if I didn't think so.'

'What sort of reply did you give to her emails? I'm thinking ahead, because this is going to become a legal battle if the ATL takes it on. Neither of us are lawyers, but it doesn't take much to see her defence would seize on any hint that you might have given her encouragement.'

'No problem. I passed them off with some excuse that I wasn't interested – not in so many words, of course – or was otherwise engaged.'

47

'I think it'll pan out OK then. What with all the other issues boiling up, it should be possible to warn her off. In fact I think it'll all end with her dismissal on at least two counts, professional malpractice and, in your case, sexual harassment. Look, Sylvia's pretty approachable. I think the best bet is to discuss it with her. Tell her you've talked to me about it. If you want me to sit in on it I will.'

Janet sagged back against the bench, her face relaxed for the first time in several weeks, 'I'm grateful for you listening. Great load off my mind. I'll tell her tomorrow.'

'Well, I'm glad you felt able to confide in me. Look, we can do this again. Meet here for coffee from time to time. It's a really relaxing place. You don't mention a boyfriend, nobody in the wings?'

'No. Did have one, lasted a while, but petered out because he moved abroad with his job. Although there is a guy who windsurfs with the group I've just joined. He seems to be paying more attention than would pass for casual on the two occasions we've been surfing. Quite like him.'

'The reason I ask is because I was going to suggest the four of us, my boyfriend and yours – if you had one - could go for a drink one evening. So many good pubs around.'

'Well, that sounds great. I'd like that. Let's see how the surfer plays his cards,' said Janet with a laugh.

The two, enjoying the friendly atmosphere of the place, sat and chatted for another quarter of an hour. But for each with a pile of school work to be marked and lessons to be prepared for the following day, meant leisure had to be rationed.

'Thank you,' Alex greeted the girl serving behind the counter as she placed her empty cup on the bar and opened her purse ready to pay.

That done, both friends filed through the narrow corridor between bar and tables. Outside Janet, again, thanked her colleague and each set off for home.

8

'Is that Dr Varcoe? ... Hi Norman, Dave Lobb here. That bloke is back, the celebrity, the one who's been causing trouble on the jetty. I've just heard from Chris Pascoe. A bit short notice, but are you available tonight? Still up for giving him the treatment? ... Good! Tim Hodge is in on it too, says he's ready to have a go at him. Bill's otherwise engaged, that's why Tim's with us. ... Well, Chris thought ten thirtyish. Its mid-week and pretty quiet, not normally anybody about anywhere near the quay that time of night. OK! ... Yeah, we've all got balaclavas and decided boiler suits the best thing to wear. ... I've got a spare suit. I'll drop it off at surgery. Fine! We're meeting at ten forty five at the back of the old chain locker. ... Look forward to seeing you.'

Dave put the phone down, went out to his garage and sorted out some rope and a roll of industrial adhesive tape. Putting them in an old canvas hold-all he added a sheathed filleting knife and a hessian sack of the kind used for holding mussels. Just the right width and length to fit snugly over a head without causing suffocation.

***

Sometime later, he greeted the other three. Doc Varcoe briefed them on a few matters he considered warranted attention and handed each of them a pair of surgical gloves. His army training gave him a perspective the others lacked, but he shared his knowledge without any air of superiority. They trickled off singly. Any recognition of one of them, should there be complications, would then be unconnected with a group of four.

They entered through the gate which accessed the quay and slipway. This would be their exit point with the victim. Dave Lobb handed the hold-all to Tim and fixed the gate open with one of a large number of pebbles previous owners had collected from the beach and left in a pile in the garden. Going to a heap of lobster pots, stacked against the harbour wall, he retrieved a driftwood plank he'd hidden there some days ago. He propped it against the pile of pots and then crossed to the small gantry crane used by the fishermen to haul stuff into or from their boats. The hook was still at the same level he'd set it earlier, seven or eight feet above the cobbled quay. A flight of granite steps, adjacent to the drop of the crane, provided additional means of controlling any cargo being offloaded.

The storm wall shielding the cottage garden provided ideal cover and various lights around the harbour gave more than enough illumination to avoid obstacles. They weren't worried about the dog. It was an accessory animal of a kind favoured by the camp fraternity, too small to be a menace. The living room curtains were open and Gaylord was slumped across a settee watching television. Chris Pascoe put his hand on the lever of the back door and tried it.

'It's unlocked.'

'Right, let's get him. Balaclavas on!'

They moved through the door into the kitchen and living room beyond. Four men bursting in on an unsuspecting resident is startling enough, but with features obscured by sinister looking headgear, the effect was magnified. Gaylord did not even leap up. His face registered the horror and fear of unknown treatment he knew must be intended for him, otherwise why the masks? He instinctively backed himself up into the corner of the settee. None of the four uttered a word, as agreed. Chris Pascoe went around the back of the furniture and put an arm lock round the cowering victim's neck. He dragged him up over the back and laid him along the edge as Norman Varcoe grabbed his legs. Dave Lobb pulled the tape out of the hold-all and quickly wrapped a length around the legs of the struggling man. He felt about for the filleting knife and removed it slowly and threateningly from its sheath, meeting the gaze of the threshing victim as he did so. Not knowing the filleting knife was merely going to be used to cut the tape, Gaylord fainted. The dog, by this time, had appeared from a bedroom and was adding to the bedlam. Tim Hodge supported the limp body in an upright position, against the back of the settee, whilst the man's arms were pinioned to his sides and tape wrapped round his body from wrists to armpits. Doc Varcoe put the mussel sack over Gaylord's head and Dave Lobb secured it with a couple of coils of tape around the neck. By this time he had come to.

Knowing the mussel sack would muffle his voice, Chris Pascoe grabbed the man's throat, 'If you don't stop struggling we'll cut your balls off. Stand up straight, can you hear me? Nod you bastard.'

Gaylord nodded vigorously. Dave Lobb fetched the plank in.

'Put it against his front,' Doc Varcoe issued the instruction quietly.

Dave laid it up against the front of their now subdued quarry. Tom held it in place whilst Dave pulled the rope from the bag. At the same time Doc Varcoe noticed a smart phone on the coffee table in front of the settee. It was switched on ready to receive. He picked it up. Flicking through the library of photographs stored in its memory, he gave a grunt of satisfaction.

'I thought as much.' The others looked at him.

'Typical of his kind, pornographic stuff of kids and young adults in various stages of sexual abuse. We'll hang on to this for insurance. There'll be a few names and addresses, I bet, the police could be interested in. D'you hear that, you miserable little toad?' He put the phone in his pocket.

It took them about a couple of minutes to tie their victim to the plank, lashing him securely round the chest and ankles. He started to whimper and sob.

'Shut up you snivelling little shit.' Norman slapped the bagged head in front of him first with the back of his hand and then the palm.

'Now you're going to get a taste of your own depraved, self-indulgence. We're enjoying it as much as you and your perverted friends do with your under-age victims. Except you and your friends think you're immune from retaliation. But think on.' Another slap. 'And don't think you're safe in London. We've got contacts who know how to get to you. We're part of a newly-formed organisation dedicated to sorting out scum like you.' This latter, of course, wasn't true, but the idea came as a sudden flash of fiction, that suggested itself as a further means of intimidating its listener.

'Right, pull his jeans down.'

Dave Lobb looked at Doc Varcoe, 'What're you going to do?'

The doctor did not answer, but walked over to a jar of kitchen implements and selected a wooden spoon. Pulling a loosely fitting cork from a half finished bottle of wine standing next to it, he walked back to their captive, trussed like a piece of game to a carrying pole. Bending down, in one swift movement he stuffed the cork between the man's buttocks and rammed it home with the handle of the wooden spoon, right up to the full length of the shaft. Gaylord shrieked beneath the hessian covering his face and urinated down the plank, saturating his jeans. The three spectators looked at each other and back at Varcoe, who stepped back and exhaled in a release of tension.

'You think that sadistic?' He addressed the others, 'It would be if you thought I got gratuitous pleasure from it. But if you had seen some of the patching up I've had to do, in A&E, on young male rape victims, carried out by bastards like him, then you wouldn't have any pity for the swine. It'll sear his memory for all time. He'll pass it in due course, but he'll have a painful sphincter for six weeks and a glowing cluster of haemorrhoids that will restrict his television performances for a long time to come. Right, let's get him out to the Quay.'

The other three, by this time, were recovering from the suddenness and brutality of the action and, with some measure of emotional discomfort, were adjusting to the reasoning that had motivated their companion. It left them with a mixture, paradoxically, of revulsion and excitement. Tim Hodge grabbed the agitated dog by the scruff and shut him in the cupboard beneath the sink.

Clearing a path between the furniture, they lowered the plank with the victim top most and negotiated the space to the door. One of them checked the quay and its environs before signalling an all-clear. Reaching the crane they put the plank on to the cobbles. Dave Lobb signalled to Tim Hodge to reach for the hook as he wound the wire cable off its drum. As soon as enough length had been freed they pulled the hook to the loop of rope at the foot of the plank. Drawing up the slack and tensioning the cable, one end of the plank rose an inch or two off the ground and swung round under the imbalance of gravity. One of them steadied the plank as Gaylord was raised, upside down, to swing out over the water.

'Right, only submerged up to his chin for no more than a count of three then out for a count of ten. That'll give time for the sack to drain and let him breathe, then back for another three. We'll do it,' here Norman held up four fingers, 'times. I'll check he's still breathing at the end of each submersion. All agreed?'

The other three nodded.

'OK, wind him up a bit more, I'll steady him over the edge.'

Their prisoner dangled like a trophy shark being weighed. Doc Varcoe went to the granite steps. Tide was high and only the top four or five steps were above water. He stationed himself on the first step above the level of the inky black sea water and signalled for Gaylord to be lowered. His passage off the quay was rapid and he was in the water within a few seconds. Lifted back out, the doc checked he was breathing, signalled the OK and allowed the remaining submersions to be completed. The final withdrawal was carried out allowing their victim to scrape his uncovered flesh up the barnacled face of the harbour wall. At the top it was an easy matter to unhitch their captive.

'That'll give him some idea of the pain his victims are in when they need morphine just to lie on their backs. Our friend won't forget this. Right, let's get him back.'

The four returned to the cottage. They propped the 'celebrity' up against the settee and removed the rope. Leaving the sack on the head of their victim, to prevent identification of the rope and plank, Dave piled the tie rope in the canvas bag and took it outside with the plank. Before returning he took the plank to the steps and immersed it, giving it a good swirl in the harbour. He then tossed it over the breakwater wall into the sea beyond. Satisfied it was afloat he went back to the group.

'I'll empty that tin of dog food on the floor,' Doc Varcoe nodded towards the open tin on one of the kitchen surfaces, 'we'll let the dog out of the cupboard when we're ready to leave. It'll keep him busy for a time. In the meantime, let's get this bastard sorted. Lie him face down.'

Chris Pascoe forced the wretch on to the three seater.

'Right, listen you bastard. One of us is going outside to watch you from the window and will stay there for anything up to ten minutes. We're cutting you free and putting a towel on your head when the sack is removed. If you move within the ten minutes we'll do worse next time. It'll be your dick then. Got it?'

Doc Varcoe did a thorough check of the room then fetched the tin and emptied the contents onto the floor in front of the door holding the dog. Knowing they had left nothing behind he let the dog out. He picked it up and rubbed its head, belly and front legs in the food for good measure.

'Sorry old boy, but that'll keep you quiet for a while, cleaning yourself up.' The dog scuttled into an alcove, hid under a wide shelf and started licking himself right away.

Dave Lobb took a chef's knife from a block and proceeded to remove all the tape. Balling it up, he removed the sack from Gaylord's head and stashed the ball of tape inside the sack. Doc Varcoe put the towel over the head of the supine form laid out on the cushions, brutally forcing the face into the upholstery for good measure. He signalled to Tim to station himself outside the window as the others followed.

Taking one last look around, he stood at the back of the settee and cast his eye over the shaking form in front of him, but he felt no remorse. Varcoe did not move. He stayed noiselessly in the room for at least a minute. His victim, thinking the room now empty, raised his towelled head just a fraction to listen. Varcoe belted him on the base of the spine with his gloved fist, 'I told you not to move,' his voice muffled as he spoke with his mouth in the crook of his elbow and a tone or two lower in pitch.

The shock and pain made Gaylord scream and for a second time he went into a faint. Satisfied their victim would not now know whether they were tormenting him further, playing psychological games with him, Varcoe knew he could rely on him not to move for the ten minutes he'd been instructed to wait. Walking soundlessly through the back door and closing it equally as soundlessly, he joined Tim, removing balaclavas and gloves before leaving the garden.

The next morning the white Ferrari departed and within a week the cottage had been cleared and was sporting a For-Sale sign. There were no follow-up enquiries by the police, so the punishment squad felt their action had achieved more than they expected. Nothing was ever discussed by the four and as far as the local public were concerned Gaylord must have got tired of the place and just upped sticks.

9

Graham got a call from Patel sooner than he expected. He contacted Bob Treloar.

'Trelawney here. Our friend has contacted me. Wants to do a run Tuesday.'

'OK, what time?'

'Leave at 23:00 and rendezvous somewhere between Falmouth and Cherbourg and to get enough fuel for the trip to Plymouth Sound and back.'

'That's a bit vague, except it pretty well points to Cherbourg, or its environs, being the departure port for the contraband.'

'Well that's all he would say. Also I'm to have company. Somebody who'll be communicating with the rendezvous vessel. Told me to make the hold ready with canvas on the floor the 'cargo' can sit on.'

'Alright. I'll contact our mob and come back to you. It could be this is an ultra-cautious run just to try you out. I still think we let you do this with no intervention from us so you get some feel for the set-up. If that's so, we fit you up without a transmitter in your flotation collar. They might be sophisticated and wary enough to have detection kit specifically set up to test you out. We'll have the two trawlers shadowing you, now we know the time slot and rough location, but they would need to be a safe enough distance, away, initially, not to arouse suspicion. Problem is your minder might insist on your AIS being switched off. In that case we're going to have to fit a transponder of some kind as a precaution. That's easy enough though. Mike Grenville can latch one up in five minutes. Kernow Marine will have an off-the-shelf job and the signal can be doctored to be outside the range of any commercially available receiver. It'll conform to an MOD spec. He'll see to that, anyway, just let him have access to the boat when he's ready. Since we met last time, we've decided to fit two micro cameras under your navigation lights. They'll focus on your port and starboard sides. That way we can use existing cabling and, with a bit of luck, get a record of the type of rendezvous craft they're using and her crew. They'll be activated by heat sources. So, automatic. No requirement for human control. Just make sure your navigation lights are on, that's all. Any questions?'

'You mentioned a Very pistol. Can you get one to me? I think I'd feel a bit more protected with one.'

'No problem, but you do know we can't sanction its use as a weapon, just as a signal for help. Call in here tomorrow sometime. If I'm not about, Phil Peters will be. OK?'

'Yep! I'll call in tomorrow then.'

'Just one other thing. If your cargo is Asian or African keep clear if any of them are coughing. We've had a few with tuberculosis slip in through these networks. It might be a good idea to have a light scarf you can pull up over your nose.'

'Bloody hell. It gets better all the time.'

'Yeah, sorry about that. We encounter it pretty rarely, but it does happen and it's only fair to warn you.'

'OK. No other surprises?'

'Only the ones we don't know about. Good luck if I don't see you tomorrow.'

***

Graham fetched the flare gun from the MCA and stayed over at Alex's the evening before the trip. The last thing he wanted was his parents asking questions and cranking the issue up to a whole new level of tension and uncertainty. The Very pistol was secreted on the lipped bulkhead running the full width of the wheelhouse and he could easily reach up to it from the wheel. It would take about four seconds, he reckoned, to open the door, reach up, grab the pistol and fire a signal into the air.

His 'minder' was to be picked up at 22:45 from the sheltered seating at the end of the quay. It turned out that sea conditions were ideal that evening. There was barely a light swell and wind was north westerly at about three knots. He made his way to the shelter with a light day-pack on his back. Alex had prepared a flask of coffee and plastic lunch box with some sandwiches. He could smell cigarette smoke while still several metres away. It wasn't a British tobacco. Turkish, or some Central European weed, so he guessed his 'companion' would be foreign. The light at the jetty's end proved him right. As the occupant emerged from the shelter and tossed his cigarette into the harbour he could see that he was swarthy. Could have been Greek, Rumanian, Italian, Balkan or from any of the islands the eastern end of the Mediterranean.

'Hodge?' There was no shaking of hands, just that one word by way of a greeting. He knew it was in his best interest to appear co-operative, but the anger he felt with Patel prevented him from being anything but cool towards these people. A monosyllabic grunt in the way of acknowledgement was all he was prepared to concede.

'Look, we're going to have to speak to each other, tough shit my friend, so pocket your anger and let's get on with it,' his criminal minder was well spoken, 'so you call me Box.'

Graham nodded and pursed his mouth with the slightest hint of a smile. He turned and went to one of the iron rings at the jetty edge. Untying a nylon line threaded through the link, he proceeded to draw in a small inflatable, large enough, just, for two people. As it neared the granite face of the quay, he towed it to a flight of nearby steps and coiled the rope as he descended to the water level. Pulling the dingy side-on to the huge stone blocks he up-ended the flimsy craft and emptied water from it then signalled Box to step in and, tossing the rope in, followed as soon as his passenger centred himself. He retrieved a small paddle strapped to the dingy wall and assumed a kneeling position to push the craft away from the steps. Within five minutes they were alongside his boat, the Tensor.

Graham started the diesel engine, powered up the navigation system and watched the screen assemble the related banks of data. He then looked to his minder for direction.

'Just take her out past the castle.'

Box positioned himself to the right of the wheel and, as soon as they left the mouth of the estuary, gave instructions for a course setting on the autopilot. As expected, his minder stopped him transmitting from the AIS unit and stood, for fifteen or twenty minutes, looking through the front windows, intermittently changing his gaze to the path being plotted on the screen. Only a few vessels showed up on the plot from the 'small craft' radar unit. It was a short range set, used mainly for navigating the harbour entrance in poor visibility conditions and to provide an anti-collision feature when out in more crowded sea lanes. The transponder, secreted in a cavity in the depths of the prow, was powered up from a remote of the size used to control garage doors. Graham had it looped on a thin cord in the bib pocket of his oilskin overall. As a precaution, Bob Treloar had told him not to switch it on until the boat was an hour or more out of port. Any unusual signal emitted, from the precincts of the harbour, coinciding with the exact time of departure of Tensor, would be suspiciously linked to that vessel. The consensus was that anyone monitoring the area would be unlikely to show much interest after five or ten minutes and would terminate their vigil. With the additional precaution of the device broadcasting to MOD protocols, detection was virtually risk free.

They must have been travelling for more than three hours, when Box took a phone from his pocket.

'Hello! Yes!' That was all he said.

'Right, cut your engine and get the hatch cover off, our visitors are close.'

Within five minutes Graham could hear the sound of twin outboard engines. A sleek, high-speed, semi-rigid power boat headed straight for them, slaloming to a slick halt by the Tensor's side. One of two men in the craft hooked a short aluminium ladder to the larger boat's gunnel and urged a group of young women to clamber onto the Tensor. There were six of them. All were suffering from the buffeting their journey had subjected them to. One of them was retching, but her stomach had nothing to offer. The contents had long been ejected into the channel.

'Come on, get your asses out of here.' The second man, holding the wheel of the power boat, spat the words out in heavily accented English. He then said something to his accomplice in what Graham took to be Arabic. The heavily accented, guttural h's gave away the language. The girls surged for the ladder and were helped up by the other minion. They were carrying an assortment of hand grips and back packs. None wore shoes. Their helper passed two bags to Box, one small, the other, it transpired, contained their footwear. Nothing was passed the other way. As soon as the ladder was removed the

59

smaller boat accelerated away into the darkness, at about forty knots Graham reckoned.

Box ushered the girls to the open hatch and told them to climb down. Graham, seeing the state they were already in, fetched a plastic bucket with a length of rope tied to the handle and passed it down. He didn't need to explain what it was for.

'Do you all speak English?'

'That's enough. Do not talk to them.'

Graham shrugged and glared at Box.

'Get going. Sail north east. I'll set course later.'

'Not before I secure the hatch. We're going nowhere.'

The deck light fixed to the rear of the wheelhouse was strong. He could see that the girls were now settled with their backs up against the hold wall. One of the girls asked for water. He guessed, by her accent, she was from one of the Baltic states, Latvia or Lithuania. He looked at Box, who just nodded his assent with the briefest of head gestures. A pack of mineral water was stashed back in the cabin. He used the opportunity to check the screen for evidence of the two trawlers. Sure enough they were in the vicinity. He ripped open the pack of water and removed two of the litre bottles. Passing back to the hold he glanced up at the port navigation lamp and gave just the slightest trace of a grin at the concealed camera.

The girl requesting water reached up for the two bottles and passed one to the girl still retching her guts up. Graham reached below the edge of the hatch to a switch and turned on armoured lights both ends of the hold. He then lowered the steel lid and slipped the locking pin in place.

Back in the wheelhouse he set off on a north easterly course. Box sat on the hatch, smoked a cigarette and tossed it over the side half finished before making his way back to the cabin. The remainder of the journey passed with boring monotony. Box watched the plot of the shipping in the vicinity for a short while, then settled on the bench backing the end of the cramped cabin. He was satisfied there was no threat of interception from any quarter. The two other boats were doing some false zig-zagging, as if engaged in genuine netting manoeuvres. Innocent trawlers as far as he was concerned.

The carpet of lights that marked Plymouth sound provided a kind of beacon to aim for. Graham called up the navigation chart, for the approach, on the screen and checked to see that the depth sounder was registering. Satisfied that all other indicators were functioning, he looked to Box for instructions.

'Keep to the navigation lane and watch out for harbour speed limits. Go as far as that creek.' Box pointed out an inlet on the screen chart. Taking out his phone he called up a number and just said, 'First buoy', as they passed the first of many channel markers at the entrance to the sound.

Graham throttled down to five knots as they threaded their way along the many navigation beacons peppering the estuary. If there was a limit, his speed would not arouse any interest. They reached the creek.

'OK, see that row of yachts, take the boat up there.'

About a hundred metres in from the main waterway, he could see a wharf with a security floodlight illuminating a number of yachts. All were resting on cradles, some with storm covers, others with no protection whatsoever from gulls, weather, or debris from the many tall trees overlooking the site. They were parked there 'til the spring, he guessed, their owners waiting for the more favourable sailing conditions that season would bring. Arriving alongside the wharf, he edged the vessel towards a flight of steps.

'Right, keep her in tight.' Box jumped across to the steps and climbed to the top of the wharf and glanced around. Satisfied, he went back to the deck of the trawler and picked up the bow painter.

He took the bow mooring rope back across the steps and hitched the line to a ring set in the stone- work several metres in front of and above the boat. Back on the boat he secured the stern to a similar link, able to reach it without leaving the deck. Satisfied with the boat's stability, he jumped back onto the steps and climbed up to the parking lot for another look around. Returning with a cigarette in his lips, he jumped back on board and signalled Graham to remove the pin from the hatch cover whilst he entered the wheelhouse. Taking the smallest bag from the floor, where he had parked it with the other, he tipped the contents on to the small chart table. Six passports, forged or otherwise, fell out. He inspected each cursorily, as if it was none of his business to know their contents and returned them to the bag.

By this time they had been alongside for about twenty minutes. The sound of a diesel engine disturbed the damp, cold silence of the creek. A Range Rover, with darkened windows, appeared above the boat. After positioning it to face the way it had entered, a man, again of swarthy appearance and stocky build, got out and opened the front and back doors. Approaching the steps he put one hand up to Box by way of greeting, as the latter left the snug comfort of the wheelhouse, before making his way down to the deck. Both men hugged each other in a way that really meant nothing other than a formality to be discharged according to fraternal protocol. Box led him to the hatch, ignoring Graham. No introductions would be made. Lifting the lid, he showed his criminal partner the girls in the hold. Going back to the wheelhouse he retrieved both bags. Giving the small one to the owner of the Rover, he tossed the large one into the hold.

'Put on your shoes and come up. Quickly.'

The girls, relieved to see sky, needed no encouragement to get on deck. The driver pulled a pistol from the back waist band of his trousers.

'Right, send them up.' Box jerked his head in the direction of the stairs and followed the dishevelled group up the stairs as his comrade in crime waved the gun menacingly and preceded them to the Range Rover.

'Get in and keep quiet.'

Graham Hodge could see all this from the deck. Box's partner turned to look down at the boat.

'OK, scram.' He nodded in the direction of the main waterway. Graham walked to the hatch and replaced the cover for the second time that day. Box paused at the open passenger door, giving a totally expressionless glance towards him before climbing in and closing the door. The Rover sped off. The whole transfer must have taken less than five minutes.

Left now to his own devices the first thing he had to do was haul a ten-litre container to the filler for the diesel engine. His attention taken by the task of topping up the fuel tank, he did not hear the footsteps on the wharf steps.

'Catch many fish?'

Graham nearly let the fuel container slip off the rim of the filler hole. He placed the can on the deck, at the same time turning to see his visitor. The man was dressed in navy anorak, navy trousers, black shoes and wearing a cap of some service denomination.

'Can I come aboard?'

The speechless fisherman just stared and lowered the fuel container to the deck.

'Ben Rogers, Customs.' His visitor held out a warrant badge as he crossed the deck, free hand outstretched. They shook hands.

'It's OK, we knew you were coming. Didn't want to let on in case you somehow let it slip by being too relaxed. Been tracking your course.'

By this time Graham had recovered from the shock.

'What about the Range Rover and the girls?'

'Ah, girls was it? We didn't know what was being brought in. Couldn't see through the tinted windows, but they're being followed to their delivery point, wherever that turns out to be.'

'The driver has a gun.'

'Not surprised, but our lot are not going to intercept them. Just going to get a fix on their operations this end. You've proved yourself as far as they are concerned, that's my guess. Anyway, come back with me. Leave the boat tied up for now, she'll be safe. We've got our wheels hidden in a farm turn-off down the track. You can come back for a shower and a sleep at our base in Plymouth.'

Graham suddenly felt the strain and fatigue of the last six hours. The same period spent at sea fishing never left him feeling as spent as he did now and he realised he hadn't touched the flask and sandwiches Alex had packed for him.

'That sounds great. I feel totally whacked. Let me slacken off the ropes first though, otherwise when the tide drops something'll give. I want to finish emptying this too.'

'Right, I'll loosen the stern tie when you're ready to sort the other.'

The boat's moorings slackened, Graham checked everything was switched off, closed the wheelhouse door and told his companion he was ready. Ben led him down the track to a navy Land Rover

Defender. On the road to the base he crashed out on the back seat and slept for the duration of the journey.

The coastguards not only provided a shower and a bed, they gave him a 'full English' for breakfast, although it was mid-afternoon and more of a late lunch by the time he was up and about. Replete and refreshed, they whipped him back to the boat to make his return, solo.

10

Falmouth coastguard contacted Bill Hawken just after four in the afternoon.

'We've got a distress call from a pleasure craft, on private charter. Small wedding party en route from Fowey. She's drifting just west of Dodman Point. Engine overheated and started a fire. Fire extinguished. Weather forecast not brilliant. I'd say we've got a two hour window to secure her. Message clear?'

'Clear Tom,' Bill recognised the voice of Tom Masters, 'I'll get on to the crew right away. Andy Cornwell will be designated cox.'

'Fine. Tell him to get in touch as soon as he's on the move.'

***

Cornwell notified coastguard and checked the intercom from the open cockpit above the wheelhouse. Satisfied the crew were in place and ready to go, he opened the engines a fraction to exit the lifeboat's mooring zone. Way out in mid estuary he increased the speed to twenty knots. The boat raised its bow and made a pretty sight as the twin plumes from her bow separated to form a V-shaped wash in her wake. He glanced back over the stern. The white trail the craft left behind always gave a boost to his mood. It was one of the most exhilarating experiences, in his mind, anyone could ever experience, sitting above two thousand horsepower of energy, his to control at the touch of a lever. He estimated their journey would take twenty five minutes at the full speed of twenty five knots. Leaving St Anthony Head on his left he called down to the wheelhouse to tell them he was coming down.

'Hello Falmouth, Andy Cornwell on. Any further news from Pixie Bell?'

The coastguard came over clearly, 'She's still not fixed her engine. Looks unfixable by the sound of it. Generator out, but reserve battery supply adequate for the radio. We've notified them you're on your way.'

'Any casualties?'

'Some with smoke inhalation. Couldn't get past some obese guy who fell on steps and blocked the exit. Space too tight to get a grip on his arms. They had to get a rope under his armpits and drag him back in to the saloon. No knowledge of his injuries, if any. Hang on, new message coming through, might be as well if you tune in.'

'Skipper of Pixie Bell. Current taking us back towards Dodman. How close is the lifeboat?'

'We reckon twenty minutes.'

Andy listened to this two-way play and visualised the coastline between Port Holland and Gorran Haven. The crew had done a number of practice shouts along that strip of coast. He didn't like the sound of it. History was going to repeat itself if the Pixie drifted in to the chin of land jutting out below Vault Beach. Some forty years earlier a pleasure boat, overloaded and warned not to sail, had disappeared somewhere between Mevagissey and Portscatho. It was believed she went down in the deep waters off Dodman. No trace of wreckage was ever found. It was one of those eternal mysteries. Ten minutes later another message came through from the skipper.

'We've scraped a rock. Think we're holed.'

'Got that Andy?'

'Yes.'

'I'm going to keep my channel open, but leave local control to you when you reach the scene.'

'Fine. I've already got visual.'

Andy took binoculars and went back up to the open cockpit. He could see the skipper with a boat hook attempting to keep the boat off the rocks as it moved up and down with each wave surge. The Pixie Bell was swinging and rotating with the kind of motion that goes with a vessel bereft of power. Even as he watched the craft arrested suddenly on one of its descents and rocked about some pivotal point. He knew what that meant. She stayed in place for perhaps five or six seconds until a wave washed her off the submerged ledge she was resting on. Half sliding, half rolling off the sloping rock face, hidden below the ledge, the hull took a further hammering from the limpet covered granite. By this time the rescue craft was less than half a mile away. The crew could see the gunwale distinctly, even without the benefit of binoculars. It was abnormally close to the water. The skipper and his mate were now on the roof of the saloon releasing a couple of rafts. As soon as they were free the two of them eased them over the side into the water. The passengers were then helped to disembark. By the time they were aboard the rafts the Tamar was within hailing distance. It was obvious the boat was unsalvageable. The hull was settling into the water at a speed Andy Cornwell guessed would leave it afloat for only a few more minutes. The skipper shouted across, 'Man trapped in the saloon. Incapacitated. Too big to get a life jacket on,' and then disappeared into the passenger space with him.

Andy could see the other passengers were safe for the time being, so swung his craft alongside the stricken boat to get a better look through the saloon windows. Looking down from the open cockpit, he could make out the shape of the over-weight man slumped against the back of one of the central bench seats, a rope still hitched under his arm pits. Making a quick decision he instructed Chris Pascoe to cross over with an axe to knock a hole in the plywood roof. 'We'll drop our anchor through and rip the top off. That's the only chance he's got. With a bit of luck he'll float out. He's got no other choice, he's too big for the helicopter. Just have to hope he doesn't get sucked down as she goes, or she bottoms up. Doc, can you take a quick look at him, but I don't want you staying? We can deal with him when we get him out. There's no time to carry out any kind of treatment at this stage. Too dangerous.'

Chris Pascoe jumped across, followed by Doc Varcoe and clambered on to the roof. Jeanne-Pierre freed up the anchor and enough slack ready to pass it to him when he was ready. By this time water was slopping over the gunnel. The crew could see it now running down the steps to slosh around the feet of the casualty. Andy gestured for the skipper to go to the saloon exit ready to abandon the boat. It was obvious he could no longer do anything useful. Staying where he was merely added to the problem. Doc Varcoe did a quick check of vital signs and came to the conclusion his patient had suffered either a heart attack, or was in a diabetic coma, or both. Until he consulted the other members of the party, he dare not give any medication anyway. He loosened the man's tie and undid the top button of a shirt too tight for its wearer. Making his way out he knew his expertise would be better served attending the passengers suffering smoke inhalation.

Using the axe and trying to keep his balance was not easy, but ironically, as the boat settled further into the water, the amplitude decreased and made Chris's task easier. As soon as the hole was big enough he called for the anchor. Jeanne-Pierre crossed over, passed it up and crawled onto the roof with him. Between them the two rammed it through the hole. Andy signalled for them to get on to the prow of the stricken boat. He ran the anchor winch to give more slack as he reversed the lifeboat bow-on to the other. Putting enough water between the two vessels, he turned to look at the set-up behind him and took up the slack, gradually putting some tension into the cable. The flimsy roof started to give. Suddenly, the anchor pulled out of the hole and shot onto the deck.

Jeanne-Pierre, quick as a flash, had an idea as he eyed the boat hook the skipper had left lying on the deck. It was a hefty pole, polished smooth with use, the grain straight and the timber toughened with years of soaking up salt and oil.

'I'll take the pole inside. Well trap it against the roof with the anchor and try again.'

'Right. I'll fetch the anchor. Let's give it a go.'

The two set about the new strategy.

'Give me a bit more slack.'

Chris lowered the steel a few more inches. Jeanne-Pierre wiggled the end of the pole into the gap between anchor tang and roof. He was sweating in the layers of kit. His right arm was beginning to ache as he supported the heavy pole with that arm, simultaneously juggling the anchor into a better angle with his left.

'OK. I think we've got it. Tell Andy to put some tension on it.'

Chris Pascoe gave the thumbs up to the Cox. He stayed in place long enough to prevent the pole dropping out. Satisfied it would hold he turned to slide off the roof. He needn't have bothered. The Pixie Bell's stern suddenly dropped and he was pitched waist deep into water on to the submerging deck. Fortunately he landed feet first, but his concern wasn't for himself, he knew Jean-Pierre would be in trouble. As he slid down the ever inclining surface his feet encountered the rear board. Now chest-high in the brine, the buoyancy aid around his chest inflated and he kicked out from the sinking boat.

Jean-Pierre had just let go of the pole and anchor and was tossed down to the other end of the saloon, along with a couple of tables of food and drinks. He hit his head against the edge of one of the rear benches and lost consciousness. His useless companion, likewise, had slid down the central bench to rest alongside him. The only benefit, if benefit it could be called, was that the entrance to the saloon of the now slanting boat was clear of the incoming water.

Andy Cornwell could see Chris Pascoe was in no immediate danger. The only thing now was to hope he could rip the roof off and give the two inside a chance of rescue. Putting some torque into the winding drum, he could see the cable tighten like a huge guitar string. The anchor was holding. He increased the torque. The plywood panel took on a slight arch, then suddenly gave. Screws ripped from the sub-frame and the stored energy in the cable catapulted the assembly of pole, anchor and roof towards the Tamar. It narrowly missed Chris treading water between the two vessels. By this time the Pixie was almost vertical. The opened roof allowed a surge of water to fill the up-ended saloon. Both occupants were swirled around in the flood of seawater now covering the benches. The canister in Jean-Pierre's life jacket discharged automatically and the cold water on his face shocked him back into consciousness. Before he could swim free from the confines of the saloon the undamaged part of the roof, still fixed to its frame and now totally vertical, travelled down into the water like a sluice gate, trapping him, cutting off daylight. The boat travelled on down into the deep water. Jean-Pierre floated up to the top of the recess formed by the for'ard wall and small bar. There must have been half a metre of air above him. He could feel the body of his unfortunate companion alongside him. Their descent was arrested as the boat hit sand and settled, keel resting at a slight downwards angle.

Feeling the tug of the flotation aid around his chest pulling him along the line of least resistance, the remainder of the now upward sloping roof, Jean-Pierre took a gulp of air and followed the trail of bubbles that had been trapped with him. He was lucky. Life jackets were killers when they prevented exit from beneath upturned craft.

Their buoyancy countered any attempt to negotiate submerged gunnels or cabins. In what little light was filtering down he could just make out the length of rope still attached to the casualty. He grabbed it as he kicked out for the surface. His ascent seemed to him to take forever, but lungs at their limit, he broke surface. Even with ears full of water he heard the cheer that went up from the lifeboat crew and the passengers on the rafts. This was soon allayed, as he handed over the tail end of rope and the immediate fate of the submerged passenger became the next concern of everybody.

Tim Hodge held on to the rope to as Doc Varcoe managed to reach down and get a grip on the Breton's flotation harness. Blood was trickling down his face and into the collar of his storm jacket. The doctor hauled him up on to the deck then turned to help Tim, who was already pulling the rope in. The burden on the other end broke surface face down. As fast as they could, they pulled the man in and turned him face up before attempting to pull him out of the water. He was too heavy for the two of them, they could only raise him a foot or so before having to let him slip back again. There was no movement from him.

'Turn him back-on to the hull, we'll try to pull him out that way.' Another crew member joined the other two. Together they each got a grip on the looped rope under the man's armpits and at last managed to drag him on to the access decking. Doc Varcoe set to work straight away applying resuscitation. After a while he eased off, knelt back on his heels, looked at his two colleagues and shook his head.

'Better get the passengers off the rafts, but do it on the other side. When they're inside we'll pull him up to the stern and cover him with a sheet. I'll check over the rest once that's done.'

Andy Cornwell set about organising the retrieval of the anchor. Roof panel and boat hook were afloat just off the stern of the lifeboat with the cable still threaded through the hole Chris Pascoe had cut. One of the crew, using the lifeboat's own boat hook, managed to retrieve the other one before the winch brought anchor and roof panel up to the boat. The Pixie Bell's boat hook would be retained as an unofficial trophy.

All finally sorted and accounted for, the rafts were stacked on the stern deck. Doc Varcoe instructed Dave Lobb to radio ahead for two ambulances to meet them in Falmouth so that passengers with smoke inhalation could be transported to Truro Hospital for examination and further monitoring. Some were in a pretty bad way and the boat's emergency oxygen supply was practically depleted by the time they reached port. He insisted Jean-Pierre should also go for the once-over. As far as he could tell, with the limited medical equipment brought with him on the boat, there were no obvious signs of concussion, but he was sporting a spectacular gash where he'd hit the saloon bench. Chris Pascoe was none the worse for wear for his ducking. In a dry change of clothes for the run back to Falmouth, he reflected on the drama as he sat back to monitor the engine and transmission system on the screen in front of him. He was angry that his colleague's life had been put at risk by a subject that had exercised the crew's conversation a number of times, that of obesity and the associated problem of manhandling overweight people, during a rescue.

Too close for comfort. It was a repeat of an experience he and his wife had undergone on holiday in Australia. Eight thirty in the evening, jet lagged and tired, compounded by a twenty four hour flight, they had gone to bed. They were awakened by the hotel fire alarm on the sixth floor of the hotel. The event turned out to be a real evacuation alert and not a practice. Hastily putting on a minimum of outer garments and grabbing passports and wallets, which fortunately they had not put in the room safe, they left their room, shoe laces undone. Across the corridor from their door was the exit to the fire escape, an internal stairway. The crowd around the door did not seem to be moving as fast as Chris imagined it should be. Eventually they were inside the door and could see ahead of them an obese woman 'crab-walking' down the steps, both hands on the bannister, rump stuck out diagonally across the downward flight so that she could then see her feet. On each step she brought both feet together before separately advancing down the next riser. This was compounded by what she did with her hands. Before moving both feet off the step she slid both hands down the bannister above the level of the following step. And so this tedious sequence of movements was repeated at

71

each stage of descent. Fortunately the husband was in front guiding her by the elbow. Seeing the build-up on the stairs he persuaded her to pull in closer to the bannister to allow people to pass.

As it turned out, the alarm was triggered by smoke from burning toast in the basement kitchen. But that, as far as Chris was concerned, was not the point. A relief medic, a GP, previously assigned to the crew was of the opinion that very few could claim glandular imbalances as an excuse. His belief was that ninety nine percent of the overweight owed their condition to gluttony and lack of exercise. That, in Chris's estimation, might have been an exaggeration. Even so, such a staggeringly increasing number of fat people to be seen in the streets clutching a sugary drink in one hand and a fistful of greasy food in the other, any time of the day, gave some considerable support to this thesis. Whatever the truth, for him obese people in certain places of public access posed a grave threat to the safety of others.

His reflections were brought to an end as the boat drew level with the headland at St Anthony.

'We'll be drawing in to the harbour in about fifteen minutes,' he said to no one in particular, knowing the wedding group would welcome some feedback.

11

Two ambulances were ready at the lifeboat station. Passengers needing treatment were put into the vehicles, the more seriously affected ushered in to the front one of the two, to be despatched with due haste. The rest, judged to be unaffected, were on phones arranging to be collected by friends for a return to Fowey, or were enquiring about a night's accommodation locally.

Jean-Pierre changed out of his gear. Doc Varcoe was going to run him across to Truro in his own car. Keeping a discreet eye on him he noticed him swaying. Just in time he was able to catch him as he keeled over. Dashing out to the second ambulance, he got some of the less affected casualties out and instructed the paramedics to bring a stretcher to the changing room. They loaded the unconscious crew member into the back of the vehicle and set off immediately. The crew's doctor rode with him freeing up the paramedics to attend the other casualties.

At the hospital Doc Varcoe was well known. He by-passed registration and got on to an internal phone right away to contact Radiography and arrange a scan. That done, he next set about checking rosters to see which surgeons were on duty. Picking up the phone again, he dialled the secretary of one on the list.

'Doctor Varcoe here. Hello Susan, look I've got a seriously injured lifeboat crew member here. Head injury. Unconscious. Have just arranged for him to have a scan, but am pretty sure he's going to need some pressure relieved in his skull.' He listened for a few seconds, 'Yes, put him on.'

'Hello Norman, I heard that, Susan put the phone on speaker as you started relaying.'

'Hello Luke, ... , yes, crewman on sinking boat, clouted his head as she foundered and tilted suddenly. ... , OK. I'll tell Radiography to get the results directly to you.'

'No, I'll get Susan to tell them. Better coming from me, although they know you well.'

'Thanks for that. Will catch up later.'

'Where will I find you?'

'In the cafe. Asleep probably.'

Pleased with his luck in finding Luke Peterson, Norman Varcoe set about addressing the registration issue, knowing the paperwork would have to be completed sooner or later. That sorted, he realised how much he needed a coffee and went to the little cafe just off reception. It was late and no visitors were about, just one or two nurses. Being early in the week A & E was quiet. One of the tables near the wall took his fancy. He sat with his back to the other tables. Although he was tired, he didn't feel comfortable. Glancing through the folding doors, to reception, he could see all the arm chairs were free.

'Mr Peterson is expecting to find me here,' he addressed his remarks to the very Cornish-looking woman who had served him earlier, 'would you be kind enough to point him in my direction. I'll be in the arm chair over there.'

'Course I will my 'ansome. You look tired out. W'av 'e been doin' to yourself?'

Not wishing to be rude, but not wishing to be involved in conversation of any length, he just said, 'Just off the lifeboat. Brought in an injured crewman,' turning away as he did so, 'need to sleep.'

Despite the fatigue, he couldn't sleep. Maybe the caffeine kept him awake. But certainly the events of the day were contributing to a state of zombie-like consciousness. The image of the Pixie Bell tipping Chris Pascoe off the roof and the vertical keel, rearing up then slicing down through blue-green depths, was as vivid in his mind as it was at the time of the event. The rivulets of sea water running off the hull and the hiss of trapped air escaping from all sorts of nooks and crannies, only a boat builder would know about, were playing over and over in his mind.

Finishing his coffee, he felt his brain clearing and went back for another, which this time he decided to make last. The friendly lady waved away his handful of coins, 'On the 'ouse, you deserve it.'

He gave her a genuinely warm grin and thanked her as much for her good will as for the cheerfulness of her manner.

Luke arrived with the results of the scan, 'You're right, there is some internal bleeding. I'm getting him into theatre straight away. Does he have a partner?'

'Yes, wife, but I don't have a contact number. Will need to ring the Coxswain.'

'OK. He should be out of theatre in, say, a couple of hours. I don't think there will be any complications, looking at the scan, but you never know. Right, I'll leave it with you to contact his wife.' Luke paused, in case Norman needed to raise anything else, then putting up a hand by way of departure, he left his friend and sped off to scrub up.

Bill Hawken was in. He'd been expecting the call from Doc Varcoe.

'Look, can you give me Jean-Pierre's number? He's having surgery any moment. Need to contact his wife. Will call her first, then come back to you.'

'Got it right here. Was expecting you to call. Haven't spoken to his wife, thought it best to wait 'til I heard from you. Her name's Jenny, by the way. Tell her I'll arrange for one of the crew to drive her over. Would do it myself, but had better stay free. It would be sod's law to get another shout straight on top of the other. Can't expect Andy to take the boat out for a second time today, if it happens.'

'Thanks Bill. Won't waste any more time. Will phone her now.'

Norman tapped in the numbers. As expected, Jenny was waiting anxiously by the phone.

'Hello. Mrs Pascal? ... Doctor Varcoe here...' The conversation carried on with the usual exchange of question and answer.

'I'll wait until you arrive and stay with you 'til Jean is out,' he used the diminutive of the name to try to engender a measure of warmth and encouragement. 'Bill Hawken is going to send someone to bring you over. Mr Peterson is a highly regarded surgeon. Jean is in good hands. Anyway, look forward to seeing you later.'

Getting back to Bill Hawken, he filled him in as far as he was able. The other crew members had told him varying accounts of the accident.

'It's likely, between you and me, that he'll be put on some form of medication as a precaution against an epileptic reaction to his injury. That's assuming surgery is successful and my instincts are that it will be. The fact that he was conscious for the whole of the trip back is a good sign. Guys I treated in Iraq, with much more severe skull damage have come through OK, so I'm optimistic.'

'That's as good as I hoped. I've asked Mike Traherne to bring Jean-Pierre's wife over. Should be there in half an hour or so.'

Soon enough, Jenny Pascal arrived with Mike Traherne. Norman settled them in the other armchairs and fetched a tea for Jenny and a coffee for Mike. They sat and waited, chatting between periods of silence that lasted longer than the bouts of conversation. Jenny was pretty stalwart. She knew there was an element of risk to being a crewman and although it wasn't a total surprise, it still came as something of a shock when the news of Jean's accident was brought to her.

Luke eventually appeared, still robed up in theatre gear, mask hanging round his throat. It seemed surreal to Jenny, like a scene from a hospital soap. She stood up, composed, outwardly, but with stomach churning she waited for Luke to speak.

'You must be Mrs Pascal. Your husband is going to be fine.'

Jenny, shoulders tight, took in a quick breath and let it go with the tension. Bursting into tears, she sobbed with relief and dropped back onto the edge of the arm chair.

Luke sat on the arm and took her hand, 'The injury is not as bad as I had expected. There was bleeding, but no damage, remarkably, to brain tissue. Just a small lesion in the lining of the skull. That's probably why he stayed conscious for the boat journey back. Tough nut your husband.'

'Thank you,' Jenny was now recovering. Drying her eyes, she took in full lungful of air this time and flopped back against the back of the chair.

'What happens now?'

'We'll keep him in for a few days observation. I'll send a report to his GP and give him some tablets to take for a week or two, just to control any temporary healing trauma. In a month we'll have him back in for a check-up, but that's merely as a precaution and to give him a chance to ask questions. He'll be back to normal once his skull has healed. Won't know any different in six weeks. The other good news is he shouldn't need any medication to prevent epilepsy. I expect you'd like to see him. If you wait a few minutes, I'll ask one of the nurses to take you along.'

Letting go her hand he got up, touched her shoulder gently and nodded to the trio with a smile that said, 'Good day's work,' and walked off.

***

The ride back in Mike Traherne's car was calmer than the outgoing journey. Conversation was infrequent as they each were lost in contemplation of the day's events. Doc Varcoe was asleep as Mike pulled up outside his home.

'Thanks for that. Be nice to get to bed.' He wasted no more time on pleasantries, except to say to Jenny that he'd call her later tomorrow to ask how Jean-Pierre was.

12

The day following the visit to Provedore, Janet Capstick spoke to Sylvia James. Not engaged in any kind of lunchtime duty, they ate sandwiches in Sylvia's classroom and Janet reported, more or less what she'd told Alex.

'That's monstrous. What a cow. Look, if we are going to make a complaint, we need to inform the area ATL rep and have all the evidence, emails, the card and, to a lesser extent, anecdotal evidence ready. Is there any particular time or place at school when she forces her attentions on you?'

'On at least two occasions she's asked me to see her in her study.'

'Right. I suggest we let the ATL know about it. In the meantime, why don't you arrange to see her, in her office. Take your phone, put it on record and tell her you're making a complaint against her. Slip it out of your bag as you sit and hold it on your lap out of sight. Can you do that.'

'I think so.'

'Right. The sooner you can do it the better. I'll wait until that happens and hope we get some damning evidence from her. I also think she's unstable. Wouldn't be surprised if she turned violent, after hearing about the episode of her turning up at your flat. Better make sure one of us is outside when you force a meeting.'

A few days later, having requested a meeting, Janet was called to the head's study. She was prepared. Her phone was charged up ready for the encounter.

'Come in Janet, have a seat.'

Janet sat. With her bag on her knees it was easy to slip out the phone already turned on.

'You're looking particularly stunning today. To what do I owe the pleasure? Want to come away with me after all, do we?'

Janet felt nauseated by the smarmy greeting, 'That's what I'm here about, Ms Brown. I want you to stop harassing me.'

'Come, come darling, an invitation to a weekend in a nice hotel isn't harassment. You don't know what you're missing. Some of my friends will be there. I like to make them jealous.'

'I don't wish to meet your Lesbian friends. The whole idea is repulsive.'

'Oh, little Miss Fussy, on our high horse are we? Remember what I said about references, you'll need one if you apply for another job and you won't get one if you don't play ball.'

'I don't think so. I've made a formal complaint to the ATL.'

At this the creature opposite Janet turned white with anger and rose from her chair. Janet brought the phone up to video the reaction, pushing her chair back as she did so.

'You bitch, you fucking bitch, I'll kill you.'

The head was too slow as she made a lunge across her desk. The chair behind Janet toppled as she now stood, still recording the outburst. Sylvia, the other side of the door could hear all this. Her sharp character assessment of the head had proved right. She was through the door in a flash followed by the only male member of staff, John Hitchens, who happened to be in the vicinity. By this time the head was trying to grab the phone, Sylvia grabbed it from Janet and carried on recording the fracas as John got between Janet and her attacker. Realising she was now in an irreversible predicament, she screamed a string of obscenities at her tormentors, as she perceived them and yelled at them, 'Get out. Get out.'

In a surreal sort of way the situation was exciting for the two women retreating through the door. They now knew the head's corrosive influence was virtually over.

'Right. Phone the police. This is a case of assault. The women is not safe to be on the premises.' The head's secretary, who suffered from the changeable moods and occasional vitriol of her superior, had taken in the significance of the situation and realised she was soon to be freed from the tyranny this woman had inflicted since her appointment. Lifting the phone she dialled the local police station. She had barely replaced the desk phone in its cradle when the head came raging out with a long bladed paper knife. Janet had her back to the door and had barely turned before the head was upon her, grabbing her by the shoulder. The weapon was a souvenir from Spain, an imitation, miniature sword in Toledo steel. It had no sharpened edge, but was thin and pointed. Too late, John Hitchens lunged for the attacker. He collided with her, but was not fast enough. Knocked off balance, the blade aimed at Janet's back, penetrated her cheek and exited through her open mouth. Man and woman fell to the floor. John lay across the stunned principal. Sylvia, fired up by adrenelin, stamped on the wrist holding the weapon. Two inches of a thin heeled shoe penetrated flesh and sinew, splintering the bone. The head gave a roar of pain, dropping the letter opener. Her nemesis kicked the liberated knife out of the way.

By this time a small crowd of teachers had gathered. Alex, amongst them, pushed through and guided Janet, blood pouring down her face, to a chair in front of the secretary's desk.

'Somebody support her. While I get the wound dressings from the cabinet.'

For a second time the secretary picked up the phone. This time to call an ambulance. The deputy head, Veronica Hill, arrived just as the call was being made. She had been deputy under the previous head and was not unpopular, just someone who carried out her responsibilities in a detached, efficient, matter of fact sort of way. Someone explained what had happened.

'Take Ms Brown into her study and keep her there,' she instructed no one in particular, 'and the children better stay on an extended break until we can sort out Miss Capstick's class.'

A couple of teachers managed to raise the moaning head teacher to a sitting position, then up on to her feet.

'Here,' Alex had returned, 'wrap this around her wrist. There'll be blood everywhere else,' throwing a bandage to one of the two escorting the woman. She didn't care whether the other caught it or not, her concern was for her colleague, now pale with shock, blood streaming from the stab wound, down her cheek and neck, saturating her blouse.

'Can you hold this gauze pad in place while I sort out some adhesive tape?' Janet nodded and put her hand up to the dressing. Sylvia, by now, had recovered her wits. Not one disposed to panic, in disarming the head she had acted instinctively in defence of anyone else in danger of further stabbing.

'God that woman's like a raging bull. Another couple of inches up or down and that might have been an eye or an artery.' The deputy asked everyone not involved in the fracas to leave the scene. No

80

murder had been committed, but she considered the police would want the site to be as free from any further disturbance as possible.

'Best to leave the knife where it is, untouched. It'll serve to justify and confirm the action you took to prevent Ms Brown stabbing John.'

Sylvia nodded, grateful that Veronica, by her comment, was supporting her.

'Alison,' Veronica turned to the head's secretary, 'might be a good idea if you can write a brief account of what happened, just for our consumption only. Try to keep it to a half page of A4. The police will interview everybody concerned, anyway. But if the head tries to bring some kind of action against anybody, at least we'll have a documented account of the event we can refer to, compiled whilst fresh in everyone's mind and supportive in our favour. You can all read it when it's done and add or subtract from it before agreeing its contents.'

Alison nodded and got typing.

'Can you open your mouth?' Janet's mouth was dripping blood. Alex, like a lot of teachers, had attended one or two Red Cross courses. What in her mind she thought she could do if she discovered anything in the way of serious trauma, was beyond her. But just to do something helped. The wounded teacher's teeth were coated with a film of blood. There was a steady trickle of the stuff dribbling down her chin. Alex mopped it up with another pad.

'I want to see if your tongue is alright.... . Looks OK. Teeth all there. Nothing else, just the wound in your cheek.'

'What kind of wound?' The injured girl only knew she had felt a stinging blow to her face and was unaware of the damage. Alex felt it probably wiser not to describe the injury. So far no one had fainted and she didn't want Janet, particularly, to pass out at this stage.

'Just a cut, but probably needs stitching. Soon have you patched up in A & E.'

A couple of police officers arrived. Veronica Hill filled them in on the events then showed them to the head's study.

The senior officer took the deputy head aside out of earshot of the group in the office, 'Might be a good idea if she goes in a separate ambulance. Injured arm or not, she could still cause trouble. Won't do her any harm to be in pain for a bit longer while she waits. Will give her something to think about. Always seems to subdue them, we've found, if these violent types stew a bit when they've been injured as well. I'll explain to the medics why she can't go in the same vehicle. Angela here will take statements. I'll go back in and caution your head and charge her with assault. Might seem callous to outside observers, while she's injured, but you yourselves know she deserves it.'

The two officers completed their assessment and waited 'til the ambulance came for Janet. They were well known to the paramedics. Both teams frequently encountering each other at RTAs, road traffic accidents.

'It won't be safe to allow these two to travel in the same vehicle.'

'We can fix that,' one of the medics replied, 'I'll give the big one good dose of sedative and strap her down on the trolley. It'll her quiet for a couple of hours.'

'I'm not sure that's a good idea,' Angela voiced concern, 'I don't mean the strapping down, but allowing her to travel with the other one. It'll cause the young one some distress to be confronted by her assailant all the way to Truro.'

'Point taken. I'll ask for another ambulance for her,' the driver responded, 'but I'll still give her a good shot of sedative.'

Janet was escorted out. Alex went to the ambulance with her, 'I'll go home for my car and follow over. I think they won't keep you in. Can bring you a clean blouse, you're about a size smaller than me, so one of mine'll fit. I'll see you soon.'

'Thank you.' The young teacher, with the early stages of shock setting in, gripped her friend's hand and burst into tears. 'That's a good sign,' thought Alex, 'better than fainting.'

13

As was frequently the case, the town's people woke up to the sight of seven or eight vessels anchored in the bay. There might be as many as three tankers, a warship, an oil-rig supply vessel or two, a drilling rig waiting for a tug tow into the harbour and even, on occasion, the unusual lines presented by the '*Airbus380onBoard*' ship, carrying Airbus sub-assemblies to Bordeaux.

For a while good weather, a lack of foolhardiness amongst the yachting fraternity and a density of shipping in the Channel, lower than usual, made for a quiet time. But when a call did come from the Falmouth Coastguard centre, all hell broke loose. The worst of all possible scenarios was about to unfold in the bay.

A giant liquid gas tanker, the Ligas Princess, had dropped anchor in the waters between Pennance and Pendennis Points. Her deck was nothing like that of other vessels. Four giant domed structures sat like huge motor cycle helmets along her deck. She needed a replacement switchgear unit and some other minor repairs that didn't require her to enter the docks. The switchgear was just a spanner job, but the other work required specialist welding and cutting equipment to be dropped on board.

A small supply boat ferried the equipment out to the waiting ship. It pulled alongside, dwarfed by the enormous hull of the tanker. A crane swung out over the little tender and dropped a hook and sling to the crewmen waiting below. In less than a minute the sling was fitted, secured against slipping and checked yet again, before allowing the crate, it was attached to, to be hoisted on board. The little boat then made for the flight of steps being let down from the deck above. Buoyancy aid in place around his neck, the welding specialist assigned to the job waited for the next wave surge to subside and crossed over to the first step. It was a long climb. He was not a fit man. Years of pies, pasties and beer exacted their price as he made his way to the top. Chest heaving, he was relieved to step onto the steel deck.

'This is a job for a young man,' he gasped as he greeted the ship's Chief Engineer, 'trouble is, got a mortgage to pay off.' What he didn't say was that he'd just received notification that the second home in Spain, one he'd hoped to retire to and paid for from the sale of the house inherited from his parents, was going to be demolished. The cause was some legal dispute between the local authority issuing the original planning permission and the regional authority now challenging its validity. The stress of that, added to his general lack of fitness, was stacking up to a major heart attack.

'Don't tell me. Know the feeling. The name's Oscar Bergsen,' putting out a hand to the other.

'Harry Baker.' The welder responded in kind.

'Like a coffee before I take you down below?'

'That'll suit me fine.' Baker, cast a glance across to where the crate was being unloaded and followed the engineer to a well-furnished mess.

'How'd you like your coffee?'

'White and three sugars, please. They look after you well here.' Harry was impressed by the comfortable and well equipped facility afforded the crew.

'Have to. An expensive piece of maritime traffic like this needs to be looked after by an alert crew. If you have a discontented crew, you have trouble. Look, lunch'll be served in an hour. Have a look at the site first and then have lunch with us, we can discuss any problems you feel need to be addressed while we're eating.'

The two finished their coffee and descended to a lower deck area. A corridor of pierced steel flooring extended for what seemed miles in front of them. Pipes and bulkheads formed an inner viscera of steel all coated in a paint, the colour not far different from that of rust. They stopped by a recess with a flange in three-quarter inch steel plate running from floor to ceiling. It was about eighteen inches wide.

'Your bosses have seen the drawings, I assume you have too.' Harry nodded.

'Right, these are the four holes we want cut.' Oscar pointed to four outlines marked in white on the steel flange. Need to pass some fibre-optic cabling through from up there. He pointed to another white outline on what Harry guessed was the underneath of the bridge decking.

84

'What are the other holes for? Fibre-optic doesn't take up that much space.'

'There'll be bundles of them and they'll feed into a junction box which will then serve the main arterial cable coming through there,' he indicated the white ring above with a gesture of his head, 'and there's stuff having to be taken through those other holes as well. The rectangular bit you cut from there we want welded back on where that white line is. The cable junction box will be fixed on it.'

'Looks straight forward.'

'OK then. Let's get back up.'

Lunch over, the Chief Engineer organised the transfer of cutting and welding gear to the site. A cable was run to the welding transformer. The trolley, holding the gas cylinders for the oxy acetylene torch, was located in the recess with the welding equipment. All set up, Harry opened the valves to the cylinders and applied his lighter to the nozzle of the torch. Turning the valves to a fine adjustment, the flame turned from an insignificant yellow flutter, to a searing, hissing, incandescent blue, needle sharp in form. He pulled the visor of his welding helmet over his face and made a final adjustment to an arc lamp positioned to pick out the white paint better. The darkened glass, protecting his eyes, made it hard to see any detail. Ideally he should have been wearing special goggles, but over the years he'd got used to the helmet. It was easy to flick the visor up or down. He cut the most accessible hole first, just to get a feel for the type of steel alloy in this part of the ship and played a little more with the fine tuning of the flame. The first hole took no time at all. Each of the other three was a little more difficult. He had to kneel for the lower two and the mesh floor left marks in his knees even though he wore leather protectors. Turning off the flame, the welder struggled to his feet, wheezing. Over the years fumes from the spent gases and molten metal had attacked his lungs.

'Right, let's have the platform over here,' it was a habit of his to talk to himself, 'we'll have a go at the hole up there.' He dragged over a rectangular platform, of about the same surface area as a broadsheet newspaper. The thing had been knocked up out of some angle iron and a redundant piece of pierced steel caging. It was a good foot and a half off the ground.

Harry Baker re-lit the cutter, adjusted the flame and heaved his weight on to the platform. He had no chance to lower his visor. The effort of raising eighteen stones that high was too much for his heart. He faltered and fell sideways on to the gas cylinders. Trolley and cylinders toppled and jammed themselves in the recess between welding gear and platform as the welder experienced the bewildering effect of his first heart attack. He lost consciousness, but only for a few seconds. Now on his back, the torch, lying across his thighs, flame upwards, slid off to wedge itself between his leg and one of the cylinders. The effect was almost instantaneous, he screamed, but his now damaged heart only permitted a croak to emerge from his wheezing throat. His body arched in a spasm, putting yet more burden on to his ruptured heart, as the nerves in his leg reacted to the searing pain of the flame. He shuddered and died as the heavy leather apron he was wearing caught fire.

It was some time before any alarm was raised. Heat sensors were located in a number of places and a console on the bridge registered the location of the sensor nearest the source. No one took any particular notice because they knew of the work being carried out in that area. It was not until smoke began to issue from the stairwell, coupled with the unmistakeable smell of burning flesh, that anyone went to investigate.

***

Bill Hawken received the call from MCA and notified the crew on standby.

'We've got a real pig on our hands this time,' he spoke as he and the crew put on their gear, 'liquid gas tanker with fire on board. Bloke with oxy-cutting gear collapsed and set fire to himself. Dead! The acetylene cylinder is taking some of the heat. They can't get at the valves to put the flame out. Seems the cylinders have fallen and wedged themselves into a recess and since it's using its own oxygen supply, any kind of fire extinguisher is useless. If the heat transfer to the contents in the cylinder is still going on, so they tell me, then they believe the gas becomes unstable and can blow. But that's just a guess. They don't really know what can happen. This just doesn't fit

86

the normal risk assessment protocols they observe. I've asked the authorities to order the captain to take her out as far as she can get on a one three five bearing.'

'So what are we supposed to do?' Andy Cornwell voiced what the rest were thinking.

'We need to go and pick up their crew. They've launched a lifeboat, but Sod's Law, its engine won't start. They've still got a couple of deck hands on board and are talking of trying to get a hose down to cool the cylinder, plus a skeleton crew, on stand-by, to assist in taking the ship out.'

'Talking? Need to get their ass in gear and get on with it. Sounds as though there's a bit of incompetence all round. Ship that size with a cargo that dangerous should be mega-safe. How far out is she?'

'Just out from Gyllingvase beach.'

'Bloody hell. If that lot blows there, the town'll be wrecked.'

Bill Hawken straightened up from pulling on his boots, 'Message coming through.' He adjusted his headset, 'MCA say the captain is going to start the engines to move her out, but we're to proceed.'

Within a few minutes the boat was making its way out of the estuary. Around Pendennis Point they could see the tanker. A waft of black diesel smoke was issuing from her funnel, but she was not yet moving. Her forward anchor chain was still visible, pulling on the steel tang fixing her to the sea bed. When they were within a few hundred yards of the ship's own lifeboat, bobbing effectively rudderless, without power, they could see the anchor chain's catenary start to change profile and shed water as it was being drawn on board.

'Easiest to give her boat a tow. Chris, we'll put you on board at the same time.' Bill Hawken addressed the lifeboat's mechanic, 'See if you can get her engine sorted. If you can, we'll not need to take her all the way back to a safe mooring. She can go under her own steam then. We'll have to hang about, anyway, for the rest of the crew if they can't fix things.'

Bill took the rescue vessel up alongside the other boat. Chris Pascoe crossed over with another crew member. He went inside the cocooned interior as his fellow crewman fixed a line to the bow of the powerless craft. Once secured, he jumped back and the two boats headed for the harbour.

They had almost reached the jetty when Chris Pascoe raised his head through the forward, Perspex roof light. He put a thumbs-up sign and signalled Bill to heave to. The engine now functioning, the ship's boat was able to draw up to its tow. One of the tanker's crew freed the tow rope and Chris jumped back on to the rescue craft as Bill instructed the merchant seaman in charge of the other boat to look out for the harbour Pilot Boat.

Heading back out again, the tanker was now underway. They caught up with it, keeping just off its port side. Both craft then travelled for fifteen or twenty minutes out towards the main sea lane of the English Channel. The water here was somewhere between sixty and a hundred metres deep and the swell made the going rougher.

'I'm going to instruct him to slow to a stop. He should be a safe enough distance out. If she does blow at this distance, then the worse likely to happen is a few hotel windows rattling. I'll get Coastguards' approval first.'

The radio traffic between the Coxswain and Falmouth Coastguard confirmed Bill's decision. The tanker disengaged its drive shaft, but kept its engines idling. Its forward momentum carrying the huge vessel forward some way until its movement was arrested by wind, current and drag. The smaller craft, in the meantime, kept its engines running, throttling down gradually as it kept pace with the monster hull it was dwarfed by.

'I'm going to pull back a few hundred metres until they signal for assistance.' Bill Hawken was beginning to feel concerned. Away from the shelter of the bay sea conditions were decidedly rougher and Bill, still controlling the boat from the outside, decided it safer to go below to the wheelhouse once he'd put some distance between the two vessels. The tanker, because of its bulk, was relatively steady, but the sixteen metre rescue craft was beginning to toss like a rocking horse. Even so, no longer under power, the larger ship was now developing a very slight but perceptible roll.

'Andy, I'm coming in. Passing control over to you.'

'I have control,' Andy acknowledged the signal.

At this point the Tamar had barely gone a couple of hundred metres when a shock wave hit them obliquely astern. The crew looked back at a cloud of water and metal debris rising above what had been the tanker. Just like a gun recoil, the explosive force into the atmosphere was balanced by an equal and opposite momentum downwards. The huge hull was forced down into the sea, before it disintegrated totally, displacing an equal volume of water and creating a wave of monstrous proportions.

'Bloody hell! The poor buggers.' Mike Traherne, who was on this shout, expressed the horror they all registered. 'Andy, that wave is going to swamp us.' The Deputy Cox looked back through the rear door. Across the transom he could see the wave bearing down. There was a few seconds of respite before it reached them. Hawken had not yet left the bridge cockpit but had just released his harness as it happened. He made a dash for the ladder, but was not quick enough. The wave caught the lifeboat and tossed it vertically, forcing its bow down into the sea. The Coxswain was thrown over the top of the wheelhouse and down onto the bow rail. The craft fell back, more or less upright, but Bill Hawken, shoulder broken and unconscious, was pitched overboard.

Andy Cornwall, safely anchored in his seat, caught a brief glimpse of the yellow garbed figure as he was catapulted in front of the bridge window and watched the unconscious form roll off the rail into the sea. He throttled back immediately. Dave Lobb had spotted it too. Quickly un-harnessing, he and Tim Hodge made a dash for the deck. The Coxswain was barely afloat. The automatic flotation aid had got damaged, it seemed and was only partially inflated, because his lower face was being alternately immersed then uncovered with each wave flux.

The Deputy Cox aligned the boat so the two crewmen could reach down to the stricken Coxswain. They got a grip on his collar and then the lifting beckets and hauled him back-first up on to the lower walkway. Lying him down on the sloping surface, they were relieved to find him breathing. His helmet must have saved him from serious head injury because the earphone had been ripped off by the rail and was hanging loosely from its locating point at the side.

'Look, we better not try to get him into the safe bay, those steps are too steep. It's not far back to base. Let's drag him gently up on to the fore deck. I'll be surprised if he's not broken something. We can't risk compounding any breaks taking him up those steps.' Tim Hodge voiced his agreement.

By this time, Doc Varcoe had joined them and also agreed with the decision, 'Let me have a look at him. It should be OK to slide him even if there are breaks and safer up on the foredeck than here, but let me give him the once over first, before we do. Obviously his neck's not broken and I'm pretty hopeful his spine is OK.'

He checked pulse, eyes for dilation and mouth for evidence of blood due to lung puncture.

'OK, gently remove his boots. Don't want drag on his hips from those. I'm going to put a neck brace on even so. Just keep him from rolling anymore whilst I get it. I'll tell Andy to make for the dock helipad and to radio for Culdrose to send their chopper to transfer him to Truro.'

The two crewmen knelt by their casualty on his seaward side and gently wedged him against the orange superstructure to prevent him rolling. Doc Varcoe returned, fitted the brace, tapped on the front side window and gave the thumbs up to Andy Cornwell. The boat's engines, idling until now, revved to a gentle cruising speed and took the craft towards the docks. The change in motion and more pronounced throb from the engines must have penetrated Bill Hawken's sub-conscious. At that point he opened his eyes.

The doctor placed a hand gently on his chest, 'Welcome back. Don't attempt to move. You know where you are?'

'Course I bloody do!' Bill Hawken gritted his teeth and grimaced as the effort of talking caused a stab of pain from his injured shoulder to inform him he wasn't going to get up.

'Can you wriggle your toes? Good. Back's OK. Now we're going to drag you up on to the bow. There'll be a trip to Treliske Hospital by helicopter. We're landing you near the helipad at the docks. Are you happy about being moved up to the bow?'

The Coxswain closed his eyes, sucked in a breath and, without thinking, tried to nod his head. Another stab of pain shot through his body.

'OK, I'll try not to ask any more questions. Before we move you I'll give you a shot of morphine, but we'll have to get under your jacket.'

Doc Varcoe managed to put a needle into the lower part of Hawken's forearm and deliver a dose of pain killer. When the dose started to take effect, they managed to slide the injured coxswain up to the fore deck. The trip back took longer than normal, as Andy Cornwell balanced urgency against the risk of causing further harm to the injured crewman. He steered the boat directly into the larger swells, changing course as necessary and throttling back with each descent into the corresponding troughs. His skill was apparent in the way the craft's speed seemed to appear constant. In fact, the sensation was an illusion. It wasn't the speed that was constant, it was the way he managed to minimise the effects of pitch change, so that the keel was kept pretty well horizontal even though the hull was traversing vertical displacements between wave crest and trough. Entering the shelter of the estuary, he took the speed up to twenty knots.

Dave Lobb, along with the Second Cox, picked up notification of the Culdrose helicopter's imminent approach. He looked across. Andy nodded and instructed the radio operator to acknowledge the call.

'Tell them we'll pull up to the slipway just below the pad and that we'll need a stretcher to get him from the boat to the chopper. He can't walk. Doc Varcoe's pretty sure he's broken his shoulder, but that's about as much as we can prepare them for. As far as he knows, there is no serious back or neck injury. Tell them he's conscious, but tranquilised with a morphine shot. Got that?'

'Yep!'

The radio operator relayed the information and was asked if the doctor wished to accompany the injured coxswain.

Andy turned to Dave Lobb, 'Slip out and ask Doc Varcoe if he thinks he should go, I'll tell them they'll have an answer as soon as we can give it to them. It might be a good idea that he does go in case Bill loses consciousness, for whatever reason we don't know about.'

Back on the foredeck, Doc Varcoe decided, without hesitation, that Bill Hawken would be glad of his attention on board the copter.

The air crew were a hundred percent competent, but the doctor knew that, psychologically, his presence would provide reassurance to the injured coxswain. The decision was relayed back to the approaching Sea King, which was now visible just west of Pendennis Castle. The lifeboat reached the slipway close to the helipad. Dock staff, who had been notified, were on hand with an inflatable craft ready to transport a stretcher to the boat.

Andy Cornwell took the Tamar side-on to the ramp. Mike Traherne slipped over the side and with the help of a couple of dock hands the stretcher was handed up to the two crewmen either side of Bill Hawken. Doc Varcoe supervised the placement of their skipper on to the stretcher and with the lifeboat's keel grounded on the ramp, they lowered him over the side, cross-ways on to the Zodiac. The climb up to the waiting helicopter was treacherous. A layer of green algae on the slipway made the going hazardous, but they reached dry concrete without mishap.

One of the helicopter crew came to meet them and took charge of the operation at that point. Bill Hawken was transferred to the deck of the red Sea King. Doc Varcoe was helped up alongside and given a helmet already connected into the intercom system. Having previously trained on ops in Iraq, he had no trouble recalling the actions required to operate the simple switching and volume controls. He gave the thumbs up to the pilot officer. The medic, responsible for the injured crewman's well-being, performed a sequence of procedures ensuring the latter's comfort and security, before giving the go-ahead to the pilot. The door was closed and the group took off. Within six minutes they were hovering above the landing pad at Treliske Hospital. The rest of the crew, meanwhile, thanked their helpers from the docks and Andy Cornwall took the depleted lifeboat back to its mooring outside the RNLI boat house.

Graham Hodge liked to meet the rescue craft whenever he was free to be at the boat house. If no one else beat him to it, he was ready with tea or coffee on hand and a plateful of biscuits. After the crew had changed they met upstairs in the small lounge to discuss what now had become an urgent need to reassess staffing.

'God, that was a close shave. But we're two men short now. We were lucky today. Those poor devils on the ship wouldn't have

92

known what hit them.' Andy now assumed the role of Coxswain, as he stated the obvious. Suddenly they all realised how tired and emotionally drained they were. No one challenged him for the roll. He was respected and had proved himself reliable a number of times under pretty demanding situations.

'We're going to have to accelerate the training schedule.' Graham took this as a cue, 'My girlfriend wants to join.'

The group turned to look at Tim's younger brother and some good-natured banter followed. The crew had met Alex a number of times, at social gatherings and no one pulled a face at the suggestion.

'Well, that'll be novel.'

Andy looked at the faces around him. 'What d'you think? We can't make a decision in front of you here Graham. Need to give anyone a chance to express objection without embarrassment. My gut feeling is the crew would welcome her for training. Do you want to go below for a few minutes while we discuss it? No time like the present. We can't afford to waste time dithering over this one.'

Graham nodded, and went down and through the connecting door to the shed housing the smaller Atlantic 75 inshore, rescue craft.

'Whatever we decide,' Andy looked around the table, 'for or against, we'll have to put our decision to Bill as a matter of procedure.'

The others nodded.

Mike Traherne spoke. 'In the two or three years she's been at the junior school, I hear she's gained a lot of respect as a teacher. I would support her nomination.'

'Anybody else got comment to make about her joining?' Andy leaned back in his chair as a general murmur of approval came from the other crew members.

'Right, I'll be visiting Bill in the next twenty four hours. I'll put the proposal to him. We still need at least one more candidate. With Jean-Pierre still under observation, we're two men short. Mike, you've seen him recently, I've seen him, he seems to me to be mending well. What d'you think?'

Mike Traherne nodded, 'He's off medication and the last scan revealed no evidence of any internal complications. The surgeon says his skull will be stronger than before the fracture. The only thing is I'm not sure how Jenny sees his role as part of the crew.'

'Yeah, got the same feeling last time I called. Anyway, at the rate we're getting casualties we're going to have to speed up the training of the existing mob. There's also the matter of you,' Andy turned to face Tim Hodge, 'and Graham. Ideally we can't have two brothers going out on the same shout, unless it's a straightforward rescue. So even when Graham's - by the way, shout to him to come back in - finished his training we'll still need two extra in the programme.'

'There's no shortage of interest, but we need people who'll commit and not give it up after a couple of years. Too bloody expensive to send people to train at Poole and then lose them,' one of the long serving crew added.

Graham reappeared. Andy nodded and grinned, 'Looks like Alex is recruited, but Bill and the Operations Manager will have to approve. You know Bill won't object without good reason. Best thing is for her to get in touch with the OM. She can drop in a letter of application. We'll get the proper paperwork to her anyway, in the meantime, so she can get it off. Well that's it, I think we better call it a day. I'm knackered. Let's get home.'

14

It was some weeks before Graham Hodge was contacted by Patel. The two default payments were progressed to make it look as though he was still two months in arrears at the current point of the calendar. When the second call came, again it was with the same arrangement. Graham notified Bob Treloar and a meeting was scheduled for the following day.

***

'I think, maybe, we should take action this time,' Bob Treloar lent back in his chair, 'I know we said it might be better to let a few trips go through to give them a false sense of confidence and give us a chance of getting a better lead to brains at the top, but they might be getting twitchy. Our contact in France reckons they're being more cautious. But that last trip gave us a fix on some big operators working out of Eastern Europe and their contacts over here. You happy with that Graham?'

'Well, that's up to you. If only Box is on board and is not armed, well, I can't see any great danger, unless he gets spooked and pulls a knife or something.'

'We don't want to take unnecessary risks, but I don't think you'll be in any kind of serious danger. Is there any way you can disable the boat's engine without him knowing how to restart it, because if you're without power he's pretty well a non-player and all we've gotta do is come alongside and take command?'

'I could fit a kill-engine switch, a bit like a kill-cord, that needs manual resetting so that the normal ignition doesn't respond if he tries to restart it. Then, as far as he knows, it'll look like an engine malfunction that needs a mechanic to put right.'

Bob Treloar looked at the rest of the group around the table, 'You reckon Graham's safe on that score?'

Mike Grenville nodded, 'Shouldn't pose a big risk. We can let things progress as far as the transfer, then trap the launch with the two trawlers. We've got the coastguard cutter factored in now. If for any reason the net goes wrong, we have a high speed RIB, rigid inflatable, deployed from the cutter, already in the water. It's a good ten or fifteen knots faster than the one they've been using. We're not normally armed, but this time, in view of the fact your Range Rover driver has a firearm, we will have a firearms team on it and will have no compunction about firing on them if they don't respond to commands to stop.'

'OK then, we'll do what we've just said. Graham how easy is it to fit the disabler to the engine? Quick job?'

'Fairly straight forward. Under the bulkhead in front of the wheel. Could reach it with one hand still on the wheel.'

'As a precaution, is it worth wiring in a reset switch as well, adjacent to the diesel so that, say, two hours into the trip you cause malfunction and then restart the engine at source, just to make him unsuspicious when the actual engagement takes place?' Grenville put the suggestion to the young fisherman.

'Well, possible, but messy. I'd have to crawl about under the deck and it's a bit of a shit hole down there. But don't need to. Can just toggle the switch, would need to do it when he's not looking, though.'

'Is that easy enough?'

'Should be. He leaves the wheel house to flick his cigarette butts over the side. I could attempt it any one of those times, before he gets to the door and his back is to me, so he doesn't think it's funny it happens when I'm out of his sight.'

'Good. OK, then, I'll brief our lot about this and hope the top brass agrees this is the time to take them. Any reservations?' Although the senior officer, he commanded without getting backs up and knew it wiser to invite other opinion in a matter where action of this sort was being planned. The others shook their heads.

Mike Grenville rocked back on his chair, 'I think we should go ahead with it. We don't know what other boats Patel has doing this for him. It's too risky to try and get details of his commercial dealings from the bank to find out. There's always a possibility his manager is taking a rake-off, or somebody even higher up, unlikely, but possible. Fewer people in the know, the better.'

'That's a thought. But a ... ,' Bob Treloar hesitated, 'we'll need to know eventually.'

Ben Rogers from Customs turned to Mike and Bob, 'We can get that, but the main thing is to hope Patel isn't notified when the transfer is intercepted and tips anyone off higher up. Chance we've got to take. We can, of course, take him into custody as soon as we know Graham's left harbour. That might be the best option.'

The group around the table pondered this, trying to think of snags.

Bob looked around. 'Right, no more suggestions? I think we've more or less exhausted the plot. I'll put our proposals to the brass and outline the cautions. Let's call it a day. Who's for a pint?'

The mood in the group changed immediately as smiles broke out all round.

15

The journey to the rendezvous took place in a calm sea. Graham was getting irritated by Box's indifferent, almost sullen company and the cigarette smoke. He had no particular wish to form a relationship with him, but, on the other hand, he would have welcomed some kind of occasional interaction in order to get a better take on his psychological make-up. In the event of any violence, Graham had no qualms about disabling him to the point of serious injury. Some two and a half hours into the trip, too late, in his estimation, for Box to want to terminate the journey, Graham reached under the bulkhead as Box turned to leave the wheelhouse with another of his cigarette ends. He toggled the engine off. The engine throb changed note and died away to silence in a few seconds. Graham let the boat run under its momentum for a few metres and feigned a look of concern as he reached for the starter button.

'What's the problem?' Box's face registered anger.

With two or three attempts at restarting and an impatient Box looking on, he shook his head.

'Dunno! Have to check the engine. Could be a drop of water in the fuel line. Happens sometimes. No big deal.'

Box went for the door, giving Graham chance to toggle the switch back to 'on', unseen, before following him out. Pretending to carry out a finger inspection of the fuel line and various other physical links and electrical connections. The trawler skipper closed the fuel tap above the engine, took a spanner lying in one of the recesses and disconnected the fuel line. He bled out the residue of diesel from the pipe and muttered, 'Water', over his shoulder to Box, whose view of the whole performance was obscured by Graham's back.

'Turn on the tap', he gave the instruction to Box as he wiped his hands in a piece of old towel, feeling a glimmer of satisfaction now that he had established a measure of control over his controllers.

Back in the cabin he turned the starter motor over until the fuel reached the engine. The thing responded after a few more presses. A relieved Box took a deep drag from a newly lit cigarette. Graham could see that his normally cool exterior had been ruffled. He didn't wait as long between cigarettes and took to making more frequent viewing of the radar screen. Graham was afraid he might ask for an AIS scan of the vessels in the area and hoped the coastguard cutter would not be transmitting on its call sign.

Within half an hour of the stop, Box's phone went. Again, 'Hello, yes', was all he said.

'Right! Slow to stop, but don't cut your engine.'

The fisherman throttled down and kept his eye on the radar track. There was a number of craft within the five hundred metre radius. Two he identified could have been the trawlers shadowing his course. They were on a parallel trajectory, to the south east, between Tensor and the French coast and oblique to the normal Channel shipping lane. A larger blip was traversing a tight curve. Judging by its speed it was unlikely to be any other than the coastguard cutter. A faster moving blip was heading straight for the centre of the screen plot. It had to be the RIB carrying the immigrants, if immigrants were for a second time going to be his cargo.

Box had the wheelhouse door open. Graham could hear the approaching launch above the quiet throb of his engine. He let go of the wheel, there was no point holding it if they weren't moving and went to the door as Box stepped out on to the deck. He could just make out the tell-tale bow wave of the boat heading towards them.

'OK, get the hatch open.'

Graham glanced around into the darkness as he stood up on the high kerb of the wheelhouse doorway. He could see the navigation lights of the two trawlers beyond the trafficker's RIB speeding towards them. Of the cutter there was no indication, it must be sailing with all lights extinguished. The launch pulled up alongside, this time with just four girls, two heavily bearded men and the two minders. The fisherman took his time moving to the hatch. Any delay would not affect the traffickers, they merely had to get their cargo on to Tensor's deck, but Graham reckoned the longer he kept his boat stationary the better, so with Box's attention taken by the transfer he made a pretext of finding it hard to slip the pin on the hatch cover and went to retrieve an offcut of steel, concrete reinforcing rod from a deck crate to give it a couple of blows.

The aluminium ladder was hooked onto the gunwale. The four girls were reluctant to move. One of the minders slapped the girl nearest the ladder a stinging blow across the face and pulled a knife.

'If you don't move, I cut your face.'

She needed no more encouragement and scrambled up, hastily followed by the other three.

The two bearded passengers sported holdalls. They embraced their two carriers, passed their holdalls up to Box and clambered aboard the Tensor. Box dropped the bags on the deck. Graham, watching from the now open hatch, heard the muffled sound of what could be no less than weaponry, of some sort, concealed in the canvas holdalls. Box again signalled for the girls to be ordered into the hold and pointed to the wheelhouse for the men. Graham fetched the bucket and placed a couple of bottles of water in it before handing it down to the girls. Again, one of the minders handed two bags up to Box and, hand-over complete, signalled his companion to take off. They had gone perhaps twenty or thirty metres when two flares in succession lit the scene. Box yelled at Graham to get into the wheelhouse and move the boat. They hadn't had time to close the hatch.

'Turn off your navigation lights,' as he said it they were dazzled by a searchlight.

Graham throttled the engine up to full speed and the Tensor moved off with a lurch, propeller cavitating until speed matched power. At the same time the two bearded men were thrown to the back of the little cabin, but managed to keep upright. Box cursed, his eyes having not adjusted to the blinding glare of the light from the coastguard cutter. In that brief moment of pandemonium, everyone's attention was taken with trying to keep their balance. The jolt was just the diversion Graham needed. In the confusion he managed to toggle the engine off and for a second time the boat glided to a halt.

Now, with the engine dead, their attention was taken by the sound of a second launch. Peering into the night they were able to see the getaway launch, illuminated by another powerful searchlight on the cutter's bridge. The traffickers' craft was now travelling at full speed and, as hoped, headed for the passage of water between the two decoy trawlers with the armed group, in the RIB, in pursuit. All of them on Tensor were mesmerised by the scene as the quarry, pursued by the faster boat, attempted to outpace their pursuers by ramping up the twin outboards to maximum speed. The increase in thrust was balanced by an increase in pitch angle as the hull reared up in response. At the same time the net between the two trawlers shot up out of the sea just as the escape boat was a score of metres from the dripping steel line supporting it. Its bow was just a few centimetres above the height of the cable. Spotting it too late, the escaping pair could do nothing to avoid it. The result was a virtuoso show of spectacular and unrepeatable dynamic. The keel engaged with the cable and proceeded to run up over the taut line tensioning it still further, increasing the slope of the hull as it passed over the net.

The trafficker holding the wheel was able to keep upright as the launch tipped up. His companion was not so lucky, he started slipping down the deck. As the keel traversed the full length of the wire it dropped as the friction between hull and wire reached a terminal value at which point the energy in the cable was released. The line catapulted itself backwards, like a bow string, to shoot up between the stern and the two outboard motors. It acted like the arrestor hook on the flight deck of an aircraft carrier. The escaping launch was stopped almost dead in its tracks and the forward momentum of the second trafficker propelled him into the back of the other. His neck was broken on impact, simultaneously shattering the spine of the other. The twin propellers cut into the netting and brought the launch to a halt.

The group on the Tensor looked on almost in disbelief. Whilst it had all happened over the space of only a few seconds, the event took on a surreal dimension as the pursuit RIB glided up gracefully to the disabled launch.

Graham pretended to try to restart the engine by turning it over a few times and turned on Box as Box fixed him with a killing glare, 'Trying to accelerate the boat too quickly has flooded the cylinders or something. It's your bloody fault. Now we're all in the shit.'

The two men from the launch talked rapidly together in a language unfamiliar to Graham. He was later to discover it was Urdu. The elder of the two pulled one of the bags towards him, unzipped it and pulled an AK47 from the interior, passed it to his companion and retrieved a second for himself, together with a pistol.

'OK, you better get this thing going or you really will be in the shit.' He waved the gun in the direction of the bow.

'What d'you think I'm trying to do?' annoyed, Graham bristled at the armed man, 'You bloody people haven't got a clue about boats have you?' and turned back to give the switch another round of pulses to the starter motor. By this time the team on the RIB had confirmed the getaway launch out of action and its crew a threat to no one. They left its recovery to the two trawlers and turned their attention to the fishing boat now drifting without power, still bathed in the beam of light from the cutter.

'Saddam, get one of the girls. Quickly. Take the pistol.' The older man gestured towards the hold.

The younger man dropped his gun onto the ledge at the back of the wheel house and took the pistol held out by his companion. He was back inside a minute with a truculent girl being prodded forward with the pistol muzzle in her back.

'Be careful,' Box showed his annoyance at the shift in events, 'we paid a lot for that merchandise.'

'So what? You think you're going to sell it again now we've got the British Navy on our backs? We're going nowhere by the looks of it.'

'What are we going to do Ahmed?'

By this time the armed group from the cutter were idling a few metres off the side of the fishing boat.

Ahmed handed his AK47 to his companion and took the pistol. He grabbed the girl round the throat in a forearm lock and forced her into the doorway with the pistol jammed under her chin. It was no good shouting to the coastguard crew, they wouldn't hear, but the message he was sending was unmistakeable. He backed into the cabin and ordered Graham to turn on his VHF radio.

'Call the navy.'

'It's not the navy. They'll be the coastguard.'

'How d'you know that? Did you bring them here?'

Graham realised he should have kept quiet, but thinking quickly his wits saved him, 'Course I bloody didn't, you can see the red stripe on their hull. That's coastguard.'

'OK, contact them. Tell them we want their RIB and we'll kill a girl every fifteen minutes if they don't agree.'

Graham switched to a transmitting channel and gave the MayDay call sign.

'Falmouth coastguard receiving you. What is your location?'

'You know my location. I've just been intercepted by your coastguard cutter. Please put me through to its captain. I have two armed men on board and four hostages, girls. They want the RIB and threaten to kill a girl every fifteen minutes if they don't get it.' Graham switched to receiving.

'Very good, very good, my friend. Now hand me the microphone.'

There was a good chance the captain was already tuned in to the exchange, but his response was not immediate and it was a good twenty seconds or more before he spoke.

'Captain Bingham here. I have just been told to contact you. What is your problem?'

'Not OUR problem. YOUR problem!' Ahmed emphasised the possessive. 'You can call me Osama. I want your launch which is circling around outside. Your crew have seen the girl. She is killed in fifteen minutes if we don't get the launch.'

'I'm afraid I can't do that, it's not my launch.'

'Don't play fucking games with me. The launch, or a girl every fifteen minutes and I want you to take off all but one of your crew before handing over.'

'OK, but I need time to get them back here and then the boat back to you.'

'Ten minutes. No more.'

'You,' Ahmed gestured to Box, 'you come with us. This clown,' he nodded at Graham, 'can stay with his pig of a boat.'

'I'm not getting into that boat with you. You're fucking mad.'

'I don't think you'll be welcomed aboard the big ship. You've a chance of getting away with us. But suit yourself, we'll go faster without you on board, infidel.'

The sound from the twin outboards on the RIB altered pitch as the crew made off towards the mother ship. It was back within eleven or twelve minutes, more than twice as long as it needed to take. But the captain played for time, in order to give thought to his next move. He knew the two armed men would see the launch approaching before the ten minute deadline was passed and would be reassured by its imminent, but late arrival. It was a tactic that carried a certain amount of risk. On the one hand it left the terrorists in a state of nervous certainty, on the other, it heightened the risk of a sudden, irrational response in the event of a panic attack that deadlines weren't being kept to.

'Saddam, you will get in first whilst I hold the girl. You take the other pistol and AK and cover the crewman whilst I bring the girl down. That way we are insured against trickery. You,' Ahmed spoke to Graham, 'you'll hold on to the line from the launch.'

The RIB pulled up alongside Tensor. Its navigator threw a rope to Graham, it was Ben Rogers, the revenue and customs officer he had met in Plymouth. He went back to the controls and kept the launch tight up against the hull of the trawler. The younger terrorist, because this ostensibly was what the two were, dropped into the boat as Ahmed watched from the cabin door. He covered the crewman with his pistol and waited as his comrade advanced on to the deck with the girl.

'Get up closer to the man and jam your gun into the back of his neck while I get into the boat.'

Saddam moved up to the launch's pilot.

'Right, you,' Ahmed prodded the girl, 'get into the boat.'

She did as she was told as Ahmed covered her with the pistol. Still covering her, he sat on the gunwale and swung his legs over the side. That was the last instruction his conscious brain gave as a bullet from a silenced sniper's rifle hit him in the forehead and spattered his grey matter and the back of his head across the side of the wheel house. His partner heard nothing above the sound of the idling outboards, but happened to turn just in time to see him topple back into the trawler. A red spot on the side of his head turned into a red furrow as a bullet from a second marksman neatly separated the front of his skull from the back of his skull. He slumped into a kneeling

104

position on to the ribbed decking and fell sideways against the launch's buoyancy tube. The girl in the launch shrieked and dropped onto the floor of the inflatable sobbing with a mixture of shock and relief. The inflatable's navigator quickly retrieved the pistol still gripped by his assailant. He took off a glove, knelt by the side of the disarmed man and checked for a pulse. The shallow channel made by the bullet was flooding with blood, but the officer could see that the brain tissue underneath had been torn. Even so, the man was not dead, but he was unlikely to regain consciousness.

The customs officer could see there was no longer any threat from this one remaining terrorist. He dragged the unconscious man away from the side down to the stern of the inflatable and laid him face down. The girl he told to sit on one of the twin jockey seats amidships.

Box, still inside the wheelhouse, no longer wore a mask of sang-froid. His response to all this was to sit on the skipper's seat and, with shaking hands, attempt to light yet another cigarette.

Graham by this time had tied the painter to the gunwale. He helped Ben aboard, 'He's not armed,' Graham nodded in the direction of the Wheelhouse. By this time the other girls knew the game was over and had clambered out of the hold.

Rogers pulled the body of Ahmed away from the door and stepped across the kerb into the cabin and confronted Box.

'Hold out your hands. What's your name?' Box, with the cigarette held firmly between his lips, kept his mouth shut. He had calmed down and was now maintaining a stone-wall face.

'Please yourself.' Taking a pair of wrist cuffs from his belt, the officer snapped them on and read him his rights. He did a thorough frisk of the man and removed the mobile from Box's inside pocket.

'Has he used this?' He waved the phone in front of Graham.

'No! Not as far as I know.'

'Well if you're lying I can soon check the call history. Right, no handcuffs for you, for the time being. You better get this thing going again, because you're being escorted to Plymouth.' He addressed his remarks to Graham, maintaining the previously agreed pretext of Graham's un-coerced involvement in the trafficking.

'You,' he pulled Box onto his feet from the rotating helmsman's chair, 'are going into the hold. The girls will be taken to the ship.'

Graham accompanied Box and the officer to the hold. With Box safely installed, the fisherman pulled the hatch cover down and pinned the tongue to the bracket, securing the lid. The girls, by now, had taken in the situation they had landed themselves in and were lined up talking to their companion in the launch.

'Right! Do you girls speak English?'

One of the group nodded, 'Yes.'

'You heard what I said earlier, you will be taken to the ship. Do you have identification? Passports?'

'Yes, but they are in a bag. The men who brought us here gave it to the man in the hold.'

Ben turned to Graham, 'You know where this bag is?'

'In the cabin, on the floor in the corner with another bag containing their shoes.'

'OK. Get the bag with the shoes. They can put them on before getting in the inflatable, but no spiky heels. I'll take charge of the passports. You will come with us.'

The officer dropped back into the RIB and waited as the girls put their shoes on. Graham untied the painter and kept it pulled in as the customs officer helped the girls into the craft, holding on to the Tensor's gunwale with his other hand. With the last girl settled in place, Graham slid off his boat and hunkered down against the side of the launch. The launch careered away from the hull and pulled up a short while later at the stern of the coastguard cutter and offloaded the girls.

'We need a body bag back on the trawler and this one,' the officer spoke to John Bingham, the captain, who had come to witness the handover and pointed to the terrorist in the stern, 'is still alive, just.' At the same time Ben Rogers took out Box's phone and tapped into the call history.

'Right, I'll detail a couple of men to bring a stretcher and a body bag. Will you want anyone to go back with you?'

'No. We've got the minder secured in the hold. We'll carry on back and rendezvous with the trafficker at the creek the other end. I've just checked our detainee's call history. He's phoned nobody since he's been afloat. So can you notify our station that we're carrying on as if nothing has happened. They'll have armed men in place around the quay and a block in the lane as soon as the contact enters the creekside. Let me know on the trawler's VHF that the station has acknowledged your instruction, if you will. Much obliged Captain for your hospitality. We should make good time back.'

The launch continued to idle as a couple of crewmen hopped across to the RIB and proceeded to drag the unconscious Saddam over a side tube and up onto the transom of the ship. There was neither care nor callousness in their action. They waited for a stretcher. One arrived and with it a body bag for the corpse on the trawler. Ben caught the bag thrown across to him and passed it to Graham.

'Right, we're away.' He reversed back from the cutter and set off towards Tensor.

'We're going to need to alert the contact the other end. The number is pre-set on Box's phone. I've already been given his pin number by GCHQ, so there's no problem over authenticity. Just hope the pre-arranged signal is still 'First buoy'. The two caught in the nets didn't have time to warn anyone, as far as we know, according to signals being monitored, again with GCHQ's connivance. They'll give us positive confirmation shortly. Anyway, we'll soon know, if the transport doesn't turn up.'

Back on Tensor the two men put the dead terrorist into the body bag and laid it under a tarpaulin between hatch and cabin. That done, they settled in the wheelhouse, relieved. Graham fired up the engine, switched on the VHF to receive and set course for Plymouth. It wasn't long before Captain Bingham relayed a message from GCHQ that the pair in the launch had had no time to warn anyone of the intercept.

'Good luck with the home run. Let's hope there was going to be no confirmation of the handover or a 'sign-in' at the French end.'

'As far as we know there wasn't with the first trip, so we're hopeful. Anyway, we've bagged this lot and put a couple of terrorists out of action. So, all in all not a bad day's work. See you in port. Thanks again for your hospitality.'

The journey back was as expected. Entering the mouth of the estuary, Ben got Box's phone out and waited until they reached the first marker. He called up the pre-set. A voice the other end merely said 'Yes?' Ben paused and muttered, 'First buoy,' and put a thumbs-up sign to Graham as the other end answered simply, 'Good,' and cut.

'Right, it looks like we're in business.'

***

Graham recognised the approach to the side creek and turned into the narrower waterway. He eased up to the granite steps and crossed over with the bow tie line. Ben secured the stern from the boat and followed Graham up the steps. A customs officer emerged from under the canvas covering of one of the front yachts and let himself over the side.

'Hallo! Good trip?' He approached the pair and shook hands with both as Ben introduced Graham.

'Pretty successful.'

'HQ let us know you were en route, but nothing else. Our target should be here in just over quarter of an hour. We've got three more men hidden on site, here and the two Defenders with a couple of men waiting in the usual place back at the farm turn-off. We've also got a naval ambulance with them. The pick-up guy had a gun last time, so we're taking no chances. I better get back under. We're all armed with small side arms and assault rifles. We'll challenge him when he moves to the steps, after he's got out of the Range Rover and has opened the doors. One of the men will break cover and go for the car keys. You OK with that?'

'Fine!'

' 'better get back in place.' The customs officer clambered back on the yacht as the two of them descended the steps back on to the trawler.

A short while later the Rover arrived. Its occupant, as before, turned the vehicle and lined it up above the boat and opened the doors before turning towards the steps. He had barely placed his foot on the first step down before he sensed something wasn't right. Box wasn't on the deck to greet him. He hesitated, half turning, one foot up the other down. At that point he caught sight of the uniformed figure approaching the 4X4 and made a dash for its cover, pulling the same pistol, as on the previous occasion, from his waist band. The two men raced for the driver's door. A warning was shouted to drop his weapon, but it wasn't heeded. The driver took a running shot at the officer, it caught the man in the shoulder. A second, sharper report rang out a fraction of a second later. The trafficker stumbled and pitched forward as the high velocity bullet from one of the concealed marksmen, penetrated and smashed his hip. He hit the edge of the open door face-on and crashed in a heap, sideways, against the leather seat of the Range Rover. Dazed and shocked, he lolled against the sill of the car staring at the blood soaking down his trousers. Another officer dashed up and barged against the door, slamming it against the still armed criminal. Pinioned by the weight of the door and totally disabled by the bullet, he was no longer a threat. The officer bent down and grabbed the gun by the barrel as the other two concealed marksmen broke cover. They ignored the trafficker and went to attend their wounded colleague.

By this time Graham and Ben were up on top. One of the officers phoned for the two Defenders and the naval ambulance to drive up to the quay. The trafficker was bleeding badly, but as far as anyone could tell no artery had been severed.

'Look, I'm going to phone for a civil ambulance to pick this one up, but we'll delay it until our man has been taken. There's only room in the naval ambulance for one and he takes priority.'

'I'd let the bastard bleed to death. It's going to cost the NHS money to patch him up and then he'll probably sue.'

'I'm not going to attempt to stem the flow. With a bit of luck he might lose enough blood to kick the bucket. We'll instruct the medics to attend our man, but to waste no time delaying his transfer to hospital.'

The group made their injured colleague as comfortable as possible. The military ambulance was on the scene very quickly and the two medics got to work on the injured customs officer.

'Get our man off right away. You can give him,' he nodded towards the crippled trafficker, 'a shot of morphine if you like, but don't spend time examining him. I don't want his treatment to delay our man getting into surgery. We'll phone for an NHS ambulance for that one, but not until you've got clear of the track in. Can't afford to have your exit blocked by a civil ambulance. One of the two Defenders can lead the way. Put the blue light up and just go for it.'

It took less than two minutes for the medics to cut the injured customs officer's uniform away from his wound, fit up a drip and load him into the ambulance. One of them then selected a syringe from his kit, filled it with dose of morphine and fixed the injured criminal with a shot of pain killer. He was then back in the vehicle with his wounded colleague in the space of about fifteen seconds.

Graham watched all this in something of a daze. He had been up for several hours now and the fatigue was beginning to kick in.

Ben turned to him, 'We'll get Box out of the hold now. You sit in the cabin. I'll cuff you to the wheel and leave the door open, with you in full view and we'll keep up the pretence of your non-involvement.'

One of the free officers accompanied them down the steps. Ben attached Graham to the rim of the wheel and the two customs men then went to the hold. Box, hunched in a corner, was blinded by the morning light flooding the fishy space he was imprisoned in.

'Right, get up!'

Dropping onto his flank and then into a kneeling position, Box raised himself up, stepped across to the rungs and climbed out. Ben led him up to the waiting Defender and bundled him into the back. A second pair of handcuffs on a length of chain were attached to his wrist and anchored to a vertical bar-hold on the side.

'OK, see you back at base. This other joker's taking his boat to the docks for impoundment. We need to do a sweep for drugs as well.' Ben said this and gave a couple of thumps on the rear of the now departing Land Rover variant.

Back on the boat he released Graham from the handcuffs.

'We're moving in on Patel immediately, at his office, you'll be pleased to know.'

'What happens to me now?'

'Well, I don't know about you, but for me a shower and a good cooked breakfast. How'd you feel about that?'

Graham grinned, 'She'll be right! Let's get the show moving!'

16

In another part of Plymouth three plain clothes Customs and Revenue officers sat along a street from where they could observe Naht Patel's home. They already knew he left for his base in the bank at a regular time, unless he was scheduled to visit one of the branches within his ambit. One of the officers alerted the other two, 'There he is.'

Patel emerged from a semi-detached house, one of a countlessly similar build all along that road. He pulled the door shut, double locked it and moved to a six year old BMW on his driveway, the tacky, plastic fascia already declaring the age of the car. The three officers allowed him to exit the drive before starting the engine of their nondescript estate car and followed him to the car park he normally used. A short while later they followed to the bank. It was already open. Before Patel had time to reach his office his three tailers had caught up with him in a rather undistinguished reception area and two grabbed him by each arm. The surprise brought with it the realisation that the latest trip must have gone wrong. Even so, he tried to bluff by putting up some pretence of affronted dignity, but the grip, the authoritative manner and determined set on the faces of each of his escorts left him suddenly weak in the stomach. Like the clichéd expression of a whole life flashing through a mind so did images of a new Porsche, mansion and expensive holidays flash through his mind. The younger of the three officers handcuffed him, stated the reason for arrest and read him his 'rights'.

By this time the manager had been alerted and had appeared from somewhere in the interior. Confronted for the first time in his life by circumstances beyond his experience he blustered out a, 'Ronald Brown, I'm the manager. Can I help you gentlemen?'

The senior customs officer flashed his warrant badge in his face, 'Sam Crozier, HMRC, Her Majesty's Revenue and Customs. I want all of your staff and I mean all, assembled here in the vestibule. How many are there?'

'Six, apart from me.'

'Right, get them here. Immediately! Sir!' It wasn't the bank manager's fault Sam Crozier didn't like bureaucrats, but dislike them he did and his tone of voice conveyed it.

Sam waited. The majority of the staff emerged from a communal office. Two, each from a separate office.

'I would like to see your mobile phones please. Put them on the table. That also means you Mr Brown. I'll take charge of them for now. You'll get them back.'

'That's a bloody liberty,' one of the staff objected.

'Not half the liberty any one of the many girls, your greedy little friend here trafficks in, is being deprived of. So, unless you have anything useful to contribute I suggest you keep quiet. Or are you also in on the enterprise?' This was enough to stall any further feelings of resentment.

'Everybody happy? Let's continue. I'm right in assuming this is an operational arm and not a public banking arm?'

'Yes! We are one of a small number of node branches that implement commercial transactions on behalf of the High Street branches,' the manager answered.

'Right, close the outside door. I would like to see Mr Patel's office now. The rest of you stay out of your offices and make yourselves comfortable here. Jim you stay with them.'

The manager led the way to the Indian's work place. There, Patel was handcuffed to a radiator pipe. A chair was drawn up for him to sit on after his mobile phone was removed and his pockets relieved of their contents. Nothing of importance was found other than a bunch of keys. Sam guessed the bunch would contain his desk key.

Sam turned to the manager, 'I want system access to all this man's commercial dealings on behalf of this bank. So I would be obliged if you would log in for me on his desktop. Also I need to search his desk and any other part of the premises where he might have secreted memory sticks or other data-recording media.' Brown nodded. Powering up Patel's desktop, the manager satisfied himself the relevant files were accessible and pointed at the mouse by way of indicating the system was now ready to be accessed.

'Fine! This might take some time. I must ask you not answer any BT line telephones.'

The manager took this as an instruction to leave. Sam followed him to the door and called ahead, 'Jim, Mr Brown is to stay out with you. I've given instruction that no land-line phone is to be answered.'

'OK boss.'

Back in the office Sam faced Patel. 'You know what this is about now, don't you?'

'Haven't a clue what you're talking about.'

'Is that so? Well, you can sit there and guess and while you're guessing I'm going to have a look at your files. But before that, let's see what's in your laptop case.'

Sam unzipped the bag. The laptop, a USB mouse and a couple of memory sticks, from a net pocket, were assembled on the desk top. He powered up the computer.

'I wonder what we have in these.' Sam played with the sticks, pushing them to and fro the desk like models in a war game scenario. The laptop signalled its readiness to work.

'Right, give me your password.' Patel kept a sullen silence. Sam got up from the chair and sat on the edge of the table, his face very close to that of the chained man.

'We have the right, not many people know this, to arrest, just like the police.' He paused, 'We also have the right, just like the police and the army, if occasion demands it, to carry side arms,' he threw this unnecessary piece of information in for good measure, 'and just like the army we can get impatient and we can show our impatience, very impatiently.' Sam reached over, grabbed Patel's tie and proceeded to pull the knot tight.

He let go and leaned back as the man started to gag, 'Now, what was I saying? Oh yes, impatience. Your password?' Again Patel kept his mouth shut. Sam reached forward and proceeded to bunch his tie into a ball. He prised the man's teeth open, with a ruler from the desk and forced the ball into his mouth. That done, he knuckled him three or four times in the ribs with considerable force and finished with a light blow to the kidneys.

'That's for the girls. The girls! You know the girls? Next time it'll be your balls I'll be squeezing. Password! Nod!'

The man sat heaving, but stayed stubbornly uncooperative.

'Password!' Sam slid off the table. He got behind Patel, grabbed the collar of his jacket and yanked him off his chair. Reaching down between his legs he gripped him by the balls and squeezed. Patel went rigid, arched up on to the balls of his feet and gave a stifled shriek. Sam let go. His victim dropped back on to the chair.

'Next time I will twist AND pull. Password!'

Patel nodded. Sam left the gag in place and pushed a pad and pen in front of the man, who was now unwilling to undergo anymore violence. He scribbled down some letters and numbers, shaking as he did so. His tormentor picked up the pad, smiled, returned to the laptop and keyed in the cipher. The screen immediately responded. The expression on Crozier's faced morphed from smile to stonewall as he focussed on the icons tumbling into position. His colleague sidled up to the desk and together they examined the trickle of files they teased from the list of documents. Much of it was pretty routine.

Sam inserted a memory stick. It contained few files. One was a spreadsheet that would not open. It was password protected. Sam turned the screen towards Patel, gestured with a hand closing in a grip, following up with a very meaningful twisting action and a jerk. He pushed the pad and pen towards him a second time. Patel hesitated, but soon grabbed the pen as Sam began to rise from the desk. The password yielded a bonanza. A list of names came up. Crozier recognised Graham Hodges name amongst them. Alongside each was a description of the transaction carried out in the name of the bank, plus an instruction of when, each month, to cover the default payment. Further columns gave what Sam took to be pay offs to Patel from his fellow criminals.

A second spreadsheet was similarly protected, on the remaining memory stick. Graham tried the previous password. It worked. Again a list of names and contact numbers. Box's name figured on this. Sam knew he had hit the jackpot. Some numbers had London, Southampton, Folkestone, Harwich, Jersey and Guernsey codes. Others had international dialling codes, French, German, Indian, Dutch, Turkish, Albanian, Greek, Italian, Russian, Nigerian and North African amongst which were some Sam was not familiar with.

'Thank you my friend,' Sam smiled at Patel, 'you are most meticulous with your book keeping, but then, that is your nation's greatest selling point, bureaucratic overkill.'

Patel blanched. He could not see the screen, but guessed, correctly, that his list of contacts had been flushed out.

'Right, let's have a look at the bank balance, so to speak.' Crozier turned to the bank terminal and pushed the laptop to the side, but not before pulling the first spreadsheet back on screen. The internal data was easily navigated. It seemed to Sam there was not sufficient protection against internal manipulation of the accounts by dishonest employees. By signing in to the bank used by Graham Hodge, Patel was able to generate a history of payments that didn't exist. All he needed was Hodge's account number. This checked out against the information on the laptop.

'Right, let's get all this downloaded on a new memory stick before we Forward it as an attachment to HQ. The sooner this is transferred the better.'

'Is anyone else out there,' Sam nodded towards the closed door, 'in on your little enterprise?' and leaned back in his chair. 'If you say 'no' when you should have said 'yes' then anything you did not disclose will be taken into account in sentencing.'

Patel shook his head.

'Even so, I think we'll take no risk. Mick, tell Bob we're holding this lot incommunicado for a while longer yet.'

Sam got to work downloading, then set about sending the data to HQ, with a brief explanation as to source and significance and instructions to alert the authority at each location who would be tasked with carrying out arrests, or further surveillance.

'OK. Let's get some coffee and tea organised. I'm starving. There's a café just down the pavement Mick, we'll get in some doughnuts as well. Use your card this time, I'll sign the req. Better take orders from that lot and bring one for Gunga Din here.'

With Mick out of the way, Sam turned to Patel, 'You really are an arrogant, despicable, evil little piece of shit, from what I've just seen, but a real pretty boy. Your fellow inmates are going to have a lovely time introducing you to prison culture and then it's back to Mumbai, or wherever it is you crawled out from. You'll be able to enjoy the pleasures of a civilisation with no national health system, water supplies of dubious provenance and, oh yes, a police force with a more robust and avaricious attitude than any matched by you. The leafy suburbs, beloved of John Betjeman, will no longer be your cosy little stamping ground. I'm going to take your gag out now. If you make any unnecessary sound it goes back in.' Sam pulled the tie out without any display of finesse or concern for the pain inflicted on his victim's teeth.

'I want a lawyer.' The look of hatred Patel gave his tormentor merely served to evince more comment from Crozier.

'Interview's finished. You don't need a lawyer, you need a miracle. There's enough here to occupy your leisure time for a few years. 'f course, Indian jails aren't quite as comfortable as English ones, so leisure's a rather relative term.'

'I'm a British citizen. You can't send me to India.'

'You're not a citizen, you're a fucking parasite and you will be surprised what we can do, despite the left wing, liberal, hug-a-tree, bleedin' hearts in Liberty.'

Sam shut down the various windows and switched off the terminal, packed the laptop in its bag and settled back to wait for coffee. It arrived with a box of doughnuts that must have been just delivered to the café. They were still warm.

'A good morning's work. Let's hope they round up big fish.'

Mick nodded, mouth too full to reply.

17

Andy Cornwell drove slowly along the lower end of Melvill Road looking for a space to park. Bill Hawken, by coincidence, happened to be the crew member living closest to the Lifeboat Station. It wasn't because of his status as Coxswain. It was so merely because his father, a shipwright in the docks, had lived in the same road. When a house had come on the market nearby, many years earlier, the recently married Bill had made enough money, as a merchant naval engineer, to put down a deposit. His father too, had been a crewman on the lifeboat and his father before that. Three generations of service had seen numerous rescues, recorded in earlier, illuminated scrolls of recognition written in quaint language ' ... awarded in recognition of ... the salvation of 317 souls ...'. There were scores of nationalities, French, Spanish, German, Russian, to name a few besides the local English, Welsh and Scottish fishing trawlers, who owed their continued existence on earth to the skill and courage of just this south westerly outpost of maritime rescue. The others, Padstow, Penlee, Sennen ... , the list went on, a list complemented by crews manning numerous other stations from Baltimore in Eire to Portrush in Northern Ireland, St Mary's Isles of Scilly to Thurso in Scotland and Longhope in Orkney to Aith in Shetland, Lowestoft and Humber on the east coast to Aran and Achill Islands on the west coast of Eire, all these could claim a similar record of rescue.

Bill's front door sported a brass dolphin knocker. Andy gave it a couple of bursts. Mary Hawken came to the door.

'Come in, the old bugger's in the kitchen having a cup of tea.'

Mary let Andy through and followed him into the kitchen.

'Don't need to ask, you'll down a cup. Milk? Sugar?'

Just a dash of milk Mary. Thanks.' Andy shook hands with Bill and pulled out one of the chairs Mary pointed to.

'What's the news on the shoulder?'

'Coming along well. No complications, but don't see myself on duty for a while, if ever.'

' 's what I expected in the short term, but surely you'll be up and running in six months?'

'Dunno. Maybe time for you to take over. Ben, the Operations Manager wants to retire, that means one of us in the line-up for his job and knowing Poole, they'll be reluctant to waste a trained crewman still able-bodied with plenty of years ahead of him. Now this has happened, I'm a likely to be proposed. Can't say I'll be sorry. I would miss the excitement, true, but injuries take longer to heal, these days and Mary's had a bad shock over this last one. Had an attack of shingles. Doc says a reaction to the accident.'

Mary placed a cup in front of their caller and took a seat along with the two men.

'I'll just finish my cup with you two, then leave you both to it.'

The conversation focused for a short while on the aftermath of the explosion. The Falmouth Packet had been running a stream of correspondence on the event. Local feelings , before this had happened, were polarised over an earlier suggestion of a properly designed and built liquefied gas facility. The 'pros' saw it as a much needed boost for local employment, the 'cons' a proposal full of risk. It had raised as much controversy as the proposed dredging of the harbour. Again, many saw the benefits that dredging would bring to the docks. Deeper berths meant larger ships having access to the repair yards. Trade in the town would benefit from large cruise ships being able to dock alongside piers, instead of having to run a continual shuttle of tenders to and fro from anchorage out in the bay. Something they were reluctant to do and thus, as a consequence, sought to avoid by by-passing the port altogether.

There was the usual conflict between the ecologists and commerce. There were plausible arguments put forward by fishermen on both divides. Some concerned that dredging would throw up silt that would harm fishing stock, others that during storms run-off from land drainage, due to heavy rain, produced silt in the river anyway, which eventually cleared and so the arguments went on. Ecologists argued the case of the displacement of an algae peculiar to Falmouth estuary. But again, local harvesters of the seaweed, since stopped, offered evidence of a history of harvesting the stuff for agricultural purposes as far back as anyone could remember. Andy and Bill discussed these things for a short while.

'Anyway, 'nough said about that,' Bill pushed his empty mug away, 'we need to talk about recruitment.'

'Yep, crew have really taken a knock this month.'

'How's young Graham shaping up, in your opinion? I know what I've seen since he was taken on and he looks to be turning into a solid player.'

'No worries on my part. Glad to have him on the boat. Time, I think for him to get tested on a real shout. He's done, what, four training runs on Sunday mornings and one night time run. They've done all they can with him at RNLI College, for the time being. No further training there 'til he's had experience in the thick of it. I think Tim mentioned it to you that Graham's girlfriend, Alex, is interested in signing up.'

'Yes, he was around early last week. From what I hear, she's reliable. Depends on how she shapes up in rough sea, like any of us. As a matter of fact I've got a photo copy of her application. Ben sent it. He approves.'

'Well then, we can get her out on the next exercise. Give her a taste before she gets pulled up to Poole. We can fit her out, temporarily, with spare gear and see how she finds it. She's done one or two fishing trips on Graham's boat in rough weather I gather and, apart from the greater speed of the Tamar, I don't think she'll find a great difference in the ride.'

'That settles that one then. But we're still a trained body short, with Jean-Pierre still under the medics. What d'you think the outcome there is? Up and running in a month or two, or permanently excluded on the basis of uncertain brain trauma.?'

'Dunno! Difficult to know. Depends on observation of his neuro-responses over the next six months, I've been told. The consultant, as far as he is able to tell, says there appears to be no side effect. That in his experience the threat of epilepsy would have manifested itself in the few weeks since he has stopped medication. There's no evidence of motor-neurone impairment, so all in all the prognosis is encouraging. The unknown factor is Jenny, his wife. Haven't had any kind of feed-back as to her feelings over the whole thing. She was pretty shaken up, who wouldn't be if they're human, but her uncle was on the crew before having to retire, so there's a bit of a tradition in the family. I believe she wouldn't stop him coming back and he's game to get back if given the all clear.'

'Hmm!' Bill sat back and folded his arms across his chest, 'I think we need to get the crew together soon. Meet in the upstairs room for a quick meeting on a Friday to see who has any proposals for recruitment. In fact, why not this coming Friday?'

'Don't see why not. If they're expecting the usual get-together in The Chisel, then a few minutes earlier in the boathouse or later in the pub shouldn't make much difference.'

'Good! It'll give me something to do, ringing round and I can tell them to come with a few names.'

'That'll be good. Well, I think we've covered a bit of ground. I'll go ahead then, shall I and invite Alex down for the next practise run on Sunday morning?'

'Yes! Go ahead. Unless there's anything really demanding my input assume you're in command - which you are - as Second Cox. So just carry on as you've always done and if you like, I can do some of the admin stuff in the boathouse now I'm up and about. Take some of the load off you for a bit and get me out the house.'

'Thanks Bill.'

'I'm still dry, could do with another mug of tea, what about you? Mary, I'm making another pot of tea, ready for another?' Bill got up as he called out to his wife, from the kitchen.

'Wouldn't go amiss. Maybe it's the talking.'

18

Alex turned up on Sunday morning ready for a baptism of sorts.

'Here you are, put this lot on. Graham'll give you a hand. Don't need to introduce you. Think you've met everybody, at some time or other, in The Chisel & Adze.' Andy passed Alex a pile of kit as he inclined his head towards the mob in the changing room.

'Yes!' Alex smiled at the crew, most of them already kitted out in the yellow storm jackets and trousers.

'I'll check you out before we move off.'

The roller door, spanning the whole of one end of the lifeboat house, gave access to the top of the slipway for the B Class Inshore Lifeboat, when it was launched. It was also used by the crew to access the gangway to the sixteen metre Tamar moored in the pool adjoining Port Pendennis. Before the door was raised, Andy addressed the crew.

'Right, no surprises this trip. It's just a familiarisation run for Alex, mainly, but we are going to rendezvous with a yacht just off Greeb Point, below Portscatho. We're putting a line on and towing her in. OK? Let's get going.'

The exercise went smoothly. No wind. No rain. Overcast sky. Alex occupied a chair behind the Second Cox and had non-operational access to the management system displayed on the screen. Chris Pascoe, the boat's mechanic, had been designated steersman for this exercise and was commanding the vessel from the bridge cockpit outside. This freed Andy to swivel around to face Alex and explain aspects of the exercise every so often.

It was just over four nautical miles to the rendezvous with the yacht. In about twelve minutes they were alongside. Dave Lobb jumped across when Chris Pascoe brought the rescue craft within half a metre of the sailing boat. A pig of a manoeuvre when wind was any more than Force 2, but in these calm conditions not much riskier than stepping off onto the steps of a solid quay. Alex was given her first task aboard: to toss a line over to Dave. She swung the ball on the leader line, letting it trace a couple of arcs before releasing it in a trajectory that cleared the rail and spanned the gap in between yacht and rescue craft. A big cheer went up as the line fell squarely between David's feet. She turned and bowed to the crew, behind, who acknowledged the gesture with good natured laughter.

Dave hitched the towline to a cleat on the bow of the yacht and remained in place for the journey back to the harbour. Inside the wheelhouse Alex listened to Andy's comments about tow protocols and warnings about the dangers of trailing ropes and broken masts fouling propellers and rudders in real rescues. It was for her, in her mind, the beginning of a liberation from the mental demands of her day job.

Back at the changing room the crew made it pretty clear they welcomed the new recruit to the team. A short de-briefing session upstairs in the lounge, mainly for the newer members of the crew, lasted just three or four minutes.

'Well, I think we've got our first, future, female coxswain. Welcome aboard.' This drew a round of applause and banter from the crew.

Alex blushed, 'I don't know about that, but I'm looking forward to being a member of The Chisel & Adze on a Friday evening.'

This drew further good natured comment and the group broke up in a cheerful mood eager for lunch.

19

The flight from Madrid was on time. Captain David Kean, of the Airbus A320, radioed Newquay airport as he passed the French port of Brest, way down to the east.

'Wind light, so'westerly, visibility good,' came the response to his request for a brief report of local conditions.

'Thank you. Over!' He acknowledged the call and looked across at his new co-pilot, 'Should be an easy touch-down. Can get rocky on approach, updraft from the cliffs pretty fierce at times. Have had to make for Exeter more than once.'

There was about a hundred and twenty odd miles still to go. His passengers were not tourists, they were a group of Spanish politicians, CEOs, economists and support staff scheduled to attend a meeting with other nationalities at Boconnoc, a secluded country house in Cornwall. Their host was the British Government and the venue had been picked partly because security there was a simpler matter to organize than at other, rather well known, conference centres. The setting also boasted a display of flowering arboreal growth that was second to none and it was known that one influential foreign minister attending was a collector of trees and shrubs.

The captain turned on the intercom, 'Ladies and gentlemen, Lizard coming up soon, off the port side of the aircraft. The most southerly tip of mainland UK. I'll be taking the aircraft down for the approach to the airport at Newquay, so you'll be getting a good view of this spectacular coast as we cross over the cliff line.'

The passengers automatically turned to look through windows. Way off to the north the clear line of the Cornish coast was now evident. As the pilot put the plane into its approach trajectory, his passengers were told to buckle-up and a short while later the Lizard could be seen off to the west. The demarcation between sea and land was clearly visible from the line of white water breaking on to the granite face of the cliffs.

'Bloody hell, what was that?' The co-pilot took his eyes from the instrument panel to look through the widow in front just a fraction of a second after the fuselage nose registered a very audible thump. Almost simultaneously a further couple of bangs was accompanied by strong vibration from the engines. At the same time warning signals indicated both engines had cut out.

'We've got bird-strike I reckon, that's the only explanation. Put out a May-Day. Shit! The hydraulics are out.'

Captain Kean hurriedly located the ram air turbine switch. This was a small wind turbine that lowered from its housing under the body of the aircraft. It generated enough hydraulic pressure to actuate the control flight surfaces. Very reliable, it was a safety provision that had saved a number of flights from disaster. A light indicated it had lowered into position and was functioning.

The chief steward entered the flight deck, 'Some of the passengers claim to have seen a formation of geese struck by the plane. I heard the bang. Engines out?'

'Yep! We've put out a May-Day. Can't listen to you now. Will have to ditch, so inform passengers to retrieve life jackets from under the seats and to brace for emergency landing in the sea. You get back and strap yourself in.'

David Kean checked the air speed indicator, the plane was well above stall speed. The horizon was still level and the instrument panel confirmed this. He put the plane into a shallow turn and chose a glide path almost parallel with the beach below him at Coverack. This took the Airbus above the deadly stretch of water between The Manacles, a cluster of rocks varying in depth of submersion, according to tide, and Manacle Point. Once beyond this, the pilot turned the rudder to steer on a zero-two-zero bearing. The plane continued, losing height, its flight path now directed towards the mouth of the Fal estuary. By this time the coastguard station at Pendennis Point had picked up on the May-Day and was in voice contact. The castle at Pendennis showed up clearly, its location a trump card in Henry the Eighth's fortification network against French invaders.

'Hello Falmouth,' David Kean acknowledged their call, 'I'm handing over communications to Rory Fraser, my co-pilot, whilst I concentrate on landing. Both engines dead. Over!'

'Understood. We now have visual on you. I take it you will remain on your current trajectory, unless advised otherwise. Falmouth lifeboat has been alerted and we have instructed St Mawes ferry and the Flushing ferry to stand by for emergency rescue. The St Mawes'll turn up anyway, it's on its way back now. How many on board? Over!'

Rory Fraser switched to transmit, 'Yes, flight path as current. We are about a third full. Fifty passengers, including crew. Spanish government officials, various academics, CEOs and others bound for a conference here in Cornwall. As far as I know most, if not all, have a good command of English.'

'Ask him if he can see if our undercarriages are up,' David Kean addressed his co-pilot, 'tell him the indicator says they're up, they should be up, but we have no means of checking.'

The officer at the coastguard station picked up the query in the three-way exchange channel.

'Yes! All three, main bogies and nose wheel are up.'

'Good! I'm taking her down. Looks as though we will be passing somewhere between the two tankers anchored ahead of us.'

'That's not good. There's a South West Gig Racing Championship being held in the bay. About forty gigs in the event. One group is about to enter the zone just beyond those two ships, should be there in the next few seconds.'

'Hell's teeth! I can see them now. They're going at a fair lick. Look, I'm going to have to do the best I can. I'm going to be able to avoid the main bunch, I reckon, but I'm close to stall speed and haven't leeway to alter course by much.'

The pilot made a slight compensating adjustment to the course, as far as he dared, away from the main flotilla of gigs. Air speed was just a few knots above critical. He settled the aircraft at a pitch angle of about six degrees and let it approach the water in a vertical descent that was faster than he wanted. But to satisfy the conflicting requirements to save his passengers and that of avoiding the main body of gigs, whilst keeping the glide-in at just above stall speed, he had no option. A quick check on attitude showed the wings still horizontal. The sea no longer appeared a static medium as the choppy waves that looked like stationary crests at altitude, now rushed past creating the impression of a ride on a high speed hydrofoil.

As the tail plane touched down David Kean managed to set the ailerons, one more time, to sustain pitch angle just as the ram air turbine was ripped from its housing. The aircraft continued to skeet across the water. Both engine housings were now skimming the waves and the braking effect caused a rapid deceleration as the front cowling dug deeper into the water. The pylons joining the engines to the wings took the full force of the landing, but miraculously stayed attached.

The landing was more like a horizontal bungey jump on stiff elastic than the kind of abrupt impact experienced in a head-on collision. Passengers were pressed violently up against the backs of the seats in front, but no one actually sustained serious injury. That was more than could be said for the two lead gigs. Both, almost neck and neck, were caught by the port engine. With both engines now totally submerged, the plane floated to a halt, then began to drift as a light breeze started to nudge it in the direction of St Anthony Head.

It was chaos in the water. The splintered wreckage of both gigs, severed in two, floated amongst the injured oarsmen and women. Some were motionless, obviously fatalities. Others, uninjured, were frantically attempting to keep the heads of their dazed or unconscious team mates above water.

Rory Fraser glanced across the cockpit as he unbuckled, 'God knows what's waiting for us out there. We hit those gigs full-on.'

David Kean got up and waited for his co-pilot to exit in front of him. The emergency doors were already open and the inflated chutes deployed and filling with passengers. A number were crouched on the wing and were pulling gig rowers up over the flight surface.

'You stay here whilst I get back up through and check everyone's unbuckled. I'll exit through the rear service door, if I need to. As soon as all the flight attendants are off you follow through door one. Let's hope those boats get here soon.'

The evacuation was fast and orderly, but even so the senior pilot had to wait before being able to traverse the aisle. Up through the gangway he quickly checked toilets and galley. The plane's interior was now clear of passengers and still horizontal. Up at the tail end water was beginning to flood through the rear service door and David Kean decided his best option was to dash back through to the wing exits. By the time he reached them a number of gigs had pulled up

126

alongside and were reaching over the sides to pull their competitors out of the water.

A sudden shift in inclination had those few passengers still on the wing, scrambling towards the leading edge. There were gigs all-round the plane by this time. Rowers eased their boats alongside the leading and trailing edges of the wings and balanced their craft as passengers knelt, then grasped the oars before rising to sit astride the gunnels and slide into the safety of the gigs. Others transferred to the now detached chutes.

By this time the RNLI's semi-rigid Atlantic 75 had put out from its shed. Three of the crew had been doing routine work in the boathouse and were amidst the gig flotilla before The Duchess of Cornwall, the so named St Mawes ferry, was anywhere near the ditched aircraft. They took a load of passengers and gig rowers still on the wings and motored off towards the ferry. Transferring them was straightforward and within a few minutes they were back with a second load until the plane was cleared. The two pilots, as expected, were last to leave. They were taken into the RIB which then waited for the ferry to draw up to the stricken aircraft.

The main lifeboat arrived with a number of GPs who had been notified of the crash. They boarded the ferry. Their first job was to identify the most seriously injured of the gig crews. This done, they set about attempting to restore consciousness to the three or four still in a coma.

'Andy,' Dave Lobb spoke before he finished climbing up to the Cox, who was keeping tabs on things from the flying bridge, 'the senior flight attendant says one of his stewards is missing. Should have exited the plane after all the passengers were out.'

Andy Cornwell turned to his radio operator, 'Has he checked with the ferry?'

'Far as I know.'

'Better check with the aircraft's captain, see what his response is. The thing is still likely to stay afloat for a while, but I don't want anyone going back in looking for anyone 'til we know for sure he's missing. It's tipped up by about another five degrees since I've been watching.'

'OK, I'll put the inflatable into the water and get on to the Duchess before the Atlantic takes the more seriously injured to shore. That meet with your approval?'

'Yeah, go ahead. I'll keep a watch on the front exit door of the 320 while you're checking, but it's possible I might be directed to take casualties ahead of the ferry. If so, I'll come back to pick you and the inflatable up later. D'you want to take Chris with you?'

'Might be a good idea.'

'OK, get crackin'.'

The plane continued to slope upwards, then suddenly went into a backwards slide, its tail plane slicing down through the waves until it touched bottom. Its nose projected above the water, both front doors now submerged. It stayed like the muzzle of a large seal inspecting its surroundings. Andy eased back. Fuel was leaking into the water. The risk of fire was low, but still constituted a hazard. He decided to do a circuit around the aircraft just as a matter of routine and was cruising slowly towards the tip of the almost submerged tail fin when a signal from Falmouth Coastguard put a totally different gloss on the situation.

'We've just received a call from a mobile phone. There's someone inside the aircraft, trapped. He says he's in the flight deck. He's still in contact. Can you see anyone?'

Andy turned round and drew up to the front windows. Sure enough, the desperate, missing steward was standing on the back of the pilot's seat looking down at him. Andy radioed back to Falmouth confirming the report.

'Ask him why he's not opening the sliding window, emergency exit in the cockpit.'

The answer came back quickly, 'He says the thing is jammed and he's nothing to free it with.'

'OK. Look, we're going to need a diver. Get on to the fleet auxiliary ship in the harbour. There are some Special Boat Service people on board. We've been doing some joint exercises with them. The only chance we've got is if one of them can be got here in the next few minutes with scuba gear to get inside. I've no clue as to how long the air in the nose is going to stay sealed keeping the plane afloat.'

'OK. I'll get on to them straightaway. They've got high speed Zodiacs, but it's going to take ten or fifteen minutes I would think.'

'Don't know much about aircraft, but I reckon it won't stay above water that long at the rate it seems currently to be sinking.'

Andy kept the boat close to the aircraft's nose.

20

Elton Charlton, to give the missing steward his name, felt the Airbus give another shift. He regretted, too late, his decision to risk a return to the interior from the wing. Nobody had noticed. Everyone had been too busy looking at the activity in the water as he slipped back in. The pilot, checking the interior of the plane, was a few yards away with his back to the wing exit at the time. The steward saw his chance and raced up the aisle to the front galley. At the back of one of the storage cupboards was a half kilo of cocaine. Releasing one of the trolleys from its bay, he slid it out and overturned it. Standing on its side he was able to reach into the back recesses of the cupboard. He pulled out the compressed, plastic wrapped powder and stuffed it into his shirt just as the plane started to tip upwards. The trolley slipped back. The motion pulled his feet beyond his centre of balance. He pitched forward catching his forehead on the aluminium door of one of the lockers and dazed, dropped backwards to fall in a heap against the back partition of the galley.

He must only have lain there a few seconds before coming to his senses. It was at this point the plane gave its lurch and slid tail-wise down into the water until its rear fuselage struck the sandy sea bed. The front passenger doorways were now practically submerged and, more than waist deep in water, his lifejacket had inflated. The trapped steward made his second wrong decision of the day. Instead of removing his life jacket and risking escape below water, through one of the two doors, he scrabbled towards the daylight filtering through from the cockpit, finding what hand holds he could. Reaching the interior he was able to pull himself up to the pilot's seat. Out of breath and in a near state of panic he managed to kneel then stand on the seat back. The catch on the sliding window was within reach. He released it, but could not budge the window. There must have been some distortion of the housing, or maintenance had neglected to check regularly for malfunction. He could see the lifeboat circling the area. At that point he remembered his mobile should be in the chest pocket of his tunic. Relieved, he fetched it out. It was still dry. Within a short while it was registering a signal. He dialled and explained his position to the emergency services.

The coastguard subsequently assigned to his case notified the unfortunate man that the lifeboat would remain on standby and that help was on its way, in the person of a team of SBS divers with scuba gear. This provided some relief to him, but it would be short-lived.

'What's happening with the SBS mob?' Andy radioed into the coastguard station, 'The plane's just moved another fraction. Don't reckon it's got more than a minute before she goes.'

'I'll give 'em another call.'

Andy put the throttles on idle so as to minimise disturbance. By this time the two in the lifeboat's inflatable had picked up the news about the steward and returned to the boat ready to be hauled aboard.

'The SBS are kitted up,' the message came through on Andy's headset, 'should be with you in about six minutes. What's it looking like now?'

'Not good! In fact she's beginning to go just as I'm speaking.'

The terrified steward mouthed something to Andy before toppling off the seat as the nose sank forward and disappeared with a swirl below the water. The light in the flight deck turned green then darker, as the sunlight streaming through the cockpit windows penetrated the interior less and less with each foot the stricken aircraft sank towards the sea bed.

The cockpit took a surge of water through the flight deck doorway. An air pocket formed, which gave the flight attendant some respite. His life jacket kept him located within the bubble of air, about a couple of feet deep, but as time passed with agonising slowness, the trapped man's thoughts alternated between hope and despair. The water inside was just above the level of the instrument panels. Fumbling inside his shirt, he located the pack of cocaine. If rescue came, there was no way he could conceal it, so he'd have to leave it. But if he was going to drown, then he might as well sniff some of the contents and die in a state of euphoria, but how to decide? He put the pack back and stared at the grey/green light filtering through the panel of glass separating him from the greater depth of chilly water outside.

Although this was a special charter flight, he was familiar with the normal scheduled flights from Spain, Barcelona or Madrid. That was why he'd been selected for this duty. His first assignment as a drug mule came about through frequent visits to a gay bar in Barcelona, a bar of questionable history. There it soon became known he was an airline attendant. His spending habits, like many a homosexual, inclined towards a hedonistic extravagance that frequently stretched his monthly pay check beyond the black. It didn't take long for the bar's regular clients to suspect his expenditure exceeded his income and during one of his more inebriated bouts, he was approached by an opportunistic local with connections to a North African drug cartel.

'Approached' might have been a rather fine way of putting it. 'Coerced' was a more appropriate term to describe his introduction to crime. An intimate encounter in an alley with an under-age rent boy was set up by a dealer. He was then 'discovered' by one of the dealer's associates, impersonating a police officer and trapped into carrying packages of cocaine to the UK. This was the start of the whole drug running saga, not that he objected to the lucrative pay off, it extended his range of indulgence.

He was beginning to shiver. The water level remained almost static as the air pressure inside the flight deck balanced the exterior water pressure. Nonetheless, he could see the surface, millimetre by millimetre even in that dim, eerie light, creeping slowly up the central strut separating the two front windows.

'Where the fuck are they?' Charlton shouted at the windows in exasperation.

The panic returned, then anger. He cursed the geese; he cursed the SBS divers; he cursed the bogus police officer. He then lapsed into a state of gibbering madness.

It was about then that an Arctic 22, rigid inflatable, slalomed to a halt alongside the lifeboat. Three men were on board. Two were kitted out in Divex Shadow diving gear, a third operated the outboard. The senior officer, Jock McLean, exchanged information with Andy.

'We're going down with emergency breathing kit. My oppo, Lieutenant Mason, is standing by as back-up. You said he was in the cockpit when he went down?'

'Last I saw. Standing on the pilot's seat I would guess.'

'OK. We'll waste no more time. What's the depth?'

'Well, you can see the top of the fin. She's in twenty five feet of water. Visibility down below not too bad, you can see from here. Sandy bottom, no muddy silt. Sand settled quickly.'

Jock ordered his helmsman to take the RIB to a spot above the fuselage where the front passenger doors were located. The two divers put their breathing mouthpieces in, checked their masks, gave 'thumbs up' and dropped over the side. The helmsman handed over a canvas sack with mask and re-breathable emergency diving kit to one of the divers, who clipped the lanyard attached to it, to a ring on his harness. Within seconds the two were peering through the flight deck windows. The trapped flight attendant was still mouthing obscenities and as he caught sight of the two divers his madness intensified. He thrashed his way towards them and screamed threats and abuse. In his mind they were more bogus police come to force him into further torment.

McLean turned to Bob Mason and made a screw movement with his index finger to his helmet. He then pointed at Charlton and simulated a knockout blow to the jaw, bringing his fist up under his chin by way of signalling intention. Signalling again, he communicated that he should enter the cockpit first followed by his junior officer. Unclipping the lanyard he handed the sack to Mason and propelled himself towards one of the main passenger doors. With one backward look at Bob, he nodded and, with a flick of webbed feet, entered the fuselage.

Charlton was up against a side window. Jock surfaced behind him, took out his mouthpiece and spoke to the still raving attendant. The man turned and flailed towards the officer. He hit out, but Jock was ready. Catching his wrist he twisted. The action forced the steward to rotate and submerge, in spite of his buoyancy aid. By this time Bob Mason had surfaced alongside his companion and put both hands on the man's shoulders, keeping his face under water. Jock McLean replaced his mouthpiece and pulled the canvas sack up from beneath his helper's legs. He nodded to Mason, who raised the struggling attendant's head above water. The ducking seemed to have restored the man to sanity. McLean retrieved the tubing and mouthpiece from the sack and gestured to Charlton to put it in his mouth. Again, Jock removed his mouthpiece so he could speak to the attendant.

'I'm going to have to deflate your lifejacket a bit so that we can bring you through the door and back up with us. Are you OK with that?'

Charlton nodded.

'Before that I need to make adjustments to the apparatus and give you some instructions as to how to breathe. Put this mask on and once you're happy about what to do, we'll get going.'

Jock gave his 'pupil' a brief explanation on how to manage the breathing gear. Satisfied the steward was breathing correctly, he told him he was to hold on to the sack attached to Bob Mason and follow him out of the fuselage when ready.

'I'm going to be behind you, so if you get into difficulties I can come up alongside and sort you out. But it'll only take about five or six seconds to reach the surface once we exit the plane and there's a boat waiting above to pull you in. I'm going to deflate your lifejacket now.'

The trio then moved under the cross-panel above the flight deck doorway and out into the darker space of the A320's galley area. Charlton panicked again and scrabbled at Bob Mason's back and breathing tube. Mason turned to face the man now threshing in his attempts to return to the cockpit. Jock sensed the problem as soon as the attendant started to force his way past him. He gave Charlton a blow to the side of the chin. The man's mouthpiece dislodged. Both divers were now faced with a dazed and choking burden to rescue. Bob wasted no time and grabbed the steward under the armpits. Jock lifted his feet and the two negotiated the space through to the nearest passenger door. Their ascent took about ten seconds. They broke surface close to the RIB. Their helmsman guided the craft up to the trio and lent over to hold the victim's head clear of the water. Bob Mason pulled himself up on to the inflated side of the Arctic 22 and, sitting astride the tube, gripped the now still flight attendant. The two in the boat, assisted by Jock in the water, heaved their man onto and into the RIB.

'He's only been fifteen or twenty seconds without air. Start on him right away, he'll be alright.' Jock instructed his helmsman to resuscitate the limp flight attendant as he heaved himself up over the side. Sam Mitchell, the boat's steersman, disconnected and removed the deflated lifejacket from the victim, checked his mouth cavity, rolled him on his stomach and applied a lung-draining technique before again rolling him on to his back in preparation for the sequence of compressions of the man's rib cage.

'Jesus, look at this!' Sam held up the package of cocaine that had obstructed his first attempt to apply the life-saving action to the steward's chest. Dropping it at his side and shaking his head, 'Bloody fool,' he muttered to himself and started for a second time to resuscitate the man. After a few pumps Charlton's lungs responded. He spluttered back to consciousness.

'So that's what it was all about,' Jock picked up the package, 'we should have let the bastard drown. With a bit of ill-luck on our part he could have done us some serious damage down there.'

By this time Andy Cornwell had brought the lifeboat alongside the Arctic and could see by their body language that the three SBS men were not in a benevolent state of mind, were not jubilant at having made a successful rescue.

Jock, sitting on the edge of his boat, looked across at Andy and nodded towards the figure lying in the RIB at the same time putting a foot on the stewards chest, 'The stupid bastard must have gone back to get this,' Jock waved the plug of cocaine in the air.

The pinioned flight attendant was devoid of energy and just lay there defeated, his mind a mix of relief at being rescued and trepidation at knowing an uncertain length of time awaited him at Her Majesty's Pleasure.

'We'd better get him in here,' Andy called across, 'he's going to be suffering from hypothermia. He can't go far, that's for sure and I'll radio the police to be ready to take him when we get back.'

Jock nodded and the two divers got Charlton up ready to slide him across to the Tamar. It was then they noticed his jaw was crooked and swelling up.

'You broke his fucking jaw.' Bob said, with poorly disguised humour, 'That'll make for a peaceful journey back.'

'Wish I'd broken his fuckin' neck. These bastards supply the likes of the one who robbed my neighbour to finance his addiction.

Widower. Knocked him unconscious, took his wife's wedding ring, other jewellery she used to own and cash. It was an honest jeweller he tried to palm it off on in the next town who shopped him. Pretended he needed to get his loupe to examine the stone in a ring. Alerted the police and they were there in about two minutes. Neighbour badly concussed.'

Two of the lifeboat crew stood by on the gangway as the two divers roughly handled the now fully alert steward and gave him a shove across the gap between boats.

'We'll follow you in and hand this over to the police,' Jock pointed to the cocaine, 'better notify Customs. They'll need to get information from our trafficking friend here. But they're going to have to wait a few days, I guess, until he can move his jaw.'

'Fine, we'll get going now. Nothing else to be done. Expect you'll need to get back to your ship, but if you want to join us in the boathouse for a decent cup of coffee, before you do, you're welcome.'

'Might take you up on that. See you back at base. I guess the medics'll be dealing with the situation from now on, at Customs House Quay.'

'Dunno! The ferrys might have been instructed to go to the other pier. Easier and quicker for the ambulances.'

'OK. See you later.'

The Arctic was gunned up, turned around and lined up to the right of the stern of the now departing Tamar.

21

'Good turn out.' Mike Traherne greeted Sam Markham, owner of the chandlery and a benefactor to the local RNLI branch. Both were at a public meeting called to air issues raised by the proposed dredging of the harbour, coupled with an unrelated issue: the siting of an experimental, floating, offshore wind farm. There were local tradesmen, fishermen, representatives of local tourist attractions, marine biologists, dock industrialists, officers from the port authority, ecologists and others. Others constituted students and what one of the audience termed 'bloody tree-huggers'.

The meeting's chairman, Bob Mitchell, an aeronautical engineer and designer of light aircraft, owned a small float plane manufacturing company. His set-up was mainly a conversion enterprise, buying in ready-made land based aircraft and replacing wheeled landing gear with floats. As a separate, currently non-profit organisation, he also had a small research and development team doing feasibility studies into water take-off drones, financed by MOD grants. He looked up from the pile of papers he was ordering on the table fronting the meeting and spotted Markham. Getting up from his chair, he skirted the table and walked up to the owner of the chandlery. They shook hands.

'Good to see you. Must be two years since we last met.'

'Honfleur. I think you had flown in the day before.'

'That's right. Delivered a plane to a local private flier. That meal we had, Blaise Pascal Square? Oysters like no other.'

Sam Markham nodded, 'This is Mike Traherne, local lifeboat crew. Mike: Bob Mitchell. Bob and I go back a long way.'

Mike stood and shook hands with Bob Mitchell, 'I've seen you drive through the docks to your factory the other end. I'm always fascinated to see a new plane doing its trials in the estuary.'

'Well, as you're that close, come around for a tour sometime. In fact, Sam, you've never been round have you? Why don't you both come Saturday afternoon, if you're free that is. I'm taking up a four-seater for a spin. Just replaced the floats and need to try her out. Look, must get back to the table. Will catch up after the meeting and fix the visit then. Promises to be a lively meeting,' he grinned knowingly at the two and made his way back to the front.

'Bob and I used to sail in the Solent. He worked for a local aircraft company, saw a niche market for float planes, got experience with a company in Canada and took off from there, so to speak. Falmouth an ideal base for him. So convenient being able to deliver fuselages and wings by ship to Falmouth for conversion.'

'I've always wanted to have a look at his set up, being on the doorstep.'

'If I know Bob, it'll be interesting and he'll suggest a meal later, at the yacht club, I'm pretty sure. Glad he's chairing. Fair, but brooks no nonsense.'

A call to order came from the table. A number of speakers were called to deliver the viewpoints of the various interests represented before questions were opened to the floor, with strict instructions to limit their delivery to the three minute slot they had previously been allocated. Discussion followed. Heat between factions with opposing opinions soon developed. The main controversy focussed on the deposits of maerl, a kind of coral, in the bed of the estuary. There were two aspects, the layers of dead maerl which accommodated various marine organisms and the clusters of living maerl deposited on the sea bed. One of the objectors was Dave Lobb.

'It seems to me, the relocation of the dead maerl won't ensure re-establishment of the fish nurseries that live in it. My livelihood depends on the fish I catch locally.'

One of the dock representatives countered. 'But it doesn't say it won't. Who's to say it might not have a beneficial effect. In any case, nature reasserts itself. The harbour used to be dredged by the bucket dredger on a regular, daily basis anyway. Nobody raised any objections then. Employment in the docks depends on a clear passage for the bigger ships. We need to keep our jobs.'

Dave turned towards the speaker, 'That dredging was done on the silt. We're talking about a different zone.'

'We're not talking about removing half of Cornwall. We're just talking about a short channel joining Carrick Roads to the Inner Harbour. If anything a slight deepening of the channel will improve the cleansing action of the sea water, making for beneficial ecological gains.'

Mike Traherne raised his hand.

'Yes?' Bob Mitchell pointed in acknowledgement.

'As one who works in the docks, my father and grandfather before that, I accept other people's concerns and support responsible development of the harbour, but our jobs are as important to us as anyone else's livelihood. I would have thought the nursery habitat would re-establish itself again in a year or two. Helford River supports protected fish nurseries and how much fishing is carried out 'round here anyway?'

'There's several of us operate out of the harbour and we want to keep doin' it,' Dave Lobb replied, glaring at his fellow crew member, 'it's no good taking a chance like this and causing irreversible damage to potential fish stock.'

Mike Traherne pursed his lips. The last thing he wanted was ill-feeling. It made life unpleasant and caused uncertainty, but he owed allegiance, not only to the lifeboat crew, but to his fellow workmen at the docks.

'I agree, but the adult fish which lay down the eggs will put them somewhere else. The experts might care to comment on the re-location of the dredged material. Also, if the dead, calciferous maerl is washed free from any silt before being re-deposited, won't the same nursery infrastructure be regenerated after a while?'

One of the research ecologists turned to Bob Mitchell and signalled his willingness to respond. His answer appeared to satisfy the questioner and at this point the conversation wilted, both opposing parties running out of steam.

The chairman saw his chance, 'Ladies and gentlemen, I think we had better move on and re-open the floor to other voices. Are there any different points that have not been raised?'

'Just one.' A voice from the back, a voice barely audible, made people turn round in their seats to identify the owner.

'Would you like to give your name and state your interest?'

'No to the first. Yes to the second.' The voice belonged to a woman whose skin appeared parchment thin and was the colour of a segment of shin bone, polished smooth from years of use as a napkin ring.

A frisson rustled through the meeting as the gathering expected the makings of a mystery and anticipated some further conflict or revelation of history long forgotten.

'The pagan rites,' she only got that far, a groan went up from various people, who, by that very reaction, must have known her. 'It's all very well you groaning, but if you change that channel, you change the Ley lines and if you change the Ley lines you change the fortunes of Falmouth.'

'What bleddy drivel,' it was one of the towns people spoke up, 'course it'll change the fortunes of Falmouth, for the better and what about the end of the world you predicted would happen three months ago? We're still waiting!'

The last contributor restored balance to the proceedings and the pagan protester glared around, muttered a few comments and stared at the front table. There appearing to be no further uptake from the floor, Bob Mitchell took the opportunity to address the meeting, 'Taking off my chairman's hat, so to speak, I have to declare an interest, as a member from the floor, in dredging, because of my aircraft interests. I note the dredge starts well out into mid-estuary. In a spirit of openness I would like to put a question to the Harbour Commissioners, will there be buoys or fixed posts marking the new channel?'

'Yes, two posts. There is a proposal that these posts will project three metres above high tide levels and will carry Port and Starboard lights for night navigation. A series of buoys will then mark the path into the dock basin.'

'I ask, because I have a license permitting aircraft taxiing and turning access within Carrick Roads at certain periods. If this is now restricted it could cause problems when weather conditions make other tests, out in the bay, unsuitable for trials.'

'Point noted,' a member of the board responded. 'This will need to be examined in due course. I'll put it on the agenda for the next board meeting. We might need to call you to discuss feasible options if there are issues arising that interfere with your existing terms.'

'Fine.' Bob Mitchell then signalled a change of subject by re-stacking the bunch of sheets in front of him.

'This seems to be a convenient time to invite questions about the off-shore wind farm. Before opening the matter for discussion, I will give a few brief details by way of clearing up some misconceptions that, apparently, are going the rounds. You have had an opportunity to look at the chart, at the back of the room, showing the location off Pennance Point, or Stack Point as it is locally known. The important thing to bear in mind is that it is not a collection of structures fixed to the sea bed, as some erroneously think, but a large pontoon carrying three turbines. I also stress the fact that it is a pilot scheme. The reason for three turbines is so they can be placed at the apexes of an equilateral triangle so that aerodynamic balance and hydrodynamic stability of the pontoon is achieved. We're also experimenting with cylindrical blade sets. These are not a common configuration, but it means we don't have to re-align blade hub axes every time wind direction changes. Their fixture to a pontoon is firstly to make routine servicing easier, secondly to avoid the safety issues associated with remote, offshore farms and thirdly to be able to tow the pontoon into the shelter of a harbour when severe storm warnings are forecast.'

Bob leaned back in his chair, folded his arms and indicated his readiness to receive comments and questions.

'Do we need a wind farm off Falmouth? It's a busy port area and centre for all kinds of nautical venues. I would have thought the bay cluttered with semi-permanent flotillas of pontoons would prove a great obstruction, if not a hazard.' The speaker looked around for support.

'Any attempt at reducing carbon consumption has to be a good thing.' One of the 'green' members of the audience countered.

'Yes, but if close proximity to a port is important, exactly how close does close mean? Five hundred metres out, a thousand, ten miles, what are we talking about?'

Bob turned to the engineer in charge of the project, 'I think this is one for you.'

'Good morning ladies and gentlemen. My name is Dick Rogers. The location of the pilot trial is, as you can see on the chart, located about two hundred metres due east of Pennance Point. This makes it close enough to the harbour for towing to shelter. If this proves successful, then twelve turbines, that means four pontoons, would be located about two miles east of Rosemullion Head. That's more or less due south of Pendennis Point. Each of two pontoons can be connected along a common edge to form a diamond shape and towed into harbour on the rare occasion when a severe storm warning is forecast. That's about the extent of the project. The other important point, is that the whole project will bring work to the docks. Also, and more importantly, the mobility of a pontoon makes the feasibility of temporary, floating, generating platforms a useful concept where non-permanent energy sources would be useful at say, the site of marine disasters such as that of the Costa Concordia. This means that production can continue within the docks, one hopes, due to an export demand, once the versatility of such a mobile energy source is recognised. I think that is about as much as I need say.'

Bob Mitchell thanked the speaker and re-emphasised the benefit, to the local work force, of the intention to create a long term manufacturing business out of the trial.

'Right, it's gone nine thirty. Unless there is any serious issue that anyone feels has not been addressed, I think this is a good time to stop.'

No one from the floor responded, so Bob Mitchell publicly thanked the various speakers, gathered up his papers and left the table to join Sam Markham and Mike Traherne. The latter was engaged, again, in a discussion, bordering on argument, with Dave Lobb. The two broke off as he approached and Dave Lobb took that as an opportunity to leave.

'Some people not happy about this dredging,' Bob greeted the two men with his remark, having caught the tail end of the discussion as he approached, 'but there seems to be a lot more for than against.'

'Dave Lobb,' Sam nodded in the direction of the departing fisherman, 'is part of the same crew as Mike here. Makes for an awkward situation.'

'Dave's a good sort,' Mike added, 'but it's a controversy that has to be faced.'

Bob nodded. 'Anyway, back to what I was saying earlier, 'You've had time to think. Saturday alright for a visit? Say, two-thirty at the dock entrance. I'll pick you up and then we can take the plane up for a spin after you've had a look around the factory.'

'Fine! Both of us on board for that.'

'Right, see you then.'

22

The RNLI Carrick Maid headed back into port after a late evening exercise. Alex Jago stood beside Andy Cornwell, on the flying bridge, as he explained the significance of various navigational lights blinking within the confines of the estuary. At eight knots, the harbour speed limit, the boat made hardly any noise.

'Wait a minute! What are those buggers doing?' Alex looked in the direction Andy was facing. It took her only a few seconds to spot a medium sized Zodiac pulled up to the side of one of the moored cabin cruisers. Two men were in the deck well. One of them was bent over the outboard motor, the other holding a torch. A third was watching them from the smaller craft.

'That's Pete Odger's boat. Owns the cafe on The Moor. Dave,' Andy called his radio operator, 'get on to the police and tell 'em we've got a theft in progress. Tell 'em we'll shadow them. They'll be heading for a cove or creek somewhere nearby, sure to be, with a pick-up handy. We'll give them directions as it pans out.'

'Right Cox!'

'Second thoughts. Contact the boat house first. The Atlantic 75 crew should still be about. Tell them what's happening and ask them to put out and meet us. Alex, you happy to stay on top?'

'Fine by me. See more from here.'

'You'll get thrown about a bit if they head out to sea and we have to follow them to a beach. That's why I ask. If they do, we'll have to get the dingy out of the stern. If they push up the river somewhere, to a creek, we'll still have to get the dingy out. So I'm asking you to give a hand if that happens. I'm going to continue on as if I haven't seen 'em and hope they're not spooked by us.'

Andy Cornwell took the Tamar on towards the berthing area, but traced an about-turn as soon as he was out of sight of the three men. He pulled alongside the St Mawes ferry, Duchess of Cornwall anchored at its moorings, switching off his lights as he put the ferry between him and the thieves, now back in their line of sight.

'Dave,If these jokers move before the Atlantic meets us, tell our mob we'll put on our navigation lights and train our spot on them as we follow. Who's helmsman?'

'Matt Henwood. He's bringing Janner and Dan. Hang on, I've got Devon & Cornwall police back on line. I'll get back to you when they've finished.'

Andy hadn't long to wait.

'They're putting a patrol car on the Roseland Peninsula, ready, in case they drop off that side and one on the A39. They say the Dock Police are without a launch at the moment, but they've contacted Culdrose. They also think this could be part of a gang operating regularly between Poole and Plymouth, but extending their range, in which case they're likely to have something like a fast Sealine or Bavaria Sport waiting outside the estuary. Pinched thousands of quid's worth of motors and nav equipment all along this coast and reckon it's worth the cost of putting up a Sea King to net the buggers.'

The outboard motor seemed to be giving the two men some trouble, but at last they freed it from its transom and heaved it up into the well of the cruiser. They dragged it across to the gunnel, took a breather, then lifted it up onto the boat's edge. The third man steadied it whilst the other two slid over the side into the inflatable with him. There, they slanted the motor and eased it over the side into the Zodiac. That done the two climbed back to the deck of the other boat and disappeared into its cabin. It wasn't long before they reappeared hefting some black electronic equipment, easier this time to lower into their boat.

By this time Andy could hear the note of the Atlantic's outboard twins as it approached from the inner reaches of the harbour.

'Right, time to make a move. Nav lights and spot, we'll show the buggers.'

Andy fired up the diesels, shot out from behind the ferry and shone the spot on the three men as he left the Duchess of Cornwall rocking in the wash of his bow wave. The two men on the cruiser leapt into the Zodiac as their helmsman fired up and pulled away, almost capsizing it. Steering for the mouth of the Fal, it was obvious they were making for the open sea.

The Atlantic raced past the Tamar with the three crewmen on board crouched low in the much faster RIB. It was easily matching the speed of the getaway, keeping to one side of the V-wave created by the latter a hundred metres or so in front of them.

Just outside St Anthony Head the escape boat turned on an easterly course. Another boat appeared from the small cove, just past the lighthouse and headed straight for the Zodiac. As the police predicted, it was a Sealine sports cruiser. Passing within two or three yards of the escaping craft a crewman in a balaclava mask tossed a line to the three men just as both boats, simultaneously, idled their engines and slowed to a halt by the natural drag of the water. A second man appeared with a shotgun.

The Atlantic 75 raced towards the pair of boats, but eased off as orange flame erupted into the air from the shotgun they could now see illuminated by the approaching Tamar's spotlight.

'I'm going to pull ahead in front of that cruiser. They can't get off a shot at us if we weave about and create a bit of turbulence in front of 'em. You happy with that?' Matt Henwood looked at the other two.

'Too bloody right.' Janner Janes grinned.

'I'm in for a bit of cat an' mouse with the buggers. Nobody's goin' to wave a gun at me and get away with it.' Dan Brewer leaned forward towards the other two by way of affirming his stand.

The VHF receiver alerted them to a call from the following lifeboat.

'I saw that. Shotgun?' Andy said more by way of comment than question.

'Yeah Cox. I'm going to get in front of them and create some rough water. Slow 'em down a bit when they get going. Any news from Culdrose?'

'I've radioed them, told them the score and the police. They put up a Sea King about three minutes or more ago. Should be here in about three or four minutes.'

The Atlantic's crew watched as the gang hurriedly secured their Zodiac to the much more powerful Sealine. As the larger cabin cruiser took up the slack, Matt throttled up and set course at seven degrees to their intended track. The guy with the shotgun found the motion too rocky and was forced to grab a side bar to steady himself. As the cruiser accelerated away, Matt cut across its path, about twenty metres in front of its bow and proceed to weave to and fro ahead of it. No way could the gunman get a clear shot. Slowed by the turbulence created by the Atlantic and the Zodiac it was towing, the larger boat altered course for the open sea instead of hugging the shoreline. It expected the pursuing craft would find the going rougher.

The fleet of vessels would have presented an interesting tableau to anyone able to see the action from the cliffs. Matt kept up the obstruction tactics as Dan, facing astern, relayed steering instructions in line with the cruiser's counter-moves. The going got rougher as both craft got beyond the relative shelter of Gerrans Bay. With the Zodiac in tow, the Sealine was unable to counter the waves that caught her broadside on. The three men being towed were hanging on to gunnel ropes, fighting each jerk and slap of their craft as it responded to the power surges of the cruiser. Spray and waves were adding to their misery as the floor of the Zodiac filled with water and vomit. Suddenly, the tow boat leapt ahead, as the towline ripped the fastening it was tied to from the front of the RIB. The cleat pulled away a substantial part of the boat. Air escaped from the inflated upper hull in a rush and the whole craft, without buoyancy, just flat-nosed into the waves. The loose motor, navigation equipment and bodies were tossed into the sea. Dan spotted the fiasco and shouted to Matt for instructions.

'We'll let Andy pick them up. He's not far behind. Call him on the VHF and tell him we'll continue with the obstruction tactics.'

The Sealine, no longer encumbered, easily matched the speed of the Atlantic 75 and surged ahead not concerned with the fate of the other three. Matt glanced behind and decided to run a straight course to keep distance between him and the cruiser. The latter headed back on to a diagonal track towards the coast and the relatively calmer water. This made for a more dangerous situation since the gunman now had a steadier deck between his feet. A spray of pellets raked the top of the Atlantic. Matt felt the impact as shot penetrated his storm gear. Dan and Janner also caught a few of the pellets. Dan in the cheek and Janner in the chest.

'Tell Andy we've been hit, but nothing serious', Matt shouted to Dan, 'if you're OK, we'll carry on, but give them a wider berth.' The two crewmen gave him the thumbs up as Matt slewed the boat away from the other craft. The two now ran neck and neck but separated by more than the range of the shotgun. A different note penetrated the sound of outboard engines and rush of water against hulls as the navigation lights of a helicopter, a few hundred yards away, signalled the arrival of the Sea King.

'Hello Ace of Clubs,' Andy called the pilot as the latter made contact with the lifeboat, 'our Atlantic crew have been fired on. The Sealine has a shotgun on board.'

'OK, I've got them in line of sight. Leave them to us. I'll hail them. We've got weapons and we'll threaten them with a capsize if they don't heave to and put their gun down. Tell your RIB crew to fall away and follow at a safe distance. There's a Royal Navy River class patrol vessel just off St Austell Bay. That's about ten or a dozen nautical miles away. She can be here in about half an hour and put a landing party aboard.'

'Acknowledged.' Andy passed the instruction on to Matt and the chase continued.

'Sealine,' the helicopter pilot trained a powerful beam of light on the cabin cruiser and hailed them through an equally powerful loud-hailer system, 'this is Flight Lieutenant Roberts. I am commanding you to put down your weapon and stand to.'

The escaping vessel showed no sign of slowing down, its occupants now out of sight inside the covered space.

'I repeat, cut your engines.'

The cruiser remained on course.

'Right,' Flt Lt Roberts spoke to one of his crew located in the open door of the Sea King, 'put a bullet into the windscreen. I'm going to pull down to twenty metres. I'll pursue at his speed and approach to within fifty metres. Give me the OK when you're ready.'

'OK skipper.'

The copter sent up a drenching storm of spray that engulfed bow, midships and stern of the Sealine, ensuring none of its crew could use the shot gun. Lining up his sight, the marksman put a single shot, side-on, into the protective shield of glass. The effect was instantaneous. An opaque pattern of crazed lines replaced the clear panel of curved glass, the damage clearly visible to the crew in the helicopter.

One of the gang rammed the pole of a boat hook against the glass and pushed out the shattered panel to make a hole for the helmsman to look through. This was a mistake. The Flt Lt banked his Sea King across the bow of the vessel and sent a plume of water through into the cockpit. Within seconds the electrics were flooded and the boat came to a halt. Hovering, again within hailing distance, the officer gave instructions for the occupants to come out of the cabin and sit aft on the stern platforms.

'There is a Royal Navy patrol ship in the vicinity. It is coming to seize your vessel. I advise you to offer no further resistance.'

Three men appeared and sat within view of the aircrew, but not before one of them tossed the shotgun overboard. Not knowing pellets were embedded in the crew of the Atlantic RIB and believing he was destroying evidence, his action wouldn't save him from a serious charge of causing grievous bodily harm.

'I'm going back to base now,' Flt Lt Roberts radioed Andy, 'these can't give you any trouble. They've tossed the gun overboard, so no threat from that quarter. The navy should be here soon. I've told them you're in place. You OK with that?'

'Yes. We'll stay until they arrive and double up when they put a boat in the water. We've got the other three here. Let them stay in the drink for a while to cool down, so to speak, before we hauled them out. Have them sitting back to back. Nice little threesome, tied together like trussed chicken. They're not going anywhere. Thanks again for your assistance. See you on the next exercise.'

'Glad to be of help. Like a bit of real action now and again. Au revoir.'

The Sea King banked away and set off back to base.

Matt Henwood brought the RIB up to the Tamar. The Sealine was a good three hundred metres off shore and the noise of waves breaking against sheer cliff and the darkness would deter any attempt by her crew of three to escape by swimming to land.

'I've just been contacted by HMS Fulmar. She's less than twenty minutes away.' Andy called down to Matt. 'Do you want to come aboard and let the doc give you the once-over. Alex will keep the spot focussed on that mob over there.'

'Well, I don't feel any pain. Don't think I've got any wounds, the storm gear took the energy out of the shot, I'm pretty sure, but there's a fair amount of blood pouring down Dan's face. Think it won't hurt for him to be looked at, although he says he's alright. Janner, like me, took a hit in the jacket and is pretty sure he's not wounded.'

'OK, send him up.'

Dan climbed up onto the deck of the Tamar.

'I'd like to give you three a kick in the balls for your trouble,' he said as he passed the still sea-sick mob tied together on the aft deck, 'but I don't like vomit on my boots.'

Doc Truman gave a chuckle as he escorted the wounded crewman into an area of the inner space that doubled as a sort of sick bay when needed.

'Keep your life jacket on, but take your helmet off. I'll give the flotation kit a check-over after to see it's not punctured. Turn your face towards the light. I need to swab the blood away, don't need to tell you it's going to sting. Looks like you've got about three pellets in your cheek. But before that I'm going to photograph the wounds.'

That done the medic dabbed at the damaged face, 'You're lucky. This one,' Dan could feel the swab Doc Truman was using to indicate the wound, 'is just on the edge of your lower eye socket, about a centimetre from your eye. The bone has stopped it doing damage to your sight. The other two are in thicker flesh. We'll have all three out in a jiffy. Do you want a shot of local?'

'No. The soreness'll come later. No point in wasting the stuff.'

Dan heard the tinny sound as the first pellet was extracted with tweezers and dropped in a metal bowl. The other two needed a bit of probing about to release them. By the time the first aid was completed Dan's face looked like he'd been pecked a few times by an angry skua. The job done, the doctor cleaned up the tweezers and tipped the pellets into a polythene bag as evidence and took one more photograph.

'I'm putting a pad over the wounds. It's pretty good sticky tape that holds it on, but I think you should go back with us, strapped in to a seat and let someone else take your place on the Atlantic. On that score we'd better swap spare life jackets for the ones Matt and Janner are wearing. They could be punctured. Can you tell them? On second thoughts I'll do it. You get inside.'

Doc Truman put his gear away and reported to Andy who had come down to the wheelhouse.

'Have checked Dan over. Nothing serious, but think he needs to come back with us. That OK. Also, what d'you think, better change the life jackets on Matt and Janner? They could have been punctured.'

'Fine! Matt can take the Atlantic back with Janner. We can take a couple of jackets from down in the respite area. D'you want to sort that? Not sure if the these jokers will be escorted back by HMS Fulmar, or if they'll take a launch in to the police at Falmouth and hand them over. My guess is they'll put them in a secure cell and take them back to Devonport, eventually.'

'How near are they now?'

'Still about ten or fifteen minutes away.'

The doctor fetched a pair of lifejackets from the storage area, below the wheelhouse and brought them up to exchange with the Atlantic's crew.

***

'Captain Simon Cameron here, Carrick Maid, I can see your navigation lights.' Andy picked up the message from the patrol vessel and signalled back immediately, 'We have you in view too, Captain. Will stay put. Presumably you will put down a tender to take this mob on board?'

'That's the intention. How many?'

'Six. Three on our deck, trussed up. Three on the Sealine. Their cabin cruiser is incapacitated. The Sea King did a good job. See you soon. ETA?'

'I would say seven minutes, according to your range.'

'OK. Await your arrival.'

23

Alex Jago took her gaze from the approaching warship and glanced across at the Sealine. What made her look she wasn't sure, but some change in atmosphere, some alteration in activity, it was probably sound, made her look in its direction. Re-aligning the spotlight on to the vessel, only two of the crew were in evidence sitting at the stern. The sound of a reluctant engine being powered up left her in no doubt, the cabin cruiser was being re-started. What little she knew about engines, car engines in particular, led her to guess the cruiser had somehow been hot-wired, by-passing its saturated ignition circuit. She called down to Andy.

'I'll be up with you in a jiffy. Keep the spot on them. The Fulmar will be here, I hope, in time to do something. I'll give them a call and let 'em know the score.'

The Sealine, now under full power, 'upped' its bow and surged away from the two RNLI craft.

'Matt, get after them. We'll follow again.' Andy shouted across to his colleague.

The Fulmar, by this time, was close enough to illuminate the scene with powerful search lights.

'Hello, Carrick Maid,' Cameron addressed the Coxswain on the radio, 'tell your Atlantic crew to pull back. We're putting a fast patrol boat into the water. We have SBS personnel ready to deal with them. We'll put a shot or two into them if they don't pull up. They're not responding to any of our attempts at radio contact. Either their gear is damaged or is not switched on.'

Andy acknowledged the instruction and relayed the message to the inflatable's crew. The two Falmouth boats then followed the escaping cabin cruiser at a safe distance. Both crews watched with mounting excitement as the Fulmar did a spectacular broadside of a turn. Straightening up and keeping a moderate speed of knots, the patrol vessel released a grey, military grade Zodiac from its deck with four SBS personnel crouched within its sinister-looking, black gunnels. As soon as they hit the water and released the hoisting harness, they were away at a speed well in excess of that of the cruiser. Catching up and drawing alongside the racing cabin cruiser, they gestured for the vessel to stop, but were ignored.

'Right you bastards,' one of the SBS spoke to himself as the two vessels travelled neck and neck, 'enjoy the ride.' With one of his comrades illuminating the craft, he let loose a stream of bullets from a 9mm submachine gun along the waterline of the planing hull all the way up to the bow. As the craft bounced up and down, alternately exposing its smooth, fibre glass under-belly to air then sea, the break in streamlined flow, caused by the now ruptured surface, led to sudden and catastrophic failure of the front of the hull as it punched the choppy water for the last time. The punishing force of impact, with the unforgiving wall of water, ripped a kayak-sized chunk from the perforated hull of the vessel. Such an abrupt braking force caused the craft to up-end as the bow submerged and unspent kinetic energy put the whole structure into a cartwheel. The cruiser slapped keel upwards and deck downwards into the waves, ripping yet more of the structure from the hull as the cabin overhang absorbed the remaining energy.

'Bloody hell,' the helmsman of the Zodiac, used to spectacular outcomes in past military operations, swung his craft around in a tight circle to examine the wreckage, 'you spoilt the paintwork on that one Mick.'

It was pretty likely the occupants were dead or seriously injured. The gaping hole in the bow flooded the lower cabin quickly. Within a space of less than ten seconds the front end submerged and the craft slid forward to sit like an up-ended mallard foraging below water. This released the three crew. There was no movement from any of them as they floated free from the wreck. Two, obviously, had suffered broken necks. Their heads were hanging as though on hinges, totally uncharacteristic of that in a corpse that had undergone drowning. The third had lost most of his clothing as the jagged remains of the windscreen had torn into his chest and abdomen as he had exited the cockpit like a human cannon ball.

'Let's get these jokers inboard.' The SBS crew set about pulling the bodies up over the side of their assault craft.

'This one's still alive, but he's bleeding like a pig.'

153

'OK, I'll radio the bridge right away,' one of the four answered, 'and tell them we've got a casualty who needs urgent treatment.'

The four re-arranged their 'cargo' to give the Zodiac a better angle of attack, so to speak and raced off to the Fulmar. Their craft was 'harnessed', lifted out of the water and the unconscious civilian rushed off to a sick bay. Captain Cameron radioed the Carrick Maid and informed them of the outcome.

'We've got the trio from the cruiser. Two are dead, the other unconscious. I'm putting a tender into the water now, to come and pick up your captives. There'll be five men, two will be armed with 9mm pistols, so there shouldn't be any resistance. They'll bring handcuffs and leg chains. The latter shouldn't be necessary, but it'll reinforce the drama they've got themselves into.'

The Tamar's crew watched as a tender appeared from around the stern of the naval ship. A few minutes later the trio of captives were hauled to their feet, freed from the rope that had stopped the circulation of blood in their arms and secured by the wrists with handcuffs behind their backs. The leg chains were long enough to permit them to shuffle along the deck to the tender. A big marine grabbed the leading one by the back of his jacket collar, ignored his complaints of rough handling and launched him over the side into the tender. The other two were given the same treatment. With brief handshakes all round, the naval escorts hopped back on their craft and set off for the Fulmar.

A patchwork of nondescript debris floated around the stricken cabin cruiser.

'Mike, we might as well tether a marker buoy to the stern of that thing before she sinks. The law can decide whether they want to do anything about raising her later. But my guess is she'll be left where she is. According to the reading, we're in thirty eight metres of water.'

Mike Traherne interpreted this as an instruction from Andy to fetch one of the orange balls stored in the refuge area, with enough line to allow the marker to float free.

'Tell you what,' the coxswain turned to Mike as he came up with the float and line, 'it'll be easier for Matt Henwood to fix it from the Atlantic. We'll cut forty metres of cord. That should be enough.'

Mike Traherne paid out a generous forty odd counts of line, each count spanning the distance from the middle of his chest to the length of his outstretched arm. By this time Matt had responded to Andy's request to come alongside. The ball and line were passed across to the RIB and ferried to the upturned Sealine. Janner Janes was given the task of fixing the marker. Matt nosed the Atlantic up to the dripping stern of the cabin cruiser. It was a quick and easy matter to attach line to one of the two exposed propellers. Satisfied it was safely knotted, the RIB was eased back a couple or three metres as its crew monitored the gradual submersion of the gutted cruiser. With a slight hiss of air it finally disappeared in a stream of bubbles as Janner let out the coiled line and finally tossed the orange ball in after it. As a precaution, Andy made a note of the GPS location.

With nothing else to be done, both rescue craft watched the now departing patrol vessel as it gave a short blast on the ship's klaxon and started its journey back to base at Devonport. The Tamar's crew settled into their places ready for the return trip as the RIB set off ahead of them. Fatigue set in like a drug as the anti-climax took hold. The practice drill had been a lengthy one and the un-programmed chase had added, by increments, its own enervating toll. Andy knew the journey back was a short one, but decided to ease off on the throttles and suggest a quick dose of coffee from the large thermos flask he'd brought. It would please his wife. She scolded him, in a good natured way, when he returned home with it un-opened.

'That was a bugger and a half,' one of the crew expressed what they all felt, as he took his coffee from the Cox.

'Too bloody right! Still, makes a change from dealing with some nut who doesn't know the front of his yacht from the back!'

'Take your time. I'll take her back gently,' Andy drained his coffee and pushed up the speed to about fifteen knots as he followed the receding light of the RIB back to the estuary mouth.

155

24

Doc Varcoe's pager and telephone went off within seconds of each other, just as he was about to start embroidering the third of a series of coats of arms embellishing a map of Cornwall. He had copied the design, an original 1836 edition by Thomas Moule, on to a piece of linen using a soft, fine leaded, draughtsman's pencil. It intrigued him that the spelling of Edgecumb, for it was a detail from the armorial bearings of the Earl of Mount-Edgecumb, was at variance with records dating back over centuries, records which gave Edgcumbe as the Earl's name. The map itself he had completed over a period of three years and from a distance it was difficult to tell it was not an original print. The intricate detail of the re-entrant coves and creeks, almost fractal, forced him to focus hand and eye on the exacting process of locating the needle with each fiddly stitch. Despite the demand such concentration placed on him, stitching for him was a relaxing pursuit. But it held a more significant purpose. The precision was as close as he could get to practising the real thing on flesh. It kept his skill finely honed and, better still, for his patients, made for neat sutures. The paging alert broke his train of thought. He quickly glanced at it as he picked up the adjacent phone, dropping linen and thread on to a side table as he did.

'Norman here. What's up? ... OK! ... Three minutes.'

His wife looked at him, expecting a brief explanation.

'Pager, the Deputy Launch Authority. Phone, the coastguard. Request from skipper of a yacht. Wife pregnant. They're encountering rough sea somewhere between Coverack and Lizard Point. She's fallen. Gone into labour and he's struggling against a head wind. Only making two or three knots. Coastguard's requested that a doctor be included.'

'See you.' He gave his wife a peck and grabbed car keys from a dish on a hall table. The journey took him under three minutes.

Nine turned up for the launch, Doc Truman was also amongst them. Andy decided two medics were better than one, so included both doctors.

'Can I go?' Alex Jago knew it wasn't protocol to request selection, 'It might be comforting if a female is on hand to give a bit of support and I've done the Red Cross Course organised through the school.'

Andy looked at Alex, then sideways down at the row of yellow boots then back up, 'Maybe that's a good idea. But this is an exception. OK?'

Alex grabbed her kit and set to donning the heavy storm gear, pleased to be part of a potential midwifery rescue.

Andy took Dave Lobb and Mike Traherne aside, 'I'm leaving one of you two out. Mike you were on the last shout, so you can stay here at base this time. Dave, take this one and miss the next. It's too much of a risk with the bad feeling between you both over this dredging business. When I feel you've sorted yourselves out, then we can get back to normal.'

The two looked at each other, then the cox and nodded their acceptance in such a way as to say they understood, grateful the remarks had not been made in front of the others.

In the time between alert and launch the sea had begun to build up half to one metre-high waves. Not too bad as far as waves went, but an intermittent, blinding spray thrown up by a wind, which seemed to change direction every few dozen yards, made for a messy search.

Dave Lobb radioed Falmouth coastguard for fresh news of the yacht.

'He's making slow headway, but is panicking about his wife. Can't leave the steering and attend to her. He's about eight nautical miles from Pendennis Point. She's manage to crawl into the cabin.'

'OK. Tell him we should be with him in about twenty minutes.'

Andy kept the Tamar at full knots. Past Manacle Point the seas were noticeably rougher. He decided to reduce speed to twenty knots. It wasn't long before the radar screen showed a point of light about two miles ahead.

'We've got him,' Tim Hodge, who was navigating looked across at the cox, 'see him?'

'Yep! He should see us soon, if he hasn't already.'

With a definite bearing to follow, Andy cranked the speed back up to the full twenty five knots. He deliberately over-shot the bucking vessel, did a u-turn behind it and drew up alongside. Alex, Doc

Varcoe and Doc Truman hitched their safety lines to the guide runner. The yacht was a good deal less stable than the Tamar.

'I'll unhook and get across as soon as Andy manages to line her up tight,' Norman Varcoe shouted to the other two, 'can make a decision about bringing the woman across. Can't see any pleasure in giving birth on that thing,' he nodded, grinning at the bucking yacht alongside.

'Right, I'm going for it.'

Lifeboat and yacht sank into a shallow trough giving the doctor a chance to half leap, half scramble across to the lighter vessel. The yacht's helmsman managed, for a brief moment, to keep the deck level as Varcoe held on to the thin wire cable that acted as a guard rail round the boat's perimeter. The yacht swung around as he straddled the twisted steel strands. He grabbed at one of the uprights the cable was threaded through as the direction of his momentum was suddenly changed. It yielded. For a moment he balanced on one leg, but the post held and he managed to cross over on to the side decking and work his way along to the cockpit.

'I'm going too,' Alex turned and gestured her intention to Andy. He nodded assent.

Of light build and athletic, Alex made the cross-over totally unfazed by the waves and foam in the gap separating the waterlines of both boats. Doc Varcoe was already kneeling on the floor, putting the patient into a more comfortable position, when she ducked through the entrance. The pregnant woman was experiencing contractions at a rate which indicated birth could be any time in the next half hour.

'Look, we're going to have to get her out of here pronto. Get back out and warn Dick. I think we had better get one of the crew over to help move her. Can't risk Dick crossing the gap. Need one doctor left on the Tamar in case I fall in. You can help steady her from behind.'

Alex needed no further urging. She smiled at the woman reassuringly and quickly turned about to emerge back on the rear deck.

'Can you send one of the crew to help get our patient across. The woman's got a lifejacket on. A standard one-fifty Newton.

Shan't need one from the boat. Norman thinks birth is close, but believes it wiser to keep you safely where you are, in case he falls in.'

'Cheerful bugger! Right, I'll ask Andy to send somebody.'

Alex turned back to the companionway.

'What's your name? I'm Alex.' Alex addressed the woman, pale and exhausted by constant retching.

'Miriam.'

'We'll have you safe, Miriam, in a jiffy. You're in good hands, Doc Varcoe does this twice a day, every day, on yachts.'

Wretched even though the sea-sick woman was, she could not help appreciating the humour and managed a weak grin.

'Right,' Norman Varcoe took the woman's arm, 'I'm going to get you up on your feet with the help of one of the crew, when he gets here. As far as I can tell you have only a bruised shoulder. Nothing broken and it'll be more comfortable and safer if we get you onto the lifeboat. Happy about that?'

'Whatever. At the moment I could cheerfully die!'

'I'll give you a light shot of something when you get across. You'll still be conscious. Need you awake to deliver the baby, but it'll relieve the nausea. You're almost full term, so any sedative won't harm the baby. You happy with that?'

'Do what you like. I just want to die!'

Dave Lobb made his appearance in the companionway, 'Where'd you want me?'

'If you can stay that side, kneel and put your arm under Miriam's armpit, we'll get her on to her knees. Alex can help steady all three of us if she holds on to something fixed. We'll wait for each lull, get her on to her feet, then through the door way. Getting her over the barrier wire's going to be the tricky bit. In fact it might be a good idea to get it cut, but we can't hang about waiting for someone to do that. Let's see how it goes when we get there.'

'No need to. It's got quick-release clips, I noticed.'

With the next descent into a trough, the yacht stayed level for a brief spell, before riding up into the next wave. The two men lifted the patient into a kneeling position. At the next arrest in pitching motion the pair managed to get her onto her feet.

'So far so good. You did well. Right, can you walk?'

'Yes, but hold on to me.'

Dave Lobb eased himself through the doorway keeping a firm grip on the woman's arm. The trio made it into the stern deck well with Alex in the rear.

Andy Cornwell brought the Carrick Maid back alongside the yacht and managed to match the rhythm of the waves. He kept one eye ahead and one to the side, so to speak, as the four struggled to keep their balance on the deck of the cockpit. Dave Lobb took the lead at this point.

'I think it's going to be easier to transfer from here rather than up on the side decking by the cabin. Too narrow and no one can stand behind Miriam up there. D'you agree?'

Norman Varcoe assessed the situation without hesitation, 'Agree!'

'Right then. I'll unclip the rail and we get her up and across.'

The husband was merely a captive operative and had been all through. He now looked ten degrees more relaxed than when the Tamar first drew alongside.

Dave Lobb turned to him, 'The cox proposes to give you a tow. We've got an ambulance waiting in Falmouth and Doc Varcoe here wants your wife inside our boat where he can provide full medical attention. I guess you don't have a problem with that.'

The yachtsman, just about all-in, nodded, 'That's what I was hoping.'

Dave Lobb hadn't even waited for the man to answer, but had gone ahead with unclipping the cable, placing himself squarely at the ready to raise the suffering woman up and across to the lifeboat. The doctor and crewman waited for the next trough to put the lifeboat and yacht in phase and lifted Miriam up onto the raised aft-deck on the side of the cockpit as Dick Truman reached over and grabbed her by an arm. The transfer went smoothly. Lobb and Varcoe waited for the next opportune moment and followed the patient back on board the rescue vessel. Alex clipped the guard cable back in place, said a temporary good bye to the yachtsman and crossed back on board.

Andy gave Dave Lobb the thumbs-up and held the boat close-to as his radio operator then went to fetch the tow rope. Hopping back aboard the yacht he fixed the line and gave a few instructions to the helmsman on towing procedure before getting back to his duty monitoring the radio.

They were twenty minutes into the return trip when a lusty yell, from the area that served as a makeshift medical station, heralded the entry of the first baby to be born on the Carrick Maid. There wasn't a great deal of room in the emergency aid space, but Alex had managed to stay within reach of the mother now lying on the bunk the medics used to treat casualties. She held on to the exhausted woman's hand whilst the two doctors set about cleaning up the baby and checking the mother for any complications.

'It's a girl.' Doc Varcoe handed the baby to Alex to wrap in a clean linen sheet as he set about clearing up what limited articles of his trade he had at his disposal to effect delivery of the child.

Alex lifted the blanket away from Miriam to place the baby in the cradle of her arm. Beat, as the Cornish would say of any one in a state of exhaustion, the mother managed a grin and kissed the infant on the side of its head.

'What did you say you were called?'

'Alex.'

'Alex,' the woman repeated the name, 'Alex. I think I would like to call her Alexa.'

Her namesake grinned, 'Well, it'll certainly remind you of this trip, that's for sure, but I should try to get some rest. It's not far to go, but with the yacht in tow we'll be a little while getting back to Falmouth. I'll look after Alexa for you.'

The woman closed her eyes as Alex took the baby and made her way carefully down into the refuge area of the boat. One of the two doctors stayed with the mother. The rest of the crew settled back into the routine of monitoring the various states of navigation and control their craft demanded.

At the boathouse, an ambulance was already backed up to the launch area. The yacht was uncoupled from the Tamar and secured close to the launch ramp. Andy helped the exhausted owner to get ashore to his wife. Alex waited at the open, rear door of the ambulance, the baby still in her arms.

'We have a tradition amongst crews,' Andy spoke to the parents before they were whisked off to hospital, 'that if a baby is born on a

161

lifeboat the child is presented with a brass, ship's bell with his or her name inscribed on it. This is the first to be born on our boat. Congratulations.'

Although both parents were beyond wanting much more than a good sleep, they couldn't help feeling a surge of pleasure at such a unique way of celebrating the birth of baby Alexa. By this time the whole crew, ambulance medics, a local reporter - who had picked up the VHF messages going to and fro - and a bunch of bystanders, had gathered round the family. A cheer went up, led by one of the more extrovert bystanders. The father, mother and baby were finally bundled into the ambulance and sent off to the hospital for a thorough check-up.

Back in the storm-gear dressing area Andy sat pulling off his boots, 'We're going to interview some candidates for crew to replace Bill and, temporarily, Jean-Pierre. Although it's possible Jean might decide not to come back. Bill is going to become Ops Manager. I've also received confirmation of my appointment as Cox.' He spoke to no one in particular.

The crew, in various stages of removing their yellow outer garments, halted what they were doing and turned to face their new skipper.

'Bloody hell! Did they know you can't swim?' It was Tom Hicks who raised a laugh, the others, knowing Andy had played water polo for Falmouth, appreciated his wit.

'Calls for a celebration in the Chisel. Better still, why don't we celebrate at my place?' Doc Varcoe looked around to see the reaction, 'I can put on a BBQ, or something a bit more formal if you like. Plenty of space inside if it rains.'

The others knew this would be a good venue. The Doc had hosted a Christmas party the previous year and had spared no cost to provide a feast the crew had talked about for weeks after. By way of a thank-you the crew clubbed together to buy a nice bouquet of flowers for Mary, his wife and a bottle of single malt for their medic. There was no resistance to the suggestion and after a few genuine comments of congratulation to their new coxswain, Andy grinned at his crew.

'Thanks boys - and girl,' he smiled at Alex, 'nothing's really changed. Business as usual. Anyway, to get back to what I was saying, Bill will be overseeing the selection, but wants the candidates to come down for a preliminary look round and a low key description of what it's all about with, initially, as many of the crew present as can make it.'

'That'll be an evening visit?' One of the crew asked.

'Probably, or a Sunday morning before we go out on a practice run. Bill wants us to meet the candidates to get some idea of their suitability, just on a social level, first. But the final choice will be made after a couple of formal interviews and that'll be before a panel of those of us who have five or more years' experience.'

'How many interested?'

'We've got three and two other possibles. If they're all suitable, we'll keep the lot. That's it. Let's call it a day.'

The group hung their garments up, tired, but in a good mood and drifted off in ones and twos.

25

'What's the problem with this ship? We don't have rough seas.'
Mike Traherne spoke to Andy as they were pulling on storm gear for
the second time in a week.

'Engine room flooding.'

'What's wrong with his pumps?'

'Dunno. That's why we're taking a heavy duty pump with us.
Pendennis Marine are lending us a spare they use in the small dry
dock. It's being loaded now. Coastguard got the call half an hour ago
and tried to get more sense out of the captain, who also seems to be
the owner. Doesn't appear to be any more than a skeleton crew on
board.'

'Sounds odd. Got any cargo aboard?'

'Again, dunno.'

With everybody kitted up, the crew got under way whilst the
pump was still being secured on the aft deck. Out beyond the 8-knot
restriction limits, Andy took the Tamar up to speed out of the mouth
of the estuary. They could see the coaster way ahead, a rust bucket if
ever there was one.

'She's out over the submarine exercise area by the look of it.'
Graham Hodge was navigator on this shout.

'That's why we've gotta stop her sinking. Bleddy Admiralty'll
have kittens if she goes down there,' the boat's mechanic commented,
'and guess who's going to have to take the pump down into the
bleddy thing when we get on and rig it up?' Chris Pascoe quipped.

The Tamar eventually drew alongside. The coaster's gunnel
was a metre and a half or so above water level and easy to get over on
to the steel deck, that's if you were a crewman having only to climb
the short ladder hanging over the side. But the pump was heavy and
the Tamar, unlike the seventeen metre Severn Class boats, lacked a
crane on the aft deck. Chris Pascoe, true to prediction, would be
tasked with getting the pump onto the deck of the ship. There were
three men on board. One was the captain, the other two Greek or
Maltese.

Andy greeted the master of the vessel, 'Got a leak then?'

'Yes! Cannot stop it. Power out, pump does not work.' The man's English was adequate, but Andy could not place the accent. Dutch or Scandinavian, maybe.

'Need to take a look. Take me down.'

Andy followed the captain along the deck to the bridge structure and stepped inside the lower deck access point. He couldn't help noticing the latter's lack of urgency as they descended the ladder into the engine room. There was something eerie about the lifeless engine room as he flashed the torch about. Water was already a foot deep and seemed to be coming in past an open, iron door ahead, the kind that has a substantial lever to secure it. That it was open seemed odd, considering the rate at which the water was pouring through.

'What's through there?'

'Nothing. Empty cargo space.'

'Right, we had better get back on deck.'

Andy could smell a rat. Something wasn't right. His instincts told him not to inform his guide of his intention to pump out the flooding hold. Emerging into the sunlight, the Tamar's skipper strode towards his boat.

'Tell coastguard we're going to use the pump and that a tug had better be on hand. In fact, better make it two. She'll need a line from the stern as well.' Andy spoke quietly to Matt Henwood, who was acting radio operator, as the latter appeared from the wheelhouse.

'Oh and,' still out of earshot of the ship's master the cox leant over the side, his radio operator turned back again to face him, 'there's something not quite right going on. Tell them the captain seems edgy. Can't put my finger on it. He could have closed what looks like a water-tight door but hasn't. Something's wrong.'

'OK Cox.'

Andy set about supervising the transfer and setting-up of pump and hoses.

'I want the portable ventilation unit set up with this gear. Connect it from the auxiliary power supply. We'll try to get those hatch covers open after that's sorted. Tell the two deckhands to do the hatches when they've helped get this stuff below.'

The ship's master adopted a belligerent pose when he saw what was happening and tried to assert some attempt to force abandonment of the ship. Andy stared at him, ignored his agitation and inclined his head towards the sizeable crew watching from the deck of the Tamar as if to say, 'Shut up, I'm in charge here.' The two foreign seamen were reluctant to help, but Chris Pascoe, intimidating, just by virtue of his size, made it pretty clear to them that they would help, or get pitched over the side if they didn't. With a length of light-weight, structural aluminium planking they managed to slide the pump, with its integral diesel generator, up and over onto the deck of the coaster. A piece of heavy duty rope attached to the plank then allowed them to use it as a skid with the gear firmly lashed to it. They dragged the pump unit to the stair-head. That was the easy bit.

'Look, we're going to have to lower it with four of us in pairs holding two ropes and someone beneath steadying it. Anyone got any better suggestions?'

'Is about the only way we can do it,' the boat's mechanic agreed, 'but I don't want those two buggers on the end of any rope if one of us is under it.' One of the coaster's crew was given a portable lantern rigged up to the Tamar's power supply and told to train the light on the stairs.

The team eased the equipment forward until its centre of gravity was pivoting on the edge of the landing. Tom Hicks, a recent addition to the crew from Port Isaac, steadied it from beneath. A bit more slack in the ropes allowed it to tilt forward and downward until the whole unit was able to slide down the stairs. At the bottom Chris Pascoe and Tom Hicks wedged the aluminium skid like a bridge across the lower transversals of a pair of gangway rails, forward of the engine. Hicks then tugged the suction hose across the engine room, with one arm round the tubing, the other free to guide his hand along the rail. He fed it through into the flooding cargo hold. The delivery hose was then connected and fed out through the stair-head door and over the side of the ship. By this time water was just below knee level. A can of diesel was passed down to the two crewmen, followed by soft, lightweight, polythene tubing to provide fresh supplies of air from a separate pump. Tom Hicks filled the reservoir with fuel and stepped away to let Chris Pascoe swing the crank handle.

'Right, here goes!' Chris Pascoe gave the crank a couple of turns. No response. He tried again. This time fuel reached the

166

cylinder head. The generator gave a few encouraging coughs and kicked over a number of times.

'This time!' Pascoe really put some aggro into the starter handle and the pump engine surged into life.

'Let her warm up for half a minute, then open the suction head,' Chris Pascoe gave the instruction to Tom Hicks, 'I'm going into the cargo area to keep the pipe in place and let's hope it does the job. She's settling a bit fast for my liking. Trouble is, the deeper she goes the greater the head of water being forced in. I'll leave the big torch with you.'

Grabbing the armoured, portable light from the rail it was now clipped to, Pascoe made his way across the space to the open, steel door. Water was cascading through by this time, in a fairly strong torrent. He stepped through the portal, across the transverse partition. He inched his way forward until he detected the edge of some steps he knew should be close to the door way.

'OK, open her up.' Pascoe shouted back through the cargo door. The suction pipe kicked into life and started thrashing about, but the lifeboat's crewman was ready for it. He made a mental note to inform the Op's Manager to include a warning with any future operation of the heavy duty pump. Holding a short handrail he felt his way down a couple of steps that brought the water level up to his waist. He moved further into the zone, sliding his feet through the inky, oily water.

Finding a convenient rib to clip the lamp to he set about locating a suitable point to locate the pipe end now that the mass of water travelling through it weighed it down and stopped the violent thrashing. Watching the surface for a few minutes, he could see the level was dropping. As his eyes got even more adjusted to the gloom he could make out two areas, on opposite sides of the deck, close to the hull plates, where water was welling up.

Unclipping the lamp he made his way over to one of the sources. Groping around in the cold, slippery water he could feel a jet of the stuff issuing from a short length of pipe. He recognized it in an instant. A spell in the merchant navy told him it was a discharge pipe used for clearing flooded bilges, or for coupling a hose to, for hosing down the cargo hold. He knew there should be a bronze cap, hanging from a chain at its end somewhere that would plug the exit hole. Clipping the lamp to a steel overhang, it took him about three seconds to locate the cap and start screwing it back on. That done he made for the second source, across the decking taking the lamp with him. Fortunately for him there were no obstacles covered by the swirling, sloshing water and he was there without mishap.

The set-up there was a similar, but he could feel the cap was in place. Again he found a convenient overhang to clip the lamp to. Nothing was escaping from the threaded area. It was on tightly and wouldn't budge when he tried moving it clockwise or anti-clockwise. Taking off his glove he slid his hand down the pipe. Part way down, he could feel water jetting through a gash in its side. His fingers could not detect any kind of welded joint that had rotted and separated. Neither did he expect to discover any such failure. His instincts had served him right. The gash was a hack-saw cut. The ship's master was into an insurance claim. Unable to unscrew the cap, which had probably corroded into place, he had hastened the flooding by sawing through the steel pipe.

Knowing the pump was now discharging much faster than the hold was flooding, Pascoe felt it safe enough to scout around for any kind of rag to wrap round the slot. There was nothing that he could see floating that would do the job. He made his way back to the door, leaving the lamp where it was. It was just as well. He found Tom Hicks slumped over the cylinder head of the ship's engine. The air was thick with diesel fumes in places and he noticed the polythene ventilation tube was no longer inflated.

'Where the hell are those deckhands,' he muttered to himself, 'bleddy hatches should have been opened by now.'

Holding his breath, he waded up to the semi-conscious crewman and dragged him off the engine. The yellow storm jacket was slippery. Oily streaks glistened even in the limited light thrown out by the torch. Getting Tom up and over his shoulders proved a wasted effort and just increased the demand to release the contaminated air fighting to leave his lungs. He dropped his colleague hurriedly against the engine casing, gulped in another lungful of air and diesel fumes, grabbed him under the armpits and dragged him towards the stairs. A little cool air filtering down from the open deck was a welcome relief. Even Tom Hicks showed some response. Pascoe leant him against the bulkhead, took in a fresh lungful of air and managed to wedge his crew mate's arms through a stair rung. Satisfied he would not fall back into the water, the big mechanic managed to climb over his friend's body and up the stairs to summon help. At the point of exit to the deck he found a cylindrical fire extinguisher resting on its side over the polythene ventilating tubing. The door had also been pushed up against the discharge pipe, obstructing any line of sight from lifeboat or deck. He pushed the extinguisher off the tubing with his foot and swung the door open with his shoulder.

'We need help below deck, quick,' Chris Pascoe shouted to Andy who was up on the flying bridge of the lifeboat, 'Tom's ill. Need to get him out. And get the police here. There's been some deliberate damage below deck. Watch that bugger,' Pascoe nodded towards the boat's captain, 'I think he's blocked the ventilation tube. Could have killed Tom. And why aren't those hatches open?' As if by magic one of the deck hands appeared from a locker with a short length of bar and started clouting one of the fastenings securing a hatch cover. Satisfied things were moving at long last, Pascoe disappeared back inside as two of the crew, hearing his shout for help, jumped across and followed him below.

Andy manoeuvred the Tamar away from the coaster, to stop the captain and his two crewmen from getting across, now that there were only two besides him on board. Matt Henwood, at his post in the wheelhouse, picked up the shout from Chris Pascoe through Andy's intercom. Within seconds he was on to the dock police, who would be picking up any of the ship-to-shore messaging going on.

'Can you send out a launch,' he instructed them after going through the usual communication protocols, 'Cox says we have a possible criminal act committed on the coaster we're attending?'

Chris Pascoe and his two crewmates reached Tom Hicks, who was now showing signs of recovery.

'Are you up to climbing out?'

'Yeah. Fumes got to me?'

'Yes. Looks like one of those three sealed off the ventilation tube. My bet is on the skipper. Anyway, I'm going back through to the hold. These two'll get you up.'

'Find anything in there?'

'Yeah. One bilge pipe cover unscrewed and one pipe sawn through. But it looks like we're beating it.'

The four turned to look at the hold access doorway. Water was now flowing back towards the suction pump hose from the engine bay.

'I'll see you guys back up on top, in a minute, after I've checked the pipe in there, but before that can one of you bring down some rope? Maybe some rag or something to tie under it to make a better seal. I can stem the flow with a few tight turns over the gash.'

With that he waded through the now diminishing flood of water to the cargo deck. There was a significant lowering in the water level. Shifting the hose to a deeper zone of water he found the shallower water easier to get through. It was not long before one of the crew made his way through to the inner flood chamber.

'Here you are,' Harry Legg, a recent addition to the crew, handed a coil of rope and a piece of rag to Chris Pascoe, 'I'll hold the lamp whilst you tackle the leak.'

Pascoe formed a hitch half way along the coil and dropped it over the pipe before wrapping the rag over the spurt of water issuing from the cut. He slid the loop back up over the saturated cloth, keeping the latter from loosening with his free hand.

'Hold the rag in place, can you, while I tighten the rope?' The big crewman then proceeded to tie a West Country whipping all the way up the tourniquet formed by the cloth. The stream of water was now blocked. Just as he finished there was a grating noise above his head as a hatch cover was being freed and slid back.

'About bleddy time! Right, let's get up on deck and wait for the law. Bring the lamp and clip it to the cargo doorway on your way through.'

Pascoe did a quick check on the suction hose and the two crewmen made their way to the stairs. There were still pockets of diesel exhaust contaminating the air, but the two men were satisfied there was little risk associated with short term stays below deck now and a down draught of fresh air from the hatch accelerated the removal of the foul atmosphere.

Back on top, the captain of the coaster had retired to the bridge. Well and truly caught, no way of escape, he resigned himself to the inevitable consequences of his actions. His two deckhands were sitting on the steel deck, backs against the raised wall of the box forming the hatch, smoking cigarettes that had a Turkish or whiff of Latakian leaf about them. Their skipper had hired them in Rotterdam. As far as they were concerned, he was the architect of his own disaster. They wanted nothing of it, nor did they expect to be part of it, judging by the way they assumed a relaxed, unaffected attitude of passive disengagement.

Tom Hicks had recovered some colour. Dick Truman, who had elected to come on this shout, declared him free from any need for urgent treatment. A short period on an oxygen mask had restored him to near normal and Dick managed to persuade Chris Pascoe to take a few whiffs just to boost his oxygen level.

The police launch arrived and Andy accompanied one of three officers up to the coaster's bridge. The door to the wheelhouse was closed. Through a window they could see the captain, lying in a gradually widening pool of blood. He had cut his wrists. The door was locked.

Andy turned to the officer, 'I'll get a jemmy. We've got one that'll force this open,' at the same time turning his back to him as he high-tailed it down the short run of steps to the deck and made for The Carrick Maid, now back alongside the coaster. He shouted to anyone listening to get the jemmy, ran for the gap between the two vessels and then for the location where the kit of rescue tools was stored. He arrived just as Harry Legg was pulling the implement from a box of tools.

'Thanks.' He grabbed the tool, gave a hurried explanation, 'Silly bugger's cut his wrists, tell Dick to get up there,' and belted back across the gunnels as fast as his cumbersome gear would allow. Reaching the locked door, he jammed the wedged end of steel between door and frame. It gave little resistance. There was still a pulse when they reached the dishevelled figure slumped against a bulkhead that also doubled as a chart table. Dick Truman appeared

171

soon after with a small bag of medical aids, mainly bandages and tape. He stripped the buttons on the man's boiler suit and had the top half off his arms and shoulders all in one slick movement.

'Keep him up.'

The medic got Andy and the police officer to apply finger pressure on the arteries as he ripped the cover off a pack of pads. Grabbing one of the charts, he laid it on the floor and dropped the pads on it. A pair of scissors soon made short work of providing some lengths of bandage. He cleaned the wounds with an alcohol solution which dried pretty well as fast as it was applied. A small pack of adhesive wound sutures provided closure for the cuts. The pads were fixed in place and bound tightly with the lengths of bandage, in turn secured by sticky tape. Satisfied with his handiwork, all completed in well under two minutes, Truman did a quick stethoscope examination of the master's chest.

'Keep him upright, but can one of you hold his arms up at chest level? We need to get the helicopter in. I'm going to put this guy on a drip immediately so I'll get Matt Henwood to radio Culdrose when I go to fetch it. That OK with you Cox? He needs treatment and monitoring at hospital. The sooner the better.'

'Fine Dick. Alan,' Andy addressed Alan Penrose, the dock police officer, 'anything you want to radio in?'

'Nothing I can think of. We've already asked Falmouth to send a van to take this mob. But judging by this one's condition he'll not be joining those two. I'm going to have to cuff them. There's a risk they might try to high-tail it when we get back. The two of us will need to search for documents. Have you been anywhere else on the ship?'

'Only the engine room and the cargo hold.'

They both turned as the external speaker announced a message from one of the two tugs now clearly visible en route from the harbour.

'Got you in our sights. ETA fifteen to twenty minutes.'

Andy shouted down to Matt now ensconced on the flying bridge, 'Tell them I'll be scouting about the ship with Roger Penrose if they call again for any instructions. Don't think it'll take us more than ten minutes or so. Should be back up before they're that close.'

172

'OK Cox.'

The two men, officer and cox, set about a quick examination of the coaster's bridge. There was nothing of any note.

'Right, let's find his cabin.'

Within the cabin space below the wheelhouse, there was a small galley, a cramped dining area cum relaxation space and two cabins. Each cabin sported two bunks which were little more than wide shelves with front fascia boards to stop bedding and occupant sliding out in rough seas. A couple of little wooden cupboards backed up against the steel bulkhead separated the two pairs of bunks. There was only a few items of clothing and other personal property in each. Two passports identified the two crew as Rumanian. The officer put them in one of the pockets on his police vest. The captain's passport was yet to be found. A door between the two cupboards revealed slightly more comfortable accommodation occupying the space forming the stern of the ship, with two bunks supported on three eighths steel plate welded to the hull. A porthole on each of the port and starboard sides let good light into the little cabin. The space below one bunk held a small chest. Andy dragged it out. There was no lock. All it contained was a few papers, the captain's passport, a wallet with some Euro notes and a plastic card issued by some European bank and a couple of spare blankets.

'No surprises there.' Penrose pocketed the passport.

Putting the blankets back, a second passport slipped from its folds, and dropped on to the floor. The officer picked it up and flicked through it. The surname was the same as that of the master of the vessel. It was a white female aged forty three. He showed it to Andy.

'Strange! Have you been anywhere else in the boat?'

'Only engine room and hold.'

'You thinking what I'm thinking?'

'Yeah. There should be some space the other end of the cargo area, in the bow behind the partition. Pretty sure I saw door there, come to think of it.'

'Let's get there quickly.'

The two men went back on deck, then down into the engine room and hold. Andy grabbed the lamp still clipped to the hold door way. Only a few inches of water washed across the floor now. It was easy to reach the far end this time. There was a door. It also had a robust lever catch securing it to its portal, just like the facing one. Andy wrenched it open. Holding the lamp inside the opening for Roger Penrose to look in, the two of them recognised immediately the body of a woman, in foetal position, lying on coils of heavy duty rope. A pile of what was probably her clothing was dumped on top of her.

'I'll check to see if she's alive, although it looks pretty ominous to me. Stay out here if you don't mind and hold the torch as close as you can.'

Penrose put on a pair of fine latex surgical gloves, turned the woman onto her back and then with one hand unsheathed, used his fingers to feel for a pulse. He got up from a kneeling position and shook his head.

'This is getting messy. We'll have to get forensics down here as soon as we dock. Right let's get out.'

They closed the door and climbed back out of the gloom into the sun. The tugs were close. Andy took back control of the flying bridge and asked Matt for an update on the helicopter's progress just a handful of seconds before the aircraft's engine signalled its approach from a north westerly direction.

The tugs held off whilst a winchman lowered a colleague with a cradle down on to the coaster's deck.

'The drip had better stay with him for the lift. Any way you can fix it above him?'

'Yeah!' The aerial crewman nodded and pointed to a support designed to suspend small pieces of equipment in transit. Doc Truman helped secure his patient to the rigid, orange frame that resembled a small kayak, then watched as the winchman raised the casualty up into the helicopter.

Roger Penrose was back on the police launch by this time radioing for a forensic team to be ready to examine the scene in the bow.

'I need to leave one of my men on board 'til we dock,' he shouted across to Andy, 'but I'll get those two over first.'

174

The two other police officers got the handcuffed crewmen on to their feet, across the gap between vessels and into the launch. One of the officers jumped back across to the coaster once the two were settled on the decking and secured by additional tethers to rings set in the launch's inflatable sides.

'Thanks for your help. See you later.' Penrose waved to Andy Cornwell and set off at speed for the port.

The departure of the dock police launch was the signal for the tug crews to prepare towing hawsers and set about hitching up to the disabled ship. One crewman from each of the sturdy little boats was sent on board to receive the tracer lines. Hitching was done in a matter of minutes, seven, maybe, at the most. When Chris Pascoe had checked the fuel level in the pump and added more diesel, cox and tugboat captains communicated agreement that all necessary checks had been carried out. The flotilla set off for Falmouth.

26

Bill Hawken handed Alex Jago an envelope with Bill's name and address printed on it.

'Go on, have a look.'

Puzzled, she pulled a letter from the already opened envelope.

"Dear Bill," it began, "Hope you have settled into your role as Ops Manager. Pass on my congratulations to Andy Cornwell now his appointment as Coxswain has been confirmed. I'm writing mainly to say we have a space available on the induction course for your new recruit, Alex Jago, if she can make it. We've fixed a number of slots during the school holidays for her to choose from. Have a word with her about preparation. We will contact her and give formal notice of the date and training in a separate letter." The rest of the letter gave details of date and programme and finished with a note of thanks for hospitality afforded the writer on an earlier visit to Falmouth.

Alex looked up and smiled at Bill, 'I've been looking forward to this and wondering when Poole would find a slot.'

'Well, now you've got it. They're a good bunch on training. All been crew at some time, or still are. You'll enjoy it.'

In the midst of the conversation, following a Sunday morning exercise, most of the crew were only half out of their gear when an alert came through.

'Yacht in trouble off The Manacles.' The message was brought down from the Ops Room upstairs.

'OK, we'll take the same crew as on exercise, except Mike,' Andy turned to Dave Lobb who had been doing some maintenance work on the Atlantic 75, 'you can replace Mike. Mike, can you write up this morning's log, but go upstairs and find out exactly what the problem is with this yacht first?'

Mike Traherne nodded and having been one of the first to get out of his kit was a natural choice to follow up on the details of the shout.

***

Rupert Royston was a prat. On a yacht he was an even bigger prat. And at the present time he was on his father's yacht with a bunch of associates celebrating the end of three years at college, a pretty cushy time financed by his mother. It was she who had chosen the name Rupert so that his initials would be RR. She had come from a wealthy family whose money had origins of somewhat dubious provenance. A social climber, she had made it her business to marry into – if not titled partnership – either landed gentry or a baron of industry, as she liked to term it. Her husband was a fleshy, red-faced boozer who had a lucrative business making castings for rail, marine and motor companies. He bullied his senior management. Although a latently violent man, he managed always to stay just the right side of the law when dealing with them. But only just. The son had many of his father's traits and combined with his mother's tendency to snobbery and a general contempt for the working public, he was liked by few people.

Two hours earlier he had put out of Penzance marina with his three college companions. The four had spent some evenings before this in Newquay, before motoring on to pick up the boat from its moorings inside the breakwater. He'd been on the yacht once before and knew just about enough to handle the rigging in good weather. His skills extended as far as using Ordnance Survey Maps, not admiralty charts, to navigate around the coast. This time was no exception.

He and some of the group had amused themselves taking turns at the wheel and running down floats marking lobster pots. This pretty well summed up their attitude to life.

'I say old chap, glass is getting low,' Royston, taking a hand off the wheel, waved in the general direction of a glass perched within easy reach.

'Sorry, bottle's empty.'

'Well get another fucker, Nigel, you twat.' Like father like son, a bully and the scion had acquired his father's ready use of obscenities.

The admonished youth slid off the side bench and went below to a case of red wine, already depleted by a third and hunted around for the cork screw. It wasn't on the table. It wasn't in the cutlery drawer and it wasn't on the floor. Reluctantly he mounted the short flight of steps leading back to the cockpit.

'Can't find the cork screw.'

'Jesus,' Royston commented, exasperated by the additional fact of having missed the last lobster buoy by about a foot, 'have I got to do every bloody thing myself?'

'Rupert, old chap,' the last two words were said by another member of the group, with an emphasis intended to highlight Royston's earlier use of the phrase, 'I think you'll find said cork screw in one's back pocket.'

This did nothing to improve Rupert's mood. He pulled it from the back pocket of his shorts and without looking at the youth, tossed it across, whilst simultaneously steering for another yellow marker. A forty centimetre, hollow globe of dense plastic. The cork-pull went wide of its intended goal, bounced off the narrow strip of wooden decking and disappeared into the crest of the V wave slanting away from the yacht's hull.

'You fucking idiot,' this from a third member of the fraternity, 'it's gone in the drink.'

At that moment, there was a solid clunk as the bow of the yacht engaged with its twentieth or thirtieth buoy. They had long since given up counting. Royston's elation at having hit the target was short lived. The vessel's speed, a comfortable six or seven knots, abruptly slowed. The yacht came to a halt. The centre board had caught the line down to the lobster pot. Sails flapped. Royston let go the wheel and turned on his critic.

'What did you say?'

Recognising he'd overstepped the mark, George Cockburn attempted to pacify his companion with a, 'No offence intended, just slipped out. I meant Nigel.' Which, of course, he didn't.

Royston grabbed hold of Nigel Tuck by the shirt front with one hand and pulled the bottle from his grasp with the other.

'We don't want you dropping this as well, do we?' With a vicious thrust to the chest, he slammed the unfortunate Nigel back onto the bench lining the cockpit's side. If the four had been a litter of pigs, Nigel would have been the runt. Turning, Royston brought the top of the bottle down onto a stainless steel cleat, snapping the neck from the shoulder. An egg cupful of wine spattered the side of the cockpit and dribbled down on to the lower decking as the neck fell into the sunken deck. Grabbing his glass, he sloshed a good quantity of the stuff into the dregs of what remained from the previous measure and took a long gulp. This restored some level of control over his bad temper. The fourth member of the group, a more savvy individual, one Bill Lang, cast a swift glance at Cockburn. He gave him the briefest of head shakes signifying a warning to add no more agro, by way of further comment, to a now tense atmosphere. Royston waved the bottle at the other three and placed it on the side bench. George Cockburn needed no encouragement, took the shattered vessel from its perch, before it had chance to slide off and topped up the glasses of the other two.

'Right, now what the fuck are we going to do?' Looking over the side, the group could see the yellow float now submerged just below the surface.

'Hand me the boat hook,' it was Bill Lang who spoke. He took the pole from George Cockburn, twisted the hook around the lobster line and endeavoured to pull it in the direction of the bow. The angle between pole and hull was too obtuse to get a good purchase and the hook just pulled free with each of three attempts.

'I'm going to start the engine. That should free us.' Royston fired up the motor and engaged the propeller shaft at full power. For a brief period the propeller cavitated, the boat then lurched forward and suddenly gathered speed as the line parted from its heavy pot on the sea bed. The group on board cheered, but their glee was short-lived. With all too recognisable finality the motor spluttered to a stop after playing a few tortured notes like a car engine at full revs beating the remaining life out of a burnt-out clutch. It could only mean one thing. Sure enough, peering over the stern they could see several metres of line floating out from under the boat. It had wrapped around the propeller until the float had been dragged tight up to the centre board and jammed. This in turn had acted as a brake. Something had to give. It was a poorly serviced key, splining the screw to its shaft, that took the full measure of torque. Sheared, it was then the engine had given about three bars of a banshee concerto and blew its gasket.

Royston annoyed with the yacht, rather than himself, picked up the partially full bottle of wine and smashed it on the deck, 'Fucking boat.'

He turned, 'What are you laughing at?'

'At you, throwing your toys out of the pram.'

Cockburn was the same height as Royston, well built, but not as fleshy. The latter was mad enough to have a go at his tormentor. Aware of Cockburn's strength, demonstrated in various ways during their years together at university, Royston was sober enough to know he was unsteady on his feet and no match for anyone in his present state. Instead he again turned on Nigel Tuck.

'I suppose you think it's funny too.'

Tuck, up until this time had kept as far away from Royston as the relatively cramped space of the cockpit allowed. Not knowing whether he was going to be physically mauled or merely subjected to oral abuse, Nigel Tuck put down his glass ready to defend himself.

'Ease up, it's not Nigel's fault,' Bill Lang had, over the last few days together, begun to develop a loathing of Rupert Royston's petulant and bullying personality, 'I suggest you take stock of your own actions rather than make scapegoats out of other people.'

The reprimand served to divert his anger away from Tuck.

'Fetch another bottle, somebody and bring up one of the packs of lager while I radio the Coastguard.' Now in a sulk he kicked one of the two other empty bottles rolling about the deck and went below to call for help.

'So what's happening?' Cockburn asked the returning Rupert.

'Coastguard are sending the Falmouth lifeboat.'

'Give any idea of arrival?'

'Said something about forty minutes. Gives us time to get a few lagers down.'

'Can't we sail to meet them?'

'Fuck that. Let them come to us. That's what they're here for. Toss me a can.'

At this point conversation petered out and the group settled down to a further session of alcohol abuse.

27

In fact, it was well over an hour before the Carrick Maid drew up alongside the drifting yacht, by which time Royston was on to his third lager and sullen with it.

'Where the hell have you been?' was his surly response to Andy's friendly greeting, 'we've been stuck here for hours.'

This did not strike the right note with the rest of the crew who could now see the broken glass and empty cans rolling around the cockpit of the yacht. Most yachts in trouble were relieved to see the rescue boat turn up. Just a few and they were a few, were content to sit back on their asses and expect the volunteer crew to provide a five star taxi service for them and tow them to the port of their original destination. RNLI crews, up and down the coast, had a way of reacting to that kind of response.

'Got here as soon as we were alerted. What exactly is your problem?' Andy addressed Royston, who from his original outburst had marked himself out as the yacht's owner.

'Pretty obvious I should have thought.' Royston belched loudly as he pointed carelessly in the direction of the stern.

'Engine won't go. Something must've fouled the propeller.'

In fact, the whole crew of the Carrick Maid knew exactly what the problem was. They could see, from the vantage point of their own craft, the yellow float trapped under the hull of the yacht and the free end of rope floating out from the stern. What they could also see and the four in their craft could not, was a pulped and frayed patch of fibre glass at the water line of the bow. A further piece of information the four were also not in possession of was a report, from a fishing boat to the coastguard, reporting a sighting of the yacht systematically running down a group of marker floats off Lizard Point. It didn't stop there. An enthusiastic birder, watching out for a sighting of choughs on the cliffs above those same floats, had been attracted by the whooping and shouting as the group celebrated each collision. Staying in a cottage next door to the lobster fisherman, whose floats he knew they were, he had the presence of mind to record the vandalism with the video function on his camera. The long range lens had picked out the yacht's name and the faces of the occupants in sufficient detail to make recognition indisputable. He had also telephoned his neighbour who in turn had also notified the coastguard. Coastguard in turn had radioed the account to the Carrick Maid, warning them to expect trouble.

'Right, I'm putting someone aboard to hitch a tow line to your bow.'

'Oh no you're not. Just clear the propeller and fuck off. We've still got sails haven't we?'

'Shut up you bloody idiot.' Bill Lang had taken as much as he could stand from his erstwhile companion and could see big trouble brewing.

'That's right, listen to your friend, and if there's any more of your offensive language I'll radio coastguard for authority to put you under restraint. Being intoxicated, a possible danger to other shipping and in charge of the safety of your passengers is a criminal offence. You're sailing nowhere. There's a hole in your bow and you'll be lucky to get as far as the next small harbour. Alex, can you take the line over.'

'Jesus! You're sending a fucking woman over.'

Royston picked up one of the empty bottles from the deck, staggered to his feet from the bulkhead side bench where he had been lounging and struck a threatening pose. He was totally out of control, swaying now in a state of blind fury. He raised the bottle, ready to throw, as Alex started to cross between boats.

Chris Pascoe, already prepared for trouble by the coastguard's warning, was ready with a boat hook. He pointed the thing at Royston's chest, 'Just try it and the last thing you'll remember is feeling this in your ribs before you go overboard.'

Bill Lang knowing Royston was oblivious to reason, made a grab for his arm. A small wave, catching the yacht side-on, threw the two of them onto the deck. Lang was first to recover and looked in shock at blood spurting from his wrist. He'd landed on the jagged base of the bottle, smashed earlier and had severed an artery. Royston still holding his bottle and now kneeling, swung it around in an arc behind him, at his assailant. The bottle caught Lang just above the ear. It happened so fast, Chris Pascoe had no time to prevent it. Instead he dropped the pole, leapt across the gap between the two boats and let his full weight drop onto the thug swaying in front of him. Tom Hicks was quick to follow and between them they held him face down. With one knee in the middle of his back and a third crew member now across to join them, they pinioned his arms and lashed the wrists together.

At this point Royston vomited, spewing the contents of an earlier snack and a mixture of wine and lager onto the deck in front of him. With three crewman obscuring the vision of the other two youths, Chris Pascoe surreptitiously and quickly, rubbed the face of the retching Royston, now struggling and kicking, into the pool of vomit. Bending forward, he talked quietly into his ear as he did so.

Chris then got up and turned the youth over onto his back. A slime of partially digested red and ochre coloured food dripped down his cheeks and ran into the hair at the nape of his neck. Whilst this was happening, Norman Varcoe was already across and dealing with the severed artery.

'Tom, get a bucket, dip it in the drink and we'll sluice this bugger off while he's flat.' Pascoe looked down with disgust at the now subdued youth.

Tom Hicks returned with a bucket and filled it from the free side of the yacht.

'You can pour, I'll keep him still.'

Royston started to complain. 'Shut up you little shit or you'll get worse. Fetch another one, we'll sluice his back. Then it might be a good idea to get these two to clear the glass and cans. They can sluice the deck down as well.'

Pascoe yanked Royston into a sitting position.

'My mother will sue you for assault.'

'I don't think so.'

It was then that he took in the scene with Bill Lang prostrate on the deck being attended by Doc Varcoe.

'You assaulted him too?'

'No! You did. I think your mummy and daddy will be proud of you,' Pascoe put his face close to the still arrogant youth, 'and I'm sure they'll visit you in prison.'

'Accident! Can't accuse me of anything.'

Pascoe said nothing, rotated the shoulders of the belligerent youth to face the lifeboat and pointed to Tim Hodge holding a video cam recorder.

'It's all on there, my friend, and somebody on the cliffs has recorded your float-smashing spree off The Lizard. So I guess you are in for a somewhat troublesome time, you and your friends.'

Norman Varcoe got to his feet and shouted across to Andy, 'We've got to get Culdrose here. This one's in a serious condition.'

'God, this is becoming a bit regular! OK. Dave,' Andy shouted to his radio operator, 'you hear that? Get on to them right away. Tell 'em we're making for Falmouth, from The Manacles and will hove to when they catch up with us.'

Alex Jago, no longer under threat, made her way to the front of the yacht and secured a tow rope to the bow. That finished, she lay across the decking and peered over the front. Reaching down, she felt the roughened surface. A portion of the resin reinforced fibre flexed. There was a definite tear, not just abrasion. The continual bombardment had created a flap of material.

'Andy, have a look at this.' She shouted across to the Carrick Maid, 'This thing's in a dodgy state.'

The coxswain jumped over and made his way across the top of the yacht, 'We can put a temporary fix on that with a few strips of heavy duty tape,' he announced after inspecting the damaged hull.

'It'll hold 'til we get back to Falmouth. Meanwhile we've got to decide about these three. These two won't cause any problems as far as I can see, but we're going to have to keep an eye on that one.' Andy nodded in the direction of Royston as they made their way back across the yacht's superstructure to the cockpit.

'Sit him up against the cabin wall. I don't want him on the Carrick. His two mates can stop him toppling over. D'you hear that you two? But before that both of you clear this cockpit. You better find a plastic sack or cardboard box to put the glass and cans in. Nothing to be thrown overboard. Then sluice down the cockpit with the bucket. I'll take the bottle our friend here used as a weapon.'

Cockburn and Tuck both nodded. The gravity of their situation had left them totally deflated, particularly now that there was a serious injury caused by their stupid antics.

'Tom, can you stay with them 'til we get back to port?'

'Yes Cox.'

'We'll have to get the stretcher to bring Norman's patient across to the boat. Easier for the helicopter pilot than trying to swing somebody down with that bloody mast to contend with. Chris, can you and Alex get the dingy out so we can patch up that hole? Fifteen hundred quids worth of damage there to put right, I reckon, not to mention compensation to the fishermen.'

Andy made a deliberate point of saying this within earshot of Royston. Knowing the precarious living the lobster fishermen made, even when weather conditions were good, he had no patience whatsoever with anyone who added to the problems and danger that life as a fisherman entailed. It was likely the arrogant pup entertained no remorse over his actions, nor concern for the cost of repairs to the yacht, but it gave Andy some satisfaction to give him thought, to dwell on, on the return journey.

As Chris Pascoe turned to follow Andy and Alex back, Tim caught Chris by the sleeve, 'As a matter of interest what did you say to him, that calmed him down, when you had him by the head?'

Chris grinned, 'I used the same polite language he used, since that's all he seems to respect and told him I'd slam his face on the deck and break his fucking nose if he continued to give trouble. But I made sure I had my body between his head and the camcorder.'

Tim laughed.

As soon as the cockpit was cleared of debris and the damage to the hull taped over, Andy set off with the yacht in tow. They were about halfway back to port when the Sea King caught up with them. The transfer was smooth. Lang was still unconscious and Doc Varcoe had no way of knowing how bad the head injury was. Royston had now taken on board the seriousness of his position. Andy's mention of the use of the bottle as a weapon had sobered him up totally. If Lang did not recover consciousness, he was in deep shit, a phrase his father was fond of using. He slumped down against the outside wall of the cabin, the mix of sea water and the sticky contents of his stomach beginning to give off a sickly smell now the heat of the sun started to dry him out. His confidence now seriously eroded, he lapsed into an almost comatose state, just fidgeting occasionally in the discomfort of his sticky clothing.

'You prick, you total prick.' Cockburn took glee in tormenting Royston now that relations were irreparably strained within the group. Any tenuous dependency that might previously have existed was now past history and Cockburn, who had always despised his college companion, now made the most of it, baiting him with great pleasure.

'I don't think dear mummy's money is going to get you out of this lot,' he was of a particularly callous frame of mind and couldn't help adding, 'especially if Bill dies.'

'Shut up you bastard. If my hands were free I'd break your neck.'

'Give it up you two or I'll douse the both of you.' Tom Hicks meant it and they knew he meant it. The rest of the journey passed in silence. Nigel Tuck, no longer a butt of Royston's volatile temper, took quiet pleasure in the latter's predicament and inched away from any possible body contact.

Andy steered the Carrick Maid up to its mooring, 'We'll let those three stew out on the yacht 'til Roger Penrose gets here. I spotted the police launch over at Flushing. He can hand them over to the local station, but I don't think they'll like the state our friend there is in. Maybe we should haul him off and clean him up a bit'. He said this with a chuckle.

Chris Pascoe crossed over again and with Tom Hicks they hauled Rupert Royston to his feet and eventually got him over on to the lifeboat slipway.

'Alex, this gentleman seemed to express his doubts about your competence earlier, as a crew member. Would you like to show how skilled you are with the hose, by cleaning him up before we hand him over to the police? Can't have him fouling up the inside of the police car, can we?' This by Andy, said with a note of mock seriousness as he addressed Alex.

With Pascoe and Hicks both holding Royston at arm's length, Alex played the hose over the squirming youth until as much of the visible residue of vomit, as possible, was removed. One of the crew went to fetch a blanket for the sodden specimen in front of them.

'That's another item to add to the compensation costs. We'll put in for a new one. Don't untie his hands until the police get here. Let's get them into the building now.'

28

The public gallery of Truro Crown Court sported its usual assortment of regulars. Basil Royston and his wife Victoria were sitting as close to the witness stand as they could get. At an earlier session, Rupert Royston had pleaded 'not guilty' to a charge of 'grievous bodily harm'. A number of lesser charges, involving compensation claims to fishermen, had been settled out of court, but Bill Lang was still in a coma and his chances of recovery considered to be fifty-fifty. A blood clot showed up on a brain scan and it was felt that an operation should be postponed until his wrist had fully healed and his blood volume back to normal after a further period of intravenous feeding. His parents were sitting well away from the Roystons close to Andy Cornwell, Tim Hodge and Chris Pascoe.

The court had been in session for some time.

'So to sum up, my client.' It was Royston's barrister speaking, 'was provoked and defending himself against an unwarranted assault. The unfortunate Mr Lang happened to be a victim of misfortune. The victim of mischance and that my Lord and members of the jury, is all I wish to say for now.' He sat down, unable to conceal a faint trace of satisfaction from his face. His delivery and its content, leading up to the summary, had been carefully scripted, measured and weighed in its preparation. Old man Royston could afford to find the best barrister and pay for services denied to the average client in a law suit. He too could not hide a smug, maybe did not wish to, smile at what he thought was a damning indictment of the crew of the Carrick Maid. Rupert Royston leaned back in the dock. His smirk did not go unnoticed by some of the jury.

The deposition in defence of the lifeboat's crew, progressed according to the same protocols. The RNLI had assigned one of their tried and tested barristers, David Sinclair, to this case. He was a west countryman, well versed over the years in the portrayal of evidence concerning risk, danger and bravery in dealing with the uncertainties rescue at sea entailed. In particular, he stressed the unreasonable expectations demanded of rescue crews by yacht owners, careless and inexperienced in the handling of their craft. Demands sometimes accompanied by an arrogant and contemptuous attitude towards volunteers they could well afford not to antagonise. Volunteers they misjudged as provincial in outlook and therefore to be dismissed as second rate citizens not worth passing the time of day with.

It chimed with the experiences occasionally encountered by the islanders on St Agnes, in the Isles of Scilly, where he spent several weeks of the year in a holiday cottage. St Agnes was a gem of maritime character with itself a history of marine rescue. An island where visitors DFL, Down From London, as they were termed, showed a similar contempt, objecting to cow pats on ancient paths centuries in the making, long grazed by cattle. Complaints about crowing cockerels in an environment dependent on rural husbandry in order to survive periods of storm cut off from the main island. This, as much as anything, fuelled his dislike of the kind of defendant he was here to defeat and gave impetus to his address to the court.

His skilful description of the wilful vandalism of the marker buoys; the events leading up to the threat to Alex Jago and subsequent fracas on the yacht, was a paradigm of legal testimony. But this was nothing compared with what followed.

'Now members of the court, I would like you to see with your own eyes,' he used the phrase knowing it was a tautology, but understood it would give a form of authority and validity to the evidence in the minds of the jury, 'undeniable evidence of the events as they actually occurred.'

Basil Royston sat up, looked at his wife with a clouded expression, then at his son, then half turned to look at his barrister as if to say, 'What's going on?' He leaned back on the bench and frowned as a video screen was wheeled into the space in front of the court recorders. The video which followed was a skilfully assembled sequence of scenes. First was the video capture from the cliffs, of the yacht systematically running down the lobster pot markers. It left no doubt as to being anything but deliberate, as the vessel zigzagged amongst a wide cluster of buoys, even to the point where it changed course twice to return to markers it had missed first time round. The faint whooping and shouting of the navigators was picked up by the camera even at that distance.

The next shot opened with a clip taken out of sequence, deliberately placed to emphasise the point of the whole exercise, that of demonstrating Royston's violent, irresponsible nature. It started with the scene showing Royston swinging the bottle around to deliver the contentious blow to Bill Lang's head. The audience winced as the dense rim at the base of the bottle hit his skull with a sickening thud. With a bit of skilful editing, the video went blank for a couple of seconds, flashed up a subliminal, still image of the point of impact for a second time, then cut long enough for the impression to remain imprinted in people's minds without being displaced by the distractions of subsequent images. It then reverted to the earlier time sequence, when Tim Hodge had first started recording the encounter with the yacht. Shots of the disgusting state of the cockpit deck, with its broken glass, empty cans and bottles also featured. It confirmed the secondary and lesser charge of drunk whilst in charge of a vessel, which had earlier and separately, resulted in a £5000 fine. A further shot showed the hole in the waterline of the cutting edge of the bow.And so the 'entertainment' continued, adding clip after clip of appalling behaviour.

Even Basil Royston squirmed. His wife gave a screech and started to sob as the whole sordid saga unwound and left few in doubt that the evidence against her precious son was becoming more and more incriminating. The court was quiet for a few seconds as the screen was turned off. The judge clasped his hands with his elbows resting on the bench and waited for David Sinclair to continue.

'I think there is little else to say. The crew of the Carrick Maid have been shown to have handled themselves with some restraint considering the abusive response they were subjected to by the defendant. The evidence you have just seen says more eloquently anything I could say to the court. So I leave you to consider and decide the verdict, bearing in mind there is one witness, William Lang, who is not here, in fact is unable to be here, even had he wished to be, to defend the action which led to his present condition.'

Sinclair nodded to the judge. He then turned and fixed an expressionless stare on Rupert Royston for just long enough to signal a personal dislike for what he saw, before sitting down beside his assistant.

The judge's summing up was brief, likewise his instruction to the jury. There was little to justify it being otherwise, since the evidence was so overwhelmingly clear. Dismissed, the twelve jurors filed out of the court to deliberate their verdict. As they left, they too delivered icy stares in Royston's direction.

The recess was brief and after fifteen minutes or so one of the court clerks signalled the jury's readiness to return a verdict. The judge called them in.

'Have you reached a verdict?'

A tall bearded spokesman appointed by the group spoke clearly, 'Yes.'

'Do you find the defendant guilty or not guilty of grievous bodily harm?'

The Langs leant forward in their seats, apprehensive, in spite of a gut feeling that the verdict would be what they hoped for. The Roystons looked ill at ease and were not so much fidgeting as manifesting body language that advertised an agony of suspense.

'Guilty.'

The audience, anticipating a guilty verdict as a foregone conclusion, nonetheless, gave a collective gasp of relief. Victoria Royston let out a howl of anguish and collapsed in a renewed torrent of sobs into her husband's shoulder. Rupert Royston could not believe, even now, that he had lost this pitch for freedom and glared hostilely at the jury. Basil Royston caught his son's eye and fixed him with a thunderous glare, willing him not to antagonise the judge with some ill-considered outburst, just prior to the stage of sentencing.

The judge waited a short while for emotions to subside and delivered his sentence.

'The jury has delivered a fair verdict. Your sentence is conditional and in two parts.'

The Roystons, at mention of the word conditional, relaxed a little, expecting some leniency to be exercised in the form of a suspended sentence or fine. This was not to be. The Judge continued.

'For the crime of grievous bodily harm you are to serve a sentence of ten years. It would have been eight, but your blatant arrogance and obvious lack of remorse justifies a higher term. Also, because of the damage to your boat and the real likelihood of sinking before reaching safe anchorage, you put the lives of your three

191

companions in danger. The conditional element I referred to is the addition of a further eleven years if William Lang does not recover consciousness within the next six months. Take him down. Court dismissed.'

The parents of William Lang, who had been sitting up, leaning slightly forward to hear the jury's verdict and the judge's pronouncement, sat back against the back of their bench taking some small measure of comfort from the sentence. Mrs Lang closed her eyes, bent her head, sagged and looked suddenly very small. She too sobbed, but quietly and with a dignity denied to the mother of Rupert Royston. Her husband put his arm around her in a genuine surge of love and concern.

Andy Cornwell got up and sidled along the bench in front of Richard and Hilary Lang and put out his hand.

'I hope that wasn't too upsetting for you. I think some justice has been delivered. What's the outlook for your son? He's obviously the sensible member of the group.'

Richard Lang reached forward and shook it, 'It's kind of you to say so. We heard this morning that he is showing signs of improvement. Apparently, starting to talk in his unconscious state, which the neurologist says is an indicator of a return, soon, to consciousness. Thank you for acting so swiftly and getting the helicopter involved. The hospital was able to stabilise him in time. He's not out of danger yet, but because of his age and good health the surgeon is certain he'll suffer no lasting effects.'

The other two crew members sidled up to join the coxswain and add their respects to the couple. By this time the court had lost its public. A few ushers hovered about whilst clerks and lawyers were busy clearing tables ready for the next session. The three crewmen made their farewells and wished the couple a safe journey home.

'I think we deserve a drink. Quill & Pen, down the road?' Andy referred to the pub at the bottom of the hill, below the courthouse.

'Aye, could do with a bite to eat as well. They do grub.' This was Chris Pascoe, who could always put away a pasty, two if they were small. The three set off. Covered by a standby crew, they were going to make the most of a period free from call-out.

29

At about the same time Bill Hawken picked up a rather formal looking envelope from the floor below his front door Jean-Pierre Pascal was doing the same in his home. The paper was of good quality, stiff parchment. Bill had seen one or two of these before and knew what it contained, but it was the first time he ever received one.

Jean-Pierre felt the smooth, crisp envelope, not your usual bill or sales flyer. Taking it into the kitchen he picked out a knife from one of the drawers and slit it open. The logo at the top of the letter was a giveaway. In formal terms it informed him he had been awarded the RNLI's Silver Medal for an act of outstanding service, namely his part in attempting to save the trapped victim of the sunken Pixie Bell.

'What is it?' Jenny, sitting having a coffee, could see the letter was important.

'Read it.'

He passed her the sheet. It only took her a few moments to get the gist of it. She read it for a second time, out loud this time and beamed at him.

'That's ... I don't know what to say ... it's wonderful, it's ...,' she broke down in tears. He pulled her up and they hugged each other.

'I want you to go back. I know you miss it, the comradeship and just being on the boat. It's in your blood.'

He said nothing, closed his eyes and gave her another gentle hug.

***

Bill, likewise, took his envelope into the kitchen where Mary was at a cupboard checking ingredients for a baking session, later in the day. He waved it at her.

'What's that?'

'If I'm not mistaken it's notification of some sort of recognition from RNLI. It's about this time in the year they make their announcements.'

'Come on then, open it.'

'No, you open it.' Bill handed the envelope over to Mary.

She took it into the living room where a letter opener lay on the sideboard. With hands beginning to shake, she opened the envelope and pulled the letter from its interior. She read it and passed it to Bill, beaming all over her face, as he leant against the back of the settee. It took him little time to take in the contents. The main part of the citation read, "For two acts of outstanding service, the rescue of the crew from and safe recovery of, the coaster Mixim and, in addition, outstanding courage in going to the assistance of the liquid gas tanker, Ligas Princess, averting serious damage and injury to the people of Falmouth by your action."

Mary took the letter from him, dropped it on the seat of the settee and gave him a great hug.

'You deserved that. I've always hoped you'd get some sort of acknowledgement for the risks you took.'

He was about to object.

'Ssh! I know you didn't do it for that, but it's a nice thing to be recognised, to finish on a high after all these years.'

Bill nodded, 'I 'spose you're right. I'm pleased for you though. You're the one waiting here, wondering if we're goin' to come back safe from a shout every time.'

'Come on, let's have a cup of tea.' Mary led him to the kitchen, the scene of so many single cups of tea every time she sat waiting for him to return from a call-out.'

***

The Chisel & Adze was crowded, even though it was early evening. All the crew members were there, wives and partners, celebrating Bill Hawken's award. It was Chris Pascoe who first noticed the two figures pausing in the open door way, 'Well look who's here,' and putting his glass down on the table he was standing by, strode through the crowd, arms outstretched by way of a greeting, as he invited Jean-Pierre Pascal and his wife Jenny into the heart of the pub.

The group opened up their circle and showed genuine pleasure at this unexpected arrival. Jean-Pierre had not been to the boathouse since his accident. A few had visited him at his home occasionally, but no one had broached his return to duty, knowing his wife had been badly shaken by the event.

'Bill gave me a call. Told me he was inviting everyone down for a celebration.'

'Yes, but what I haven't told them is that you have been given a clean bill of health and are coming back on the boat. He's had permission from the chief petticoat.'

This raised a laugh.

'This calls for a toast,' it was Andy Cornwell who spoke.

'Yes, but there's something else to celebrate,' Bill put his hand up, 'can I tell them?'

'Tell us what?' It was Tim Hodge, recently appointed Relief Cox.

Jean-Pierre nodded.

'Jean's also been awarded Silver Medal for his part in the Pixie Bell shout.'

A great roar went up from the crew. Other drinkers turned as the embarrassed crewman was patted on the back and congratulated by the now excited and genuinely delighted group.

Bill let the excitement settle to a cheerful banter. Tapping his glass with a coin he got the group's attention again, 'Hold your horses, we haven't finished yet. I told you not to have a meal before you came,' Bill nodded towards a figure quietly standing at the edge of the group, 'Mr Markham, some of you already know him, has laid on a feast in the back room. For those of you new to the crew, Sam has provided a lot of gear for this lifeboat station. We've got a lot to thank him for, the Atlantic 75, for a start, is one of them.'

'That's enough Bill,' said Sam Markham, 'you'll be putting me up for holy orders next. Let's get into the other room and celebrate in comfort.'

Sam led the way. The crew and their partners made a leisurely shuffle towards the inner room, some stopped on their way by visitors wanting to know more. One of the local journalists, Ron Brewer, made a practice of using the pub as 'his front room', as he called it. A focal point for local gossip, a popular meeting point for yachtsmen, or women, finishing solo Atlantic or round the world yacht races, this was fertile ground for news. He had been listening in to the exchanges going on and caught Bill before he left the bar.

'Can I get a few photographs down at the boathouse Sunday morning, before or after training? Whatever suits you. Will make a good front page spread and feature inside.'

'Give me a buzz tomorrow, I'll be in all morning. Have a word with Andy, just to let him know. Although I'm Ops Manager, effectively he's king pin and I don't like to interfere with his arrangements other than to point out clashes or possible consequences of certain decisions.'

'Fine! I'll do that. Enjoy your party.'

30

Bill Hawken went to the back of the shed where the Atlantic 75 was housed. The crew were still out on exercise and the journalist he was waiting for wasn't due for another twenty minutes or so. It was nearly a year since the Mixim was rescued. He went up to an old blanket and uncovered what was concealed beneath it. The bronze propeller, almost the Nemesis of the Carrick Maid, was propped against the wall. The Mixim had been condemned by the Board of Trade as totally unseaworthy on a number of counts. It was considered not worth repairing and had been towed to a breaker's yard somewhere in the Baltic, several months back. Nobody had raised the issue of its propeller and he certainly wasn't going to remind anyone of its existence. He'd give it another year. If no one asked about it, then he would make arrangements for it to be sold through some marine agents. A new one that diameter would cost, easily, eight or ten thousand pounds, maybe more. So reconditioned, re-polished and shaft taper re-bored, it should make a tempting snip for five thousand pounds.

He didn't know what he'd do with the money other than make sure the crew would benefit in some way. Maybe purchase a decent coffee-making machine, a couple of new swing chairs for the computer stations and some easy chairs for the open plan area alongside. The rest would go into a general account to fund the crew's annual party over the next few years. Legal or not, the thing had nearly done for the crew and he felt the worst that could happen was HQ asking for the proceeds to be handed over, that is, of course, if they got to hear about it. It wasn't quite the same as 'smuggling brandy for the parson', or 'Free Trade' as the Cornish referred to the ancient profession of 'cross channel trade'. No, they had a moral right to the proceeds even if they didn't have a legal right and he was going to do his damndest to see that it happened.

He studied the screw for a few more seconds. The dent in the leading edge of one of the uppermost blades took his attention. He ran his finger along it. It was quite shallow, but it caused him to give an involuntary shudder as his brain replayed the events of that night. The juddering impact, the sound of the rail being mangled, even through the howl of the wind and that of the boat's hull as it slammed into the waves, was still fresh in his mind. He dropped the blanket, turned and walked out into the daylight.

'Hello!'

Bill turned. Ron Brewer and photographer were out in the road approaching the slipway from the side of the boathouse. Bill raised his hand and advanced to meet them.

'You're a bit early. Crew's not back yet, but we can fill in a few details while we wait, if you want, here or up in the lounge.'

'Don't mind being outside,' said Ron as the two shook hands with the retired coxswain, 'no time like the present. Might as well get a bit of background info, while we're waiting for the crew to return,' and produced a spiral, reporter's note book, ready to record.

'Where'd you want to start?'

'Perhaps you could tell me a bit about the shout involving the rescue of the coaster's crew. What was her name?'

'The Mixim.'

'Ah, yeah, I remember. Left her propeller stuck into your decking, didn't she?'

'That's right.'

'What happened to it? If I remember it was about four or five feet in diameter. Caused quite a stir on Youtube.'

'I dunno,' said Bill, 'total mystery. Ah, here's the boat comin' back. Just wait here while I go to give a hand with the mooring ropes.' With that he grinned to himself as he turned his back on the scribbling journalist and made his way to the landing jetty, knowing damn well he wasn't needed.

Printed in Great Britain
by Amazon